Paws for Murder

A PET BOUTIQUE MYSTERY

Annie Knox

AN OBSIDIAN MYSTERY

OBSIDIAN
Published by the Penguin Group
Penguin Group (USA) LLC, 375 Hudson Street,
New York, New York 10014

USA | Canada | UK | Ireland | Australia | New Zealand | India | South Africa | China
penguin.com
A Penguin Random House Company

First published by Obsidian, an imprint of New American Library,
a division of Penguin Group (USA) LLC

First Printing, January 2014

ISBN 978-0-451-23950-1

Printed in the United States of America
10 9 8 7 6 5 4 3 2 1

A FASHIONABLE VICTIM

As gently as I could, I flipped the lid of the container open and heaved the bags up over the side.

I sidled around the trash container to get a good grip on the lid so I could close it without making an almighty racket. The light over Richard's back door flickered on when I stepped into the range of its sensor.

And I froze.

The new light revealed a still form sprawled across the alleyway. At first, I mistook it for a bundle of rubbish strewn across the bricks, as though perhaps an animal had ripped open a trash bag and rifled through the contents, looking for something choice.

But then I saw a hand, its fingers curled upward, as though grasping for something just out of reach.

As I slowly approached, I began to make out additional details: a brown paper bag discarded by the body, dark shadows, pieces of something spilling forth. A loose purple scarf trailed over the outstretched arm. A curl of dark red hair glowed in the harsh yellow light. A shoe—thick-soled and square—dangled off a foot clad in woolly tights.

Another step brought me close enough to make out the features on the still, pale face: Sherry Harper, her face contorted in a rictus of pain, her eyes glassy and flat in the harsh glare.

I couldn't tear my eyes from her face.

While I stood there, trying to process what I was seeing, the motion-sensitive lights suddenly flicked off.

And I screamed.

For Kim Lionetti.
Thank you for believing in me.

Acknowledgments

This book would not be here without the support of a great many people. First and foremost, I would like to thank Elizabeth Bistrow for creating Merryville and its residents and then giving me the freedom to make the characters my own. I couldn't have asked for a better editor. Thanks, too, to the Lit Girls (Misa, Kym, Marty, Jessica, B, Kim, Mary, and Jill) for providing wine and brilliant ideas; Bethany and Elizabeth for allowing me to borrow their pets for my book; and my mother, sister, and in-laws for their love. Finally, as always, thanks to my husband for being my rock: He's supported me through more than anyone will know, and deserves credit for every good thing I do.

CHAPTER
One

Sherry Harper blew into Trendy Tails like a late-summer tornado.

"It's just plain wrong, Izzy."

She'd marched up the steps of 801 Maple Avenue like Joan of Arc charging the English, righteous fire in her eyes . . . and a baby sling strung across her chest. As she shifted her weight to better stare me down, her guinea pig, Gandhi, poked his quivering nose out of the sling to get a look around. Like all guinea pigs, he had a perpetually startled expression on his face, an effect heightened by the forward tilt of his auburn ears and the ring of pale blond fur around his button eyes.

Little guy would be adorable in one of my hand-knit sweaters. A-dorable.

"Animals aren't meant to wear clothes," Sherry continued. "It isn't natural."

I didn't bother pointing out that guinea pigs didn't

"naturally" travel in canvas slings. Or live in Minnesota, for that matter.

Sherry Harper, trust-fund baby and Merryville's resident reactionary, didn't trade in logic or reason. The woman flitted from cause to cause, most of them half-baked. If she wasn't picketing city hall over the deplorable conditions of the town park benches, she was writing a letter to the editor of the *Merryville Gazette* about how city hall spent too much on frivolous things . . . like park benches. True story.

No, now that Sherry had set her sights on my brand-new pet boutique, logic wouldn't dissuade her.

"I get where you're coming from. Really, I do. But people are going to dress up their pets. They buy ridiculous and demeaning costumes from those big box stores. Those things are made overseas out of who-knows-what. I'm offering them a local, nontoxic alternative."

Sherry opened her mouth to answer, but then froze, her face twitching as she fought a sneeze. With her thick auburn hair, freckled nose, and wide dark brown eyes, she bore a striking resemblance to her furry friend . . . especially when her nose quivered.

I reached behind the counter and pulled out a box of tissues, quickly handing one to her.

The sneeze arrived with enough bluster to set the tiny brass bells around her neck tinkling. She emitted a barely audible squeak as she sucked in air, and another sneeze nearly shook her out of her custom-cobbled earth shoes.

Packer, my pug-bulldog mix, whined pitifully from his fleece-lined dog bed and buried his nose beneath his paws.

"God bless," I muttered.

Sherry honked into the tissue and, seemingly without thought, stuffed it into the baby sling.

Poor Gandhi.

"Thank you," Sherry said. "I think I'm catching cold. Change in the weather, you know."

We'd had an unseasonably warm spell during the first half of October, but it had finally broken. The chill that day was as crisp as a Granny Smith, and News 5 had predicted our first snowfall within the week. By Thanksgiving, we'd be buried.

"Look," I said, trying one last time to woo Sherry to my side, "I don't expect you to love what I'm doing here. But what's worse: dressing a dog in a Black Watch rain coat or dipping him in flea poison like they do at Prissy's Pretty Pets?"

I felt a twinge of remorse at deflecting Sherry's ire onto Prissy. But Pris had made no bones about the fact she saw my boutique as a direct competitor for her pet spa . . . or that she would do anything to destroy her competition. Besides, she had a mountain of her husband's money to cushion her, while I would be lucky to pay my rent for the next few months.

Sherry's wide brow wrinkled in thought.

"Flea dip is definitely worse. But that doesn't make what you're doing right."

"But I'm selling natural alternatives to those chemicals. And Rena's going to be making fresh, organic pet treats." The pastry skills of my oldest and dearest friend, Rena Hamilton, knew no bounds, and she could satisfy the hankerings of man and beast alike. I'd talked her into setting up shop with me, baking pupcakes and kitty canapés for our in-store "barkery."

Sherry cocked her head the way Packer does when he spots a squirrel. "Rena? Rena Hamilton?"

"Yeah, she's setting up shop over there." I pointed toward a corner of the house that had once been a dining room, and still had a doorway into an old kitchen.

Eight-oh-one Maple had been built as a single-family residence, back when many Minnesotans had about a zillion children. My landlady, Ingrid Whitfield, had inherited the house when her husband, Arnold, died. She had converted the third floor into an apartment—where I happened to reside—and the first floor into a gift shop, while she continued to live on the second floor. When she renovated the house, though, she didn't want to disturb the beautiful tiling and cabinets in the original kitchen, so she'd kept it intact. Now, Rena could use the kitchen for creating her pet treats.

"I didn't know you were in business with Rena," Sherry said. I thought I detected a tremor in her voice.

"Do you know Rena well?"

Merryville was a small town, and Rena had lived there for the entirety of her flamboyant life. Everyone knew Rena, but few people knew her well.

"Oh, we, uh, worked together," Sherry said. She waved her hand dismissively. "It was a long time ago."

Curious. I couldn't imagine Sherry Harper engaging in any labor, much less the sort of minimum wage job Rena tended to have.

But before I could push Sherry further about her past with Rena, a violent sneeze tore through me.

"Oh dear, excuse me!" I grabbed a tissue and pressed it against my nose to stave off another sneeze.

"Are you catching cold, too?"

"I don't know. I certainly hope not." With the grand opening of Trendy Tails kicking off in just over twenty-four hours, I couldn't afford to slow down.

"I've got just the thing," Sherry said, her hand snaking into the baby sling and rooting around. She pulled out a black cell phone with a pink anarchy sticker on the back, its corner nicked up with tiny tooth marks; a dog-eared paperback; and a handful of crumpled tissues before finding what she wanted and stuffing everything back in the sling.

"Here," she said, "try this." She held out a cellophane package with a crimson paper label, covered with Chinese characters in metallic gold. One shriveled tan disk nestled at the bottom of the bag. It looked like an ancient potato chip.

"It's ginseng," Sherry said. "Great for your immune system."

The nails of her short, blunt fingers were square and unpolished, but they were buffed and the cuticles trimmed, like she'd recently gotten a manicure. She shook the bag at me, and a mismatched clump of ornaments slid down her wrist to drape across her hand: two brass bangles, three macramé bracelets adorned with jade stones, and a knotted red string. A whiff of patchouli tickled another sneeze out of me.

I shook my head. "Oh, I couldn't take your last one," I insisted.

"Nah, go ahead. I drank some ginseng tea this morning, so I'm all set. I was just in Sprigs this morning, and they were out of dried ginseng, so if you don't take mine you're out of luck for a couple of days. By then, it will be too late. The cold will have set in, and the ginseng won't help at all."

I looked at the desiccated bit of plant matter. Mulch. It was mulch. And she wanted me to eat it.

"Are you sure?" I held my breath, hoping she'd retract the offer.

"Absolutely. It's good Karma for me."

Fighting a shudder, I took the bag. I didn't want to eat the ginseng—even if it would keep me healthy—but if I turned down Sherry's offer, I'd alienate her for sure.

And I couldn't afford to alienate Sherry Harper.

My landlord and former boss, Ingrid Whitfield, had assured me that a pet boutique was a viable business. Only a stone's throw from the Mississippi's headwaters, Merryville was almost an island; it nestled between the banks of the Mississippi, the Perry River (one of the Mighty Mississippi's tributaries), and the sloping shores of Badger Lake. Its quaint inns and rental cottages attracted all manner of tourists from Minneapolis, Madison, and even as far away as Chicago: outdoor enthusiasts, antiquers, and aficionados of the town's peculiar blend of austere Prairie architecture and Victorian whimsy. Ingrid reasoned that the customers who'd bought folk art and tchotchkes from her Merryville Gift Haus would be delighted by canine couture and feline fashions.

I wasn't so sure. Besides, I had a few obstacles standing in my way. Numero uno? I didn't know diddly about how to run a business. My sisters never ceased reminding me that I bounced checks like a Harlem Globetrotter, forgetting to transfer my money from savings to checking, and I always overtipped at restaurants. I certainly didn't have the financial savvy to negotiate with vendors, manage payroll for a couple of employees, or keep adequate records for tax season.

I also worried about getting support from the rest of the Merryville merchants. My neighbor, Richard Greene, had expressed displeasure about the possible noise and mess an animal-related business might produce. (His own German shepherd, MacArthur, had such a wicked bite he didn't bother with barking.) Priscilla Olson, owner of Prissy's Pretty Pets Spa and Salon, had been agitating against her perceived competition. And half the residents of Merryville thought my business partner, Rena, might be a witch.

Bottom line, I didn't think Trendy Tails could possibly survive the winter if Sherry decided to picket the store or, worse, wage an online campaign against me by posting scathing articles and reviews on the blogs and Web sites promoting the local charm to would-be travelers.

So I took the withered chip of ginseng between two fingers. The scent of the stuff, like someone had tried to cover the smell of overheated compost by burning incense, made me gag a little. I steeled my spine, squinched my eyes, held my breath, and popped it in my mouth.

Agggh. It tasted like dirt. Bitter dirt.

I chewed it as quickly as I could and choked it down.

When I opened my eyes, I found Sherry watching me, the ghost of a smile playing at the corners of her generous mouth. "Takes some getting used to," she said.

I managed a smile in return. "It must. But thanks."

A measure of tension drained from her posture, and I started to think I'd talked her off the warpath.

But just then the small brass bell tied to the front door of the shop jingled merrily, and we both turned to see Ken West wiping his loafers on my welcome mat.

Thanks to the cosmopolitan tastes (and money) of our many tourists, Merryville residents had a host of wonderful restaurants to choose from, offering everything from Tex-Mex to pizza to down-home American food. We even had a fantastic Korean barbecue. Ken West, though, was the only chef in all of Perry County to have an actual degree in culinary arts. He'd moved to town a few years earlier to open a fine dining restaurant called the Blue Atlantic. I admit it took chutzpah, opening a high-end seafood restaurant when Merryville couldn't be farther from an ocean if it tried. There's plenty of walleye in Minnesota, but not much in the way of edible shellfish. When the business failed, he stuck around, doing informal catering and scouting for an investor to back another restaurant venture.

I'm a disaster in the kitchen, and when it comes to people food, Rena only cooks vegetarian. Despite the questionable provenance of crab served in rural Minnesota, my aunt Dolly had been a regular patron of the Blue Atlantic. As a favor to her, and likely in hopes of securing her backing for his next restaurant, Ken had agreed to cater my grand opening. He would provide suitably omnivorous nibbles for my small-town Minnesota clientele, and charge me just a smidge above cost. Ken gave me the heebie-jeebies, but I couldn't say no to such a generous offer. Especially since Aunt Dolly—the only member of my family who seemed to consider my business a genuinely good idea—was footing the bill for the whole grand-opening shindig.

"Oh, I should have known," Sherry spat. "You're in league with *him*."

Ken, who had been focused on his shoes, looked up in alarm. When his gaze settled on Sherry, he heaved a sigh and his lids drooped in resignation.

"Hi, Sherry."

"What's going on?" I asked. "You two know each other?"

Ken's mouth quirked in a tiny smile. "Actually, we've never been formally introduced. But Sherry here devoted herself to picketing the Blue Atlantic for what? Three months?"

"Three and a half," Sherry said. "And I was prepared to stay out there with my sign for as long as it took to close you down."

I felt a little sick. I remembered Aunt Dolly lamenting the loss of the Blue Atlantic, but the restaurant had closed right around the time my boyfriend of fourteen years had announced he was riding off into the sunset without me. I'd been buried too deep in self-pity to follow local news. I hadn't realized that Sherry had been involved with the restaurant's demise.

"You picketed the Blue Atlantic?"

"She sure did," Ken said. "Every afternoon at five o'clock, she showed up with a huge sign—'murderer' written in red dripping letters. Very catchy."

"You were serving foie gras," Sherry said, punctuating her statement with an accusatory finger. "Do you have any idea what they do to the geese to fatten their livers?"

I didn't know. I didn't particularly *want* to know. Like Rena, I ate vegetarian, though my meatless life had started more as a way to keep the pounds from creeping on in college, while Rena was a true believer. Still, pureed goose liver didn't appeal to me in the slightest.

I was spared the details by Ken throwing up his hands in mock surrender. "Yes, yes, Sherry. It was a grievous sin, and grievously hath I answered it. The geese lost *their* lives, and I lost mine. All is right with the world once more."

Ken came further into the store, carefully skirting Sherry's position by the rack of kitty capelets, and propped himself against the front counter. He and I were now clearly squared off against Sherry, two against one. Whether I liked it or not, I was part of "Team Ken."

He unbuttoned his corduroy-trimmed barn coat and let his leather knapsack slide from his shoulder. The man looked like he'd stepped out of an Orvis catalog. "I have the final menu for tomorrow night, Izzy. I just wanted to go over it and get an update on the estimated number of guests. Didn't mean to intrude."

"You're not intr—"

"Well," Sherry huffed, throwing up her hands in mock surrender, "I see how it is. You're trying to tell me that you're worried about the welfare of animals, but you've got this monster catering your party. You're just another cog in the corporate-farming, habitat-destroying, animal-torturing machine."

"Sherry, I really don't thi—"

She cut off my effort to restore the peace. "Don't even bother. You've shown your true colors. I'll see you tomorrow night."

She turned on her heel, her gauzy saffron-colored skirt billowing around her tights-clad legs, auburn hair swishing dramatically about her shoulders, and stormed out of the store.

Ken chuckled. "She's a piece of work."

"No kidding. I thought maybe I could talk her out of protesting the grand opening."

He shook his head. "No way. She's like a terrier. Once she's got hold of something, she just won't let go."

A terrier, maybe, but I still thought "tornado" was a more appropriate metaphor: arbitrary, unstoppable, destructive.

All I could do was take shelter and hope that her wrath would skip over my little store without doing too much damage.

CHAPTER
Two

Ingrid Whitfield lifted the rhinestone-encrusted glasses from her nose so she could peer closely at a tiny set of fuchsia snow booties. "Are these for a cat?"

I paused in the act of dusting a glass case filled with bejeweled collars and multicolored toenail tips to contemplate my long-haired Norwegian forest cat Jinx. She looked so sweet, curled in a sleepy spiral atop an old oak armoire, her tail swishing lazily with her soft kitty snores.

She looked sweet, but I knew better.

Jinx was eighteen pounds of solid cat, and she would claw me to ribbons if I tried to put shoes on her massive, tufted paws.

"Definitely not for cats," I said. "Those booties are designed for toy dogs, like Chihuahuas and min-pins. The snow and ice can do terrible things to their paw pads."

Ingrid clucked softly as she let her glasses settle back

into place. "Never did understand why people wanted those silly, shivery dogs," she huffed. "Give me a good retriever or hound any day of the week. A dog that can handle a Minnesota winter without fussy little shoes."

"When Packer wore those camo boots last month, you said they were adorable."

"That's totally different," Ingrid insisted. "Packer looked dashing and rugged in his hunting outfit. He's such a handsome fellow."

I harbored no illusions that Packer the Wonder Dog was handsome. A pug-bulldog mix, he had a dour, wrinkly face with drooping jowls and mournful eyes. Casey, my former fiancé, had fallen hard for him the minute he saw him at the shelter, waggling his stubby tail, tongue lolling like a curl of strawberry taffy. I'd actually been a little jealous of Casey's infatuation with the dopey dog—until, of course, he left us both. Packer was cute, yes. But handsome? No.

"Packer's going to miss you," I said. I swallowed hard, fighting off another bout of tears at the thought of Ingrid's imminent departure. "So am I."

"I'm going to miss you, too, dear. But this old broad can't take another Minnesota winter. I need to get myself to sunny Florida before we get snowed in. Leave November first. I'm officially a snowbird now."

"You want to take Packer with you? I'm pretty sure he loves you even more than he loves me."

Ingrid laughed. "Oh, I could never break up your team, Izzy. But you and Packer are always welcome to visit us in Boca. Jinx, too. Harvey loves animals, and Packer might enjoy running on the beach."

I pictured the pooch galloping across a stretch of

sand, bouncing in and out of the surf, wheezing with asthmatic delight, while Jinx basked in the melting Florida sun. "You've got yourself a deal. As soon as I get Trendy Tails up and running, we'll all come visit you two lovebirds."

"Speaking of the store," Ingrid said, "I've already picked out my outfit for tomorrow night."

I smothered a smile. Apart from her sparkly glasses, most of Ingrid's clothes were better suited for a lumberjack than for an eighty-two-year-old woman. At the moment, she wore a pair of faded jeans, a red checked flannel shirt, a blaze orange hunting vest, and a pair of scuffed hiking boots. I couldn't wait to see what she'd chosen for the big party.

"What about you?" she asked. "Are you ready for the grand opening?"

"I don't know."

"What do you mean? The place looks great."

I had done a lot of work on the space since Ingrid had locked the door of the Merryville Gift Haus for the last time at the end of September. The solid plaster walls boasted a fresh coat of sky-blue paint, the refinished oak plank flooring gave off a mellow glow, and countless small hats and harnesses had replaced the snow globes and duck decoys in the glass display cases, which had been polished until they shone like new.

All the pieces were in place for Trendy Tails Pet Boutique to open, but I had mixed feelings about the opening.

After all, this wasn't part of "the plan."

The plan evolved the summer between my sophomore and junior years of high school, about five months into my romance with Casey Alter. The night of the closing cookout for the Soaring Eagles Adventure Camp, where we worked alongside half the kids from Merryville High, we sat beneath a lemony August moon and laid out our future: college together, followed by medical school for Casey, then a general and plastic surgery residency back in our hometown of Merryville, which would allow us to live cheap and pay off debt, and then on to New York City, where Casey would make the beautiful people even more beautiful and I would break into the world of fashion.

For years, I thought we had it all figured out. We both earned substantial scholarships to the University of Wisconsin, where Casey committed himself to his studies in biochemistry and molecular biology and excelled. I did my part, studying textile and apparel design and forgoing the final year at F.I.T. in New York so I could make him dinner, do his laundry, and save him from anything that distracted him from his work. While he attended medical school and I played Suzy Homemaker, I also made ends meet by designing costumes for community theaters, belly dancers, strippers, clowns . . . anyone who couldn't buy off the rack in south-central Wisconsin.

In Madison, the plan worked. Then we moved back to Merryville for Casey's residency, and it started to unravel.

During our first few months back home, I'd puttered around our apartment on the third floor of Ingrid's house, sewing curtains for the windows tucked beneath the gingerbread eaves and slipcovers for our thrift store furniture. But I wasn't prepared for the lonely life of a surgical resident's partner. Other than Rena, most of my high school friends had moved away, and the rest were busy starting their families.

We added Packer and Jinx to our home in an effort to ease my loneliness, but it wasn't enough. Bored and broke, I'd taken a job at the Gift Haus on the first floor of the house. I thought I'd be moving on soon. I was just biding my time until my fabulous life in New York got started.

But then, when Casey completed his residency and got the cushy position in a cosmetic surgery practice on Park Avenue, he announced "the plan" had changed. He'd still be moving to New York to make the beautiful people more beautiful, but he'd be going with Rachel Melbourne, the cute young dietician from Merryville General.

Not me.

For the next two years, the house at 801 Maple Avenue contained my whole life. Inertia and grief had kept me working at the Gift Haus on the first floor and living in the third-floor apartment. I knew I needed a new plan, one of my very own, but it was so much easier to lean on Ingrid's plucky strength, share Sunday dinners with my parents (toting home baggies of leftover pot roast and baked chicken for my pampered pets), and spend my free time stitching up designer duds for Jinx and Packer.

Ingrid was the one who kicked me in the pants when she announced her decision to close down the Gift Haus and move in with Harvey, the high school beau she'd reconnected with through Facebook. The retired lovebirds had already purchased a cozy condo on the beach in Boca, and were talking about getting hitched in Vegas before the year ended. They were going to live the Midwestern dream, spending the six months of winter in Florida and the six months of summer in Minnesota. Even though Ingrid would be back in May, she couldn't keep the Gift Haus running with her new vagabond lifestyle.

Ingrid suggested I should start selling my pet fashions full time. She even offered me a discount on the rent for the store until I got up and running, and my aunt Dolly offered to loan me the money to purchase inventory. Faced with the alternative of unemployment and a return to my old floral-wallpapered bedroom in my parents' house, I'd said yes.

Still, I couldn't help but think that the shop was just another layover on the way to my real life. The sidelong glances my parents shared when I told them about Trendy Tails made me worry that it would be an epic failure. And my sisters, my darling sisters, kept pointing out that I'd gotten a fancy college degree to design clothes for two-legged clients, not furry ones.

I heaved a steadying sigh.

"Are you having second thoughts?" Ingrid asked.

"It's a little late for second thoughts." Aunt Dolly's money was already spent, and Ingrid had passed up a half dozen offers on the house to keep it open for me and for Trendy Tails. I couldn't go back now.

"It's never too late for second thoughts," Ingrid replied. "What has you worried?"

"Oh, I don't know. Maybe just that I don't have the faintest idea how to run a business," I quipped.

"Business schmizness. You put a smile on your face, offer people a good product for a reasonable price, and you've got a business. All the rest, you just lean on your friends and family. That sister of yours, Dru, she's an excellent accountant. Been handling my books for years now. She'll keep you on the straight and narrow."

"I guess you're right."

"Of course I am. Now, you're not disappointed about making clothes for pets instead of people, are you?"

Actually, *I* wasn't disappointed at all. I loved sewing the tiny garments, figuring out how to take the latest fashions in the glossy magazines and cut them down into smaller versions that were practical—easy on, easy off, and easy clean—as well as trendy. And I loved the animals themselves, not to mention spending time with people who adored their pets.

"No, I'm not disappointed. But I'm worried other people are disappointed in me."

"Nonsense," Ingrid huffed. "Who would be disappointed? Your parents? They've got a beautiful daughter who's bravely tackling a new project and who gets to live her dream without moving all the way across the country. Your sisters? They're sisters, and they'll always fuss, but they love you like crazy. And your friends? Well, we all think you're the bee's knees."

I threw my arms around Ingrid in an impulsive hug.

"Well, then. I guess I'm as ready as I'll ever be," I said. "I just need Rena to stock the cases for the barkery, and we'll be set for the big party. Soon, we'll file the incorporation papers, and Trendy Tails will be official."

"'We'? Did Rena change her mind and decide to make your partnership legal?"

"No. I feel bad that she's thrown so much of her own money into the business—buying packaging, cookware, and all the ingredients for her organic pet treats—and I told her I'd love to have her as my partner, but I guess her heart's just not in it. She's just helping me with the filing so I don't screw it up. She was working at Spin Doctor when Xander incorporated, so this isn't her first rodeo." The Spin Doctor was the record shop across the back alley from Trendy Tails. With his gentle nature and subtle sly wit, its owner, Xander Stephens, had become a good friend over the last few years.

As if on cue, the brass bell tied to the front door handle jingled merrily as my oldest and dearest friend, Rena Hamilton, used her hip to force her way into the store. A mountain of sunny orange cake boxes teetered in her arms, hiding all but her spiky purple hair.

"Little help?" she called from behind her burden.

I hustled over to assist her, plucking the three top boxes from the stack, and her elfin face emerged. "Holy cow," she wheezed. "Wasn't sure I'd make it."

"What have you got there?" Ingrid asked.

Rena slid her stack of boxes onto the farm table we'd salvaged for the old dining room. Rena had sanded down the worn pine table, painted it a luscious cherry red, and decorated the whole thing with whimsical birds and flowers. She popped open the first box. "I've got pumpkin-banana pupcakes, carob canine cookies, and salmon kitty crackers.

"Tonight," she continued, "I'll package the suet cakes for the birds, ball the melon for any reptiles who happen to join us, and whip up a bunch of my human chow."

"Human chow?" Ingrid wrinkled her nose.

"It's fantastic," I assured her. "A sweet cereal mix with peanut butter, chocolate, and powdered sugar. Once you start munching it, you just can't stop."

Rena opened a second pastry box and started arranging bone-shaped cookies on a plate. "Technically, the people could eat these, too." To prove her point, she popped a cookie in her mouth. "They're really good," she mumbled around a mouthful of carob cookie.

I laughed. "That's okay. We can save them for the critters. Ken stopped by a few hours ago, and he has enough fancy people food to feed the Packers' defensive line."

"I don't suppose he's making anything vegetarian, is he?"

"Of course—bruschetta, hummus, some sort of roasted eggplant thingie." Ingrid was making a face. She couldn't grasp the notion of human beings not eating meat and didn't understand why Rena and I would voluntarily consume so many vegetables. I grinned at her. "He's also making little chicken skewers, crab-stuffed mushrooms, and beef pasties."

Ingrid sighed. "I'm going to miss pasties." Thanks to the Cornish population of northern Minnesota, pasties held a prominent spot at most local celebrations. Tall, raw-boned, and formerly blond, Ingrid could have been a poster girl for the Sons of Norway. But she still loved pasties.

Rena finished setting out her pet treats and joined us in the main part of the showroom. "Ingrid, do you think you can survive in Florida? No pasties, no lutefisk . . . and you'll have to give up all your flannel."

Ingrid huffed good-naturedly. "Smarty pants. Yes, I'll survive. I know exactly what I'm giving up: snow shovels and rock salt for the sidewalk. And I'm getting my Harvey."

Rena and I sighed in unison. Ingrid and Harvey had a romance for the ages. Ripped apart when his parents shipped him off to military school, they'd lived their separate lives but never forgotten their first love. Then, sixty years later, a mutual interest in Johnny Mathis and a facility with social networking brought them back in touch. They'd picked up their affair right where it left off.

"I want a Harvey," Rena moaned as she sank down to sit tailor-style on the floor. She clicked her tongue against her teeth, and Jinx leapt down off the armoire, rolled her shoulders in a graceful stretch, and then draped herself across Rena's lap like a heavy blanket. Rena was the only person who could call Jinx like that. I won't lie . . . It made me a little jealous.

"You'll get a Harvey someday, dear," Ingrid said, her lips curling in a knowing smile. "I had to wait until I was nearly eighty for mine."

"So another forty-five years? I guess I can swing that."

Rena had worse luck with love than I did. Sure, my breakup with Casey had been tragic and spectacular, but our relationship had been reasonably strong. Rena, however, had bounced from boy to no-account boy since high school, mostly flirting and fighting without any real commitment at all.

Her problem, as I saw it, was that her outsides and her insides didn't match. Rena Hamilton stood five foot nothing, but she had enough attitude for a half dozen normal people. She dressed in ripped T-shirts, grungy jeans, and Doc Martens. A row of skull-shaped studs marched up the curl of her ear, and her hair looked like it had been cut (and colored) by a hyperactive six-year-old. In short, she looked like she'd knife you in a dark alley to score a fix of heroin.

That outside tended to attract guys who wanted to live fast and hard, guys who weren't interested in forever, guys who liked their women the way they liked their beers: cheap and numerous.

But inside, Rena possessed one of the sweetest, most loyal souls I knew. She cried at sappy movies, but she'd deck you if you ever commented on it.

Rena wanted—*needed*—the boy next door, but she kept getting Sid Vicious over and over again.

I held out a hand and pulled Rena up into a hug, reaching out to clasp Ingrid's hand, too.

"Ladies, we're all turning a page in our lives. Here's hoping the next chapter is more wonderful than the last."

CHAPTER
Three

The night of the grand opening, Jinx, Packer, and I got decked out in our best duds. Packer wore his green-and-gold hoodie in honor of the Green Bay Packers, for whom he was named. Jinx endured a posh purple capelet, to satisfy the Vikings fans in the crowd, and a jeweled dangle on her collar. I was the Switzerland of local football, so I slipped on my one and only little black dress.

Even Rena dressed up for the occasion in a fitted red satin dress and fishnets. She still sported her Doc Martens, but she spiffed them up with red ribbon laces, and she exchanged her usual messenger bag for a tiny black patent cross-body purse. Her ferret, a chocolate roan named Valrhona, wore a ruff of black velvet edged in rhinestones around her neck.

We opened the doors to Trendy Tails promptly at six o'clock. The sun had just set, and the streets of Merryville were draped in indigo twilight, the old-fashioned streetlights slowly humming to life. The air smelled of frost and woodsmoke, and the golden light from the antique chandeliers inside the store beckoned warmly. Postcard-sized announcements about our pet costume contest at the annual Halloween Howl were scattered about the store, and the scents of Ken's delicious hors d'oeuvres wafted through the shop.

Within the hour, guests poured in, many with their pets in tow. Xander Stephens had wisely decided against bringing his brilliant green iguana. But all the furry beasts were in attendance.

I was in the middle of greeting my sister Dru and her tabby, Poppy, when Rena grabbed me by the arm.

"Look who just showed up," she hissed. Rena jerked her head toward the front of the store where I saw Priscilla Olson and her husband, Hal, had shown up with their Persian, Kiki. A perfectly coiffed silver chinchilla, Kiki looked like a puff of dandelion fluff. Her mommy, Pris, held her draped over one shoulder of her cobalt dress. Limp and passive, the cat could have passed for a fur stole. "After all the trash she's been talking about Trendy Tails, I can't believe her nerve."

"Actually, thanks to the Halloween Howl, we've been forced to declare a sort of cease-fire in the pet wars," I explained.

Every year, the Merryville merchants hosted a safe alternative to trick-or-treating for the kids in town, the Halloween Howl, at Dakota Park. Lots of candy for the little ones, more substantial fare for the adults, face painters, apple bobbing, even hay rides around the park's perimeter. Most of the businesses in Merryville's historic district would be involved this year:

the Grateful Grape, the Happy Leaf Tea Shoppe, Joe Time Coffee, and the Thistle and Ivy were providing refreshments, and Xander was reaching into the Spin Doctor's vaults to DJ some spooky music. The *Merryville Gazette*, which sponsored the event, had asked Prissy's Pretty Pets and Trendy Tails to coordinate a new feature of the Howl: a pet costume contest.

"I don't expect the cease-fire to last past Halloween. Still, I should go make nice," I said.

I made my way across the store and greeted Pris and Hal with a tiny wave.

"Hi, Prissy. Thanks for coming."

I extended a hand in greeting. Pris barely brushed her long delicate fingers over mine, as though she didn't want to be rude but was worried she might catch something from me. As if to confirm her worst fears, I picked that moment to sneeze, which sent me scrambling for the tissue I had tucked in the sleeve of my dress. Pris's glossy peony pink lips slid into a close-mouthed cocktail party smile.

"We wouldn't miss it," she oozed. "And bless you."

Hal Olson, the RV king of the upper Midwest, leaned in to shake my hand properly. His massive hands enveloped mine. A few stray hairs, bleached gold by the sun, curled around a chunky signet ring on his right hand. "Always happy to support new business in Merryville. Lifeblood of the community. If I have my way, this little burg will be growing like gangbusters over the next couple of years."

Hal's smile was all teeth, square, white teeth that contrasted sharply with the permanent tan of a veteran golfer. He was a solid man, stocky and barrel-chested, his thick sandy hair cut brutally short to eliminate any hint of a curl.

Hal was only a few years older than me. But two decades spent walking the largest RV lot in all of Minnesota and the Dakotas had pickled his features to a sort of indeterminate middle age. Near as I could tell, he had two modes: the "damn glad to meet you" enthusiasm he was exuding that night and a grim-faced, no-nonsense, businesslike bustle. On, or off, nothing in between.

In contrast, Pris had mastered a carefully neutral grace. She glided through rooms, bestowing the blessing of her smile on the privileged, not deigning to acknowledge those she found unworthy. She presided over church socials, hospital guilds, and the garden club like one to the manor born. Pris had been homecoming queen our senior year in high school, and it seemed she'd never really gotten off the float.

She still looked like a homecoming queen, too. Wide cornflower eyes, upswept wheaten hair, the sort of willowy figure only granted to the young and the genetically gifted . . . the only thing missing was the sash.

"Well," I said, "I'm glad you two could make it. And thank you for bringing Kiki along."

"Oh, she's just our precious, precious baby," Pris oozed. "Isn't that right, Hal?"

"Yes, dear."

"In fact, we just had her portrait done. Hal, show Izzy the pictures."

Hal sighed, but did as he was bid. He fished around in his back pants pocket for his wallet and flipped it open. He let the little plastic picture sleeve unfold, accordion-style. There were three pictures: one of Kiki wearing a big blue satin bow, one of Kiki wearing a tiny tiara (that I have to admit I admired just a bit), and one of Pris holding Kiki up like some sort of Olympic medal.

"They're lovely," I said. "She's beautiful."

I reached out a hand to stroke Kiki's silky white head.

Either the cat was psychic or had some sort of bionic sense of smell, but somehow she knew I was close before I touched her. She reared back in Pris's arms, bending like a world-class gymnast, claws spread wide and teeth bared in a crazed hiss.

"Whoa!" I jerked my hand away as Pris stumbled to keep hold of her off-balance little bundle.

Hal laughed, a booming chortle. "I don't think I've ever seen that cat move so fast in my life. Usually just lies there like a pelt."

Pris snapped at him. "Hal!"

"Oh, well, you know what I mean." He cleared his throat and patted his stomach, obviously discomfited by his wife's anger. "Always been more of a dog person."

I took that opening and ran with it. "Would you like to meet Packer? Or my sister Lucy's dog? Both Packer and Wiley are extremely friendly." In fact, Wiley was a bit too enthusiastic for a party environment, always jumping and leaping and lunging. As much as I loved the dopey guy, I half wished Lucy had left him at home. I couldn't shake the fear that he'd snatch a canapé off someone's plate or try to French kiss one of my guests.

Hal's eyes lit up, but Pris put a restraining hand on his arm. "You don't want to smell like dog, dear."

"No. No, I suppose that's right. Wouldn't want to upset the, uh, cat."

Poor Hal, I thought. Everyone should be allowed to smell like dog now and then. But then, I got the distinct impression that Kiki wasn't the only member of the household who would be offended by a dog-smelling Hal.

"Well, I should mingle," I said before I got stuck negotiating a marital spat.

I beat a hasty retreat to the barkery area, where Rena was busy feeding bits of a canine cookie to a tiny schnauzer.

"Good heavens," I said, "that cat's out for blood."

"Where?" Rena craned her head to see where I'd come from. "Who, Kiki? She looks like she's asleep."

Sure enough, when I glanced over I saw that Kiki had once again collapsed over Pris's shoulder.

"Huh. Go figure. Cat must be schizophrenic."

"If I had to live with Pris and Hal, I'd be a little crazy, too."

"Oh, I don't know . . . *Hal's* all right," I muttered.

Rena chuckled. "You're right. Pris is a special kind of horrible. But Hal's no prince himself. Kinda handsy, you know?"

"Really?" I was genuinely surprised. Hal had always been a straight arrow. Eagle Scout, deacon at Trinity Lutheran . . . and I heard he was thinking of running for mayor of Merryville.

"Oh, he'd never make a pass at *you*," Rena said.

"Thanks," I deadpanned.

Rena gave me a gentle shove. "That's not what I mean. Hal's not stupid. He'd never try anything with you, because he knows he'd never get anywhere. But girls he thinks are easy? That's a whole other story. It's never anything big, just a touch that lasts a little too long or a gaze that drifts below the neckline. That sort of thing. No overt come-on, but his interest is still unambiguous."

"I can't imagine Pris putting up with that."

"Meh." Rena shrugged. "Who knows what goes on behind closed doors? Or what people can ignore if they don't want to see?"

"I guess you're right." Who was I to judge? I didn't notice that Casey was carrying on an affair with six-percent-body-fat Rachel until their moving truck hit the Perry County line.

I scanned the room to make sure everyone was having a good time. A commotion by the front door caught my eye.

"Oh heavens," I moaned. "Speaking of things you want to ignore."

Sherry Harper stood in the open doorway of Trendy Tails, letting the biting night air inside, a crudely painted sign in her hand: NAKED IS NATURAL. Ingrid— who had surprised us all by donning a lovely green plaid shirtdress for the evening—blocked Sherry's way, but I knew she couldn't hold her off for long.

"I'll be back," I said.

I managed to make it through the milling crowd of partygoers with a smile on my face. But the moment I reached Ingrid's side, I let the mask slip.

"Sherry, honestly? I can't stop you from protesting my store, but you certainly can't come inside with that sign."

"I just wanted to warm up," she said. Her gaze shifted, and she eyed a passing mug of steaming hot cider with a look of raw yearning.

"I know it's cold, but if you want to protest, you have to do it outside. On the sidewalk. Otherwise, I'll call the cops."

"Of course you will," Sherry said, a smile of grim satisfaction on her face. "You'd let Gandhi freeze, wouldn't you?"

That's when I saw that Sherry once again had her baby sling draped across her chest. The white canvas shifted, betraying the living being nestled inside.

"Well, geez, Sherry. Why would you bring him out on a night like this?"

Her smile faltered. "I couldn't just leave him home alone."

I suspected it was Sherry who didn't want to be alone. In my experience, guinea pigs are perfectly content with the occasional hour of downtime.

"Be that as it may, you cannot bring your protest inside, Sherry. If Gandhi is cold, you need to take him home."

"Fine," she snapped. She struggled to get back out the door, fumbling the unwieldy sign.

"What was that all about?"

I turned to find my older sister, Dru, hovering behind me.

"Nothing," I said. "Just a misunderstanding."

Dru narrowed her eyes, clearly unconvinced.

Everyone said the McHale sisters could pass for triplets. Lined up in family photos, we were three Irish lasses with dark wavy hair, moss green eyes beneath straight raven brows, skin as pale as moonlit snow, and identical left-tilting smiles. But the instant we opened our mouths, our distinctive personalities left little room for confusion over who was who.

"Don't mess this up, Izzy," Dru chided. "Mom about died when Aunt Dolly said she was loaning you so much money. She's a widow on a fixed income. If you don't pay her back, you know Mom will, even if Mom and Dad can't really afford it."

"Thanks for the vote of confidence."

"I'm just being honest," my sister said, lips turned down in a familiar scowl.

In Dru's eyes, honesty justified all manner of mean and hurtful comments. Normally, I would just brush off one of her nuggets of sisterly honesty, but a part of me suspected she was right. Uncle Ned had actually left Aunt Dolly with a comfortable nest egg when he passed away, but I still felt awkward about borrowing money from family. Whether I liked it or not, my parents' well-being was in my hands, because my parents weren't as well-to-do as Aunt Dolly, but Mom would give her last dime to pay my debt to Dolly if I could not.

"Be careful, Dru," our baby sister, Lucy, quipped, as she sidled up with a glass of wine dangling loosely in her grip. "If you're not careful, your face will stick that way." Lucy twisted her mouth in an exaggerated frown, then laughed. "Lighten up. It's a party."

"Life's always a party for Lucky Lucy and Dizzy Izzy," Dru snapped, invoking our much-hated childhood nicknames. Lucy had a particular knack for never getting caught doing the wicked things she did, a knack that had encouraged her to be impulsive and a little bit spoiled. In my case, my naïveté and overall gullibility had earned me my moniker. Well, that and the time in fourth grade when Rena challenged me to a playground spinning contest and I ended up puking all over Sean Tucker.

Dru stood a little straighter in her sensible, accountant-appropriate low-heeled pumps. "Some of us have to be responsible grown-ups."

Lucy rolled her eyes. "Yes, thank heavens Dru the Shrew is around to save us from our silliness."

Lucy and I didn't care for our nicknames, but Dru positively hated hers. She turned on her heel and stalked off in a huff.

"You shouldn't have called her that," I said. "She's not a shrew. She's just . . ."

"Uptight?" Lucy suggested.

"A little. But she means well."

"So," Lucy said, craning her neck to take in the entire party, "this is what you do now, huh?"

"What do you mean?" I narrowed my eyes, studying my crafty little sister. Dru came right out and said mean things. Lucy tended to be more subtle, and I often missed the subtext of her comments. But even I could tell there was something snarky on the tip of Lucy's tongue.

"It's just that I thought you wanted to be a fashion designer."

"I am a designer."

"For dogs."

"Not just dogs," I said.

"Right. Dogs and cats."

"What's wrong with that?" I asked, cringing inwardly at the needy note in my voice.

"Nothing," Lucy said with a casual lift of one shoulder. "If that's what you want to do."

She leaned in close and cocked her head. "*Is* this what you want to do? I mean, you don't even like dogs."

"I do too like dogs," I huffed. "I live with one, don't I?"

"Casey bought that dog. You just got stuck with him."

That was true. And it was also true that dogs—big dogs, at least—made me a little nervous. Once, when I was about eight, I went to a sleepover at a friend's house. She had a Great Dane, almost as tall as I was. While the dog put up with all the other little girls patting it and wrapping ribbons around its neck, it took an intense dislike to me. When I touched it, the dog set off for the kitchen, ran two vigorous laps around the house, then ran past me, leg up, peeing on me as he went. True story.

Ever since, I had been a bit wary around big dogs.

"I like dogs," I insisted.

"Still," Lucy said, letting the word drag out like a fisherman's line.

And like a fish, she hooked me. I felt the heat rush to my face in a ferocious blush.

Why was everyone so skeptical that this was what I wanted to do? I admit, when I dreamed of a career in fashion, I had imagined designing clothes for a New York Fashion Week runway, clothes that would grace the pages of glossy magazines, clothes that would wow the paparazzi at red carpet events.

I had *not* imagined myself designing hamster hoodies and canine car coats.

But while my family, my former design school colleagues, and basically the whole wide world seemed to think I should want something more or different or better, I couldn't imagine having more fun than I did sewing teeny tiny jackets for pugs and bejeweling collars for pampered Himalayans.

If only I had a better grip on the business end of things, I'd be over the moon with joy about my new venture.

"Maybe this isn't what I imagined my life would be like," I ground out, "but did you imagine you'd be working as a court reporter? I mean, what happened to law school?"

Lucy laughed. "Oh my. Touché, sister. I didn't know you had it in you."

"Izzy!" My friend Taffy Nielson, owner of the Happy Leaf Tea Shoppe just down the street, hustled over to my side. "Tim Hodges said his wallet's gone missing," she hissed.

"Oh, that's got Val's name written all over it." I sighed. Rena's ferret had a tendency to pick pockets. Thankfully, the rodent always stashed her loot in the same spot, in the fleece-lined hammock we'd strung up for her at the back of the barkery. "I'll take care of this."

I suggested Lucy get another pupcake for her amiable border collie, Wile E. Collie, Super Genius, and sent Taffy off to rescue my mother from the clutches of Diane Jenkins, a bartender at the Grateful Grape and one of Merryville's most talkative souls.

After I returned Tim Hodges's wallet to him, verified that all of its contents were still in place, and apologized profusely, I threw myself back into the happy mix of my guests and finally came to rest by the cash register. With Jinx nestled in my arms, her rumbling purr lowering my blood pressure with every passing minute, I'd settled into a quiet tête-à-tête with Taffy, picking her brain about whether the local penny saver was a better advertising bargain than the *Gazette*, when a ruckus outside drew people to the front window of the store.

I passed a squirming Jinx to Taffy, pushed my way through the growing crowd, and yanked open the front door.

Right there on the sidewalk, Sherry was having a screaming match with a gawky man in a Vikings sweatshirt. The man—Nick Haas—held a massive Rottweiler on the end of a leash.

I made my way toward the arguing couple, careful to give the dog with his blocky head and pugnacious stance a wide berth.

"What the holy heck is going on out here?" I hissed.

"He's deranged," Sherry barked.

"I've changed, Sherry," the man pleaded. "I've changed for you. We've been apart for a couple months now, so you don't know. But if you'd give me another chance, you'd see. I've cut back on the booze, cleaned out my apartment, got rid of the weed. I've done it all because I love you. Why don't you get that?"

"Oh, I get it all right. You're a pathetic loser, Nick. You say you've cut back on the drinking, but you reek of whiskey right now. You're thirty-six years old, and your 'apartment' is in your mom's basement. Pathetic.

I've told you a thousand times, it's over." She glanced at the curious faces pressed against the front window of Trendy Tails. "Please just go, before you ruin everything."

"Sherry—"

"Loser!"

In a blink, Nick's mournful expression morphed into one of pure rage. He raised his arm, hand curling into a fist, and I instinctively drew back.

Sherry, however, lunged at him, pushing him away with outstretched hands.

And that's when the dog sprang forward, snarling and gasping as it strained against the leash in an effort to attack the person who threatened its master.

A terrified bleat escaped my lips, and I instinctively scrambled backward, away from the dog . . . even though I knew that was exactly the wrong thing to do.

Nick yanked hard on the leash. "Razor! Down! Heel!"

At first I thought there was no way the commands would seep through the bloodlust in the dog's brain, but Razor must have been well trained at some point, because with one more "Down!" he dropped back on his haunches.

I looked at Sherry and saw she had stood her ground, wrapping her arms protectively around Gandhi. I had to give her credit for thinking of the safety of her pet before her own, though she'd been supremely foolish to go on the offense against a man with that kind of dog.

"Listen," I said, "you both have to leave. Right now."

"I'm engaged in a lawful protest," Sherry said. "You can't make me leave."

"I can call the cops and report a fight in front of my store. Disturbing the peace? Assault? Half a dozen people saw you push this man." I pointed at the row of faces pressed against the glass, watching the drama unfold.

"Sherry, please, come with me," Nick said.

"I don't think that's a good idea."

I'd been so wrapped up in the fight, I hadn't realized Rena had joined us.

"You two both need to cool off." Rena handed Nick a white paper bag. "Some pupcakes for Razor. Take her home, Nick. Get some sleep."

Her? That behemoth of a dog was a girl? I was impressed.

To my surprise, Nick smiled wistfully at Rena and took the bag of treats. "You're good people, Rena Hamilton."

"Thanks, Nick. Tell your mom I said hi."

His mom? How on earth did Rena know Nick Haas's mother?

He walked off, tugging at the leash to keep Razor in check. He looked back over his shoulder at Sherry once, but he never stopped.

Rena then turned her attention to Sherry. "Go home." Rena's voice was hard, urgent.

Sherry's brows knit and her lower lip softened, quivered ever so slightly. "Rena," she said softly.

"I'm not messing around. Leave. You've done enough damage for one night."

Sherry sneezed, then straightened her spine and hoisted her sign. "I can't do that. Putting animals in clothes just isn't right. I have to stand up for what I believe."

"Right. You stand up for your principles as long as it's not an inconvenience. Is that it? I mean, you sure didn't have any trouble backing down in Minneapolis."

Minneapolis? I had no idea what Rena was talking about. But Sherry sure did. Even in the weak light of the street lamps, I could see the color drain from her face.

"That's not fair, Rena."

Rena laughed harshly. "No, you know what's not fair? You coming around here trying to run us out of business. You've never had to work a day in your life, but the rest of us have to. So we can pay our bills. So we can eat. So we can keep a roof over our heads. You get to play at being the great crusader without any thought at all as to how your behavior affects other people."

Rena's words took me aback. I knew she hadn't had a steady job in years. Rena didn't have much of a filter. If it was in her brain, it was on her tongue. That candor made her a delightful friend, but it got her in lots of trouble with bosses. You can't expect to keep your job at a high-end boutique when you tell a customer she needs to dress like a grown-up, or continue to wait tables after you dump a bottle of ketchup in the lap of a guy who grabs your tush.

Still, while I knew Rena needed a job, I hadn't realized how passionate she was about our business venture succeeding. In fact, she'd shrugged off the idea of putting her name on the incorporation papers I'd be signing the next day, insisting that she was just along for laughs.

"You can work without hurting animals," Sherry bit out.

Rena threw her hands up. "We're not hurting animals. Did you see what was going on in there?" She gestured wildly toward the store. I glanced over her shoulder and saw that the partygoers were still glued to the entertainment we were providing.

"There are dozens of animals inside, all of them getting love and attention from their people, enjoying tasty snacks, being coddled. Not one of them has been hurt tonight. Not one."

Sherry, too, started yelling. "How would you know? You can't talk to them. How would you know if they were miserable?"

"You're right, I can't talk to them. But neither can you."

This fight was going nowhere fast.

"Both of you, enough's enough." I looked Sherry square in the eye. "As long as you don't cause another scene, I won't call the cops on you. And you"—I turned to Rena—"let's go back in there and show these people a good time."

Rena screwed up her face like she was prepared to argue the point with me further. But I held out my hand, and she took it.

Together, we walked back into our boutique. Together, we were going to get our grand opening back on track.

CHAPTER
Four

After I made the rounds inside, assuring all my guests that the fuss was over and that there was nothing to be concerned about, I pulled Rena aside to make sure she was okay.

"I'm sorry I lost my cool out there."

"It's okay, Rena. She got on my last nerve, too."

Rena hoisted Jinx in her arms and pressed her face into the cat's downy fur. Jinx went limp, allowing her big body to relax into the curves and angles of Rena's frame.

"You might have been angry at Sherry, but you didn't go off on her," she moaned. "She really knows how to push my buttons. But I shouldn't have gotten into an argument with her. It doesn't accomplish anything. It's like hitting your head against a wall."

Taffy joined us, handing me a cup of mulled cider. "There's only one way to deal with nut jobs like Sherry. Kill them with kindness."

Rena snorted. "Or just plain kill them."

"Taffy's right," I said. "I probably should have let her come inside when she wanted to." A sleepy Packer, worn out from frolicking with all the other dogs (and maybe toying with a cat or two), waddled up to me and pressed the top of his head against my calf. I dropped to one knee so I could massage his wrinkly head and give his ears a good scratch. "Maybe if Sherry'd seen how happy the animals were, she would have backed down. Or I could have introduced her to Mom. Mom would have worn her down to a nub, taken all the fight right out of her."

If you really could kill people with kindness, my mom would be the equivalent of a nuclear bomb. Forget lemonade . . . Mom could turn lemons into a meringue pie with nothing but a smile and the cheery force of her will.

"I made amends," Rena said. "I asked Ken to make a plate for Sherry. He wasn't very happy about it, but he fixed a plate and wrapped it in foil to keep it warm. I took that, a bag of my human chow, and a couple of melon balls for Gandhi out to her."

"Really? Rena, I'm proud of you. That was remarkably mature of you."

She rolled her eyes. "Geez, I'm in my thirties. You shouldn't be shocked that I acted like a grown-up."

"That's not what I meant. It's just that I get the sense there's bad blood between you and Sherry. It must have been tough to swallow your pride and make that peace offering."

She shrugged, but I could see a hint of color in her cheeks. She began futzing with Jinx's collar, tucking it beneath the edge of the kitty capelet.

Keeping my head down and looking up at Rena through my lashes, I casually posed the question that had been eating at me all evening. "What happened in Minneapolis?"

She paused, midtuck. "It's a long story. And old news. We were both there for a few months about ten years ago, while you were in Madison. I'd rather not dredge it up."

We're all entitled to our secrets, but it hurt to have Rena shut me out. We'd drifted apart when I'd left for college and Rena had stayed in Merryville to look after her dad, a chronic alcoholic with a failing liver and a nasty disposition. I knew, objectively, that we'd both had lives during those years. Friends, adventures, highs, and lows.

But when Casey started his residency and we moved back to town, it felt like Rena and I slipped right back into "best friend" mode. She had been with me during Casey's great defection, had seen me at my most pitiable, had matched me spoon-for-spoon as I drowned my misery in ice cream. I thought we were transparent to each other, but now I learned there was a shadow, a part of Rena I couldn't see.

"Okay," I said, trying to mask the note of hurt in my voice. I stood up and smoothed down the skirt of my dress with my palms. "Well, whatever it was, I'm glad you moved past it," I added briskly.

"Who says I moved past it? I took the woman a plate of food. We're not BFFs."

I bristled at her snappish tone. Whatever had happened between Sherry and Rena, it brought out the worst in my friend: the mercurial mood swings she'd inherited—or learned—from her unstable dad.

"Girls," Taffy clucked. "Don't let Sherry's nastiness ruin the evening. It looks like she's gone now, and I, for one, am having a wonderful time."

I craned my neck to peer out the front window. Sure enough, there was no sign of Sherry or her doom-and-gloom placard.

I forced a smile. "I'm having fun, too. And I want to thank you both for helping me out tonight. I couldn't have done it without you."

Rena had checked out of our conversation. She had retreated into her own grumpy little world. Her narrow shoulders slumped, and she let Jinx slither from her grasp.

The faint sound of an old-fashioned phone ringer prompted Rena to fish her cell out of her little purse. She looked at the screen, her frown deepening at whatever message she saw there.

She blew out a heavy sigh. "I need some air," she said. "I think I'll take Packer for a walk. Poor little guy's been holding it for hours."

I resisted the urge to snatch the phone from her hands and read the text myself. The urge to insist that she stay put until we'd closed the breach between us. The urge to demand she spill her guts to me right then and there.

"Sure," I said, forcing a cheery tone. "His leash is hanging behind the counter."

She tucked her phone back in her bag and headed toward the back of the store, pausing to grab Packer's leash and her own down parka and to call my dog to her side.

"Wow," Taffy said. "She's in a funk."

"I know. I wish I knew why."

Taffy looped her arm through mine. "She'll come around. You know Rena."

"That's the problem," I muttered. "I thought I knew Rena. But now I'm not so sure."

The party was winding down, guests drifting away in ones and twos, while those who remained settled into exhausted camaraderie. Ingrid, Aunt Dolly, my mom, and my older sister, Dru, formed a knot around Ingrid's photo album, *ooh*ing and *aah*ing over pictures of Harvey as a young man. Paul Haakinen, Ingrid's erstwhile handyman, and my dad were passing a flask back and forth like a couple of delinquents at a high school dance while they traded fishing tips. Xander and my little sister, Lucy, shared a set of earbuds, their heads bobbing in time to something on Xander's MP3 player.

As I gathered empty cups and plates into a trash bag, Taffy followed behind me with a damp cloth, mopping up stray crumbs and the occasional puddle of spilled cider.

I dropped the last of the cups into the trash bag at my feet. It wasn't quite full, but I suddenly needed a breath of air, a minute away to think about the inexplicable tension between me and Rena and how I might make it better when she and Packer returned.

I cinched the yellow plastic drawstring on my bag and took Taffy's bag from her, too.

"I'll be right back. I'm just gonna run these out to the Dumpster."

Taffy offered me a small smile of sympathy.

Next to Rena, Taffy was probably my best friend. The Nielson family had owned a cottage on Badger Lake for three generations. Taffy and her sister, Jolly, though, had moved into the cottage as year-round residents a half dozen years before, after their parents were struck and killed by a drunk driver while walking the family dog.

Taffy and Rena were both short, making me feel Amazonian in their company, but where Rena was all spikes and angles, Taffy was as soft and tender as a buttermilk biscuit. With a halo of golden ringlets, eyes like pools of melted toffee, Cupid's bow lips, and Rubenesque curves, she defined comfort. Her smile felt like a hug, and I needed one about then.

Returning her smile with a weary one of my own, I hefted the bags, one in either hand, and pushed into the kitchen.

Ken was still puttering around, packing leftover chicken and pasties into tinfoil trays to send home with the last guests.

"Everyone gone?" he asked.

"Just about. The inner circle is still hanging around, but all the customers have left. You can head out whenever you want."

"Great. I just need to wash up the last of the trays. Everything else is packed and ready to go."

He leaned his hip against the edge of the kitchen sink and wiped his hands on a candy-striped tea towel. The dainty towel looked out of place in his large, square hands. He had the beefy build of a former football player, the sort of physique that seemed to fill up the room, consume all the air. He was carefully polished, dressed like an urban accountant playing at country squire, with his khakis pressed, his loafers spotless, his braided belt looped just so. Still, there was something vaguely threatening about him. Something that made me want to take a step back.

"You had a great turnout," he said.

"Thanks. Yeah, I'm happy with how it all went."

I found myself seeking the doors with my eyes, as though my subconscious was plotting my escape. I forced myself to meet his gaze.

"The food was great," I said. "I handed out your cards to everyone."

His lips flattened in a grim smile. "Great. Two years ago *Midwest Magazine* listed me as one of the top ten rising stars in the culinary world, and now I'm passing out cards, hoping to cater a company Christmas party or a sweet sixteen bash."

I didn't know quite what to do with that statement. After all, we weren't friends.

"Well," I said, "we do what we have to do."

He laughed. "Ain't that the truth. When you were a little girl, did you dream of designing clothes for spoiled schnauzers?"

His question hit home, and I felt a rush of warmth to my cheeks. As if my sisters weren't bad enough, now this total stranger felt the need to question my life choices. "Honestly? No." I hoped that would end the matter.

But then he nodded like I'd confirmed his grim worldview. For some reason, I didn't like the idea that he and I were on the same side of some philosophical divide. "Life doesn't always go as planned," I argued, "but that's not always a bad thing."

Ken quirked one thick brow.

Well, Ken might not believe in the guiding hand of fate, but I sure did. I wasn't about to let his sour mood put another layer of tarnish on my grand opening.

"Would you get the door for me?" I asked. I hefted the trash bags a little higher to emphasize my need to keep moving.

He strolled across the kitchen, that irksome half smile still on his face, and pulled open the heavy oak door.

I scooted past him, pushing open the storm door with my hip. Three concrete steps carried me down to the brick paved alleyway that ran between the houses on Maple and those on Oak, one block over. Now that many of the houses in the historic district had been converted to shops and galleries, the alley was lined with trash receptacles, stacks of wooden pallets waiting to be recycled, and the occasional storage shed.

The light in the alley came primarily from a number of security lights rigged with motion sensors. Down the block, a light blinked on as a stray cat skulked along the wall. My own movement tripped a light on the back of the Oak Street building that housed Xander's Spin Doctor record shop and a salon called Shear Madness.

I paused to take a deep breath, letting the cool, damp air fill my lungs. From inside, I heard Ingrid's shockingly deep belly laugh, and the thud of someone knocking something over. Maybe a chair.

The homey sounds, muffled by the warm redbrick walls, served to emphasize the delicious silence in the alley. I gave myself a moment to simply enjoy the peace.

I hadn't done that much over the past couple of

years. When Casey had packed up his boxes and moved out, I'd filled the space he left with friends and family: Rena's biting wit, Taffy's gentle chatter, Packer's silly antics, Jinx's insistent snuggling, my mother's endless stories, my sisters' toothless bickering, Ingrid's bluff advice. The constant stream of words and laughter kept me upright during some challenging times. But I'd forgotten the singular pleasure of solitude.

Now that I had taken this first tottering step into a future that was mine and mine alone, I felt like I could bear the silence again, like I could be alone without feeling lonely.

Another crash from inside broke my moment of quiet meditation. If I wasn't careful, Dad and Paul would get tipsy and start "fixing" things.

I shared a Dumpster with Richard Greene, who sold rare books and military memorabilia out of the house next door. As I picked my way across the uneven brickwork in that direction, I found myself up on my tiptoes, careful not to disturb my curmudgeonly neighbor.

As gently as I could, I flipped the lid of the container open and heaved the bags up over the side.

I sidled around the trash container to get a good grip on the lid so I could close it without making an almighty racket. The light over Richard's back door flickered on when I stepped into the range of its sensor.

And I froze.

The new light revealed a still form sprawled across the alleyway. At first, I mistook it for a bundle of rubbish strewn across the bricks, as though perhaps an animal had ripped open a trash bag and rifled through the contents, looking for something choice.

But then I saw a hand, its fingers curled upward, as though grasping for something just out of reach.

As I slowly approached, I began to make out additional details: a brown paper bag discarded by the body, dark shadows, pieces of something spilling forth. A loose purple scarf trailed over the outstretched arm. A curl of dark red hair glowed in the harsh yellow light. A shoe—thick-soled and square—dangled off a foot clad in woolly tights.

Another step brought me close enough to make out the features on the still, pale face. Sherry Harper, her face contorted in a rictus of pain, her eyes glassy and flat in the harsh glare.

I couldn't tear my eyes from her face.

While I stood there, trying to process what I was seeing, the motion-sensitive lights suddenly flicked off.

And I screamed.

CHAPTER
Five

MacArthur arrived on the scene first, bounding from Richard Greene's back door the instant he opened it. As usual, the dog didn't bark, but in his excitement, his breath rushed from his body in deep, rasping pants. He took up a position at my side, head raised, alert for danger. Normally, the proximity of such a huge dog would have sent me into a tailspin, but I found myself grasping his collar and holding on for dear life.

"Who's there? What's going on?" I found Richard's sharp demands strangely reassuring.

By that point, other doors onto the alley had opened, including 801 Maple's, and security lights had snapped on everywhere.

"Call nine-one-one." There's no way anyone heard my faint plea, but all around me the cry of "Call nine-one-one!" rang out.

Richard leapt from his back stoop, not bothering

with the stairs, and rushed toward me. I felt a momentary flicker of worry for the impact of his old joints on the cold, unforgiving bricks, but age didn't seem to slow him at all. He drew up short when he reached my side. "Sweet mercy," he muttered.

His big, callused hand wrapped around my upper arm, and he gently tugged me away from Sherry's body. "What happened here?" he barked.

"I don't know. Is she dead?"

Richard glanced past me, to Sherry's still form, and nodded. "I'm no doctor, but I've seen enough corpses to know one when I see one." He frowned. "Is that Sherry?"

I nodded weakly.

"What on God's green earth is she doing in our alley?"

"I don't know. She was protesting in front of Trendy Tails earlier, but I thought she'd gone home."

He cursed under his breath. "That girl never could mind her own business. Should have known she'd meet a bad end."

I could hear sirens now, and a small crowd had begun to form, keeping a respectful distance from Sherry's body.

"Do you know her?" I asked Richard.

He nodded grimly. "Her father was a regular customer of mine before he passed. Collected first edition military histories. Knew more about the French and Indian War than anyone I ever met. Good man. Sherry's shenanigans caused him no end of grief. But he loved her more than his own life."

With an ear-splitting crescendo of sirens, the police and paramedics arrived simultaneously, the cruiser pulling into the alley from the south side and the ambulance pulling in from the north.

Richard kept his grip on my arm and angled his body between me and the approaching officers. I knew Richard didn't exactly like me. Not only did he worry that my business would destroy the peace and order of his world, but he'd made it clear he thought I didn't have the sense God gave little bunny rabbits. That animosity made his chivalrous behavior all the more touching.

While I normally thought of myself as a twenty-first-century independent woman, I gladly let Richard deal with the first responders, only answering questions aimed directly at me.

Yes, I'd found the body. Yes, I knew Sherry. No, I hadn't seen anyone else in the alley. No, I didn't know what had happened to her.

As the police shepherded Richard and me away from Sherry's body, I glanced over to the little knot of people who'd spilled out the back door of Trendy Tails. Their reactions, written plainly on their wonderful, familiar faces, ranged from Lucy's morbid curiosity to my mom's hand-wringing concern. But two people—Ken and Rena—stood apart from the others, and they were the ones who drew my attention.

I couldn't read Ken's expression clearly, but I could have sworn I saw the ghost of a smile brush his lips. And that seemed like a very strange reaction to a crime scene.

But Rena's reaction seemed stranger still. The strobing lights from the ambulance glittered as they struck her face. My feisty friend wept for Sherry Harper, a woman she claimed to despise.

*   *   *

Mom and Ken West passed around warm mulled cider while the police took statements from everyone still lingering around Trendy Tails. Most were short and sweet: Everyone had seen Sherry acting like a crazy woman early in the evening, no one knew where she'd gone after she gave up on picketing Trendy Tails, and no one had the faintest idea how she came to be dead in our alley.

Poor Rena sat tailor-style on the floor by the big oak armoire, Jinx curled in her lap and Valrhona draped across her shoulders. She looked so forlorn, I finally suggested she take the animals up to my apartment until it was her turn to give a statement.

When it was my turn, my mom, Aunt Dolly, and Ingrid formed a feminine phalanx around me, each resting a gentle hand on me as I sat at the cheery folk-art table. Officer Jack Collins, who'd stolen the valentines from the brown lunch bag taped to the back of my chair in third grade, tried to ask me pointed questions, but every time he got a hint of steel in his voice, my bodyguards stared him into blushing silence.

"It's okay," I insisted. "I want to help. I just don't know anything. I mean, how did she die? Did she have a heart attack or something?"

"The coroner will have to determine the cause of death." Jack cut his eyes to the side, like he wanted to make sure it was safe to share a secret. "No blood, though. Hard to say."

"So you don't suspect foul play?" Aunt Dolly asked. Aunt Dolly read a lot of mysteries, and I'm sure her mind was racing through a list of possible whodunits and howdunits.

"We can't rule anything out at this point. But really, I should be asking the questions here."

"I think we have a right to know what happened," my mom chimed in, her voice ringing with the righteous indignation she'd used on many a school board member who had threatened to cut funding for the humanities. "Sherry Harper was in my honors English lit class when she was a junior. She worked with Dolly on the committee that planted all those flowers on Main Street. That child was a part of our community, and we have a right to know what happened to her."

"Mom," I soothed, "Jack's not trying to keep a secret. He just doesn't know. He's trying to do his job."

"Maybe I could speak with Izzy alone," Jack suggested.

"Young man," Ingrid barked, "are you trying to eject me from my own dining room?"

Of course, the room hadn't been a real dining room in years, and Jack would have been well within his rights to ask Ingrid to leave so he could interview a witness in peace, but that didn't stop him from blushing to the roots of his buzz-cut hair.

"No, ma'am. I j-j-just . . ." he stuttered.

"We'll hush up while you go on and ask your questions," Ingrid said, more than a hint of old-fashioned schoolmarm in her voice. "But we're going to stand right here while you do it. Taffy! Go make Izzy a cup of that stress-relief tea of yours."

And with that, Ingrid declared me too distraught to handle the police on my own. I gave Jack an apologetic smile and nodded encouragingly.

He started with simple questions, getting the order

of the evening's events down on paper. He took careful note of the time of Nick's fight with Sherry, when Rena took out the plate of food, when we noticed Sherry had left, and what I'd seen (absolutely nothing) when I took out the trash.

"So the last person at the party to actually speak with Ms. Harper was Rena Hamilton?"

I felt a twinge of nameless unease.

"As far as I know. I, uh, don't remember anyone leaving between then and when we noticed that Sherry had left, but I might have missed someone. It was a big party."

"Uh-huh," he muttered, making a note in his spiral-bound notebook. "And Miss Hamilton and Miss Harper had words earlier in the evening?"

The sense of unease intensified. "Well, yes. We both had words with Sherry. We weren't happy about her making a ruckus during our grand opening."

Jack nodded and made another note in his book. I craned my head, trying to read his scrawl upside down. I glanced back up to find him glaring at me.

Busted.

I offered him a smile. "It was just a disagreement. We were okay with the picketing. Or mostly okay. But the screaming match with Nick? That was just too much."

I had noticed that the tenor of his interrogation had changed from simple who-when-where sorts of questions to questions about feelings and fights. That sense of unease coalesced.

"You don't think she was murdered or anything, do you?"

He sighed.

"Right," I said. "Too early to say."

My mom shook her head. "I can't imagine anyone hurting Sherry. She was a bit of a pill, but everyone knew she was harmless."

She wasn't harmless to Ken West's business, I thought . . . but I had the good sense to keep my mouth shut.

At that moment, Taffy came bustling in with a tray bearing a half dozen stoneware mugs and a teapot covered with a quilted cozy. She offered cups all around.

"This is a special blend," she said. "Chamomile, valerian, and just a hint of lavender. Very relaxing." Taffy's tea shop sold all manner of traditional and herbal teas, and she could usually be counted on to have some blend to treat whatever ailed you.

Officer Collins declined her offer—truthfully, he would have had a tough time asserting a commanding presence while grasping a steaming mug of tea—but the rest of us accepted. Jack tapped his pen impatiently while we passed around sugar and wedges of lemon.

"Now," he said, trying to regain control of the situation, "who was still here when you found the body?"

"Sherry," my mom insisted. "When she found Sherry. Don't call her a body. She was a person."

Jack blushed. "Sorry, ma'am. Who was here when you found Sherry?"

"Everyone here in the room, my dad and Paul, Ken West, Xander, and Rena," I said.

"No," Taffy interrupted. "Rena was out with Packer."

Jack paused midnote. "Miss Hamilton wasn't here?"

"No," Taffy continued, apparently oblivious to the

hard edge of his question. "She'd been in a funk after the whole brouhaha with Sherry, and then she got a text that irked her even more, and she offered to take Packer for a walk."

"A text? Who from?"

"She didn't say," I responded. "But I'm sure it wasn't from Sherry. I don't think the two of them had spoken in years."

"Uh-huh. And *why* hadn't they spoken in so long?"

I felt a blush licking up my neck and across my cheeks. "They just hadn't," I said, hoping I didn't sound defensive. "Besides, if Sherry texted Rena, you can just check Sherry's phone."

"We didn't find a phone with her," Jack said . . . and then he blushed, because surely he shouldn't be providing us with such details.

Jack frowned and flipped back through his notes. "Miss Hamilton threatened Miss Harper earlier in the evening, didn't she?"

"What?" I gasped. "Absolutely not. Like I said, she was peeved, and so was I. But there were no threats."

"'Or just plain kill them,'" Jack read from his notes.

This time, Taffy gasped. "Oh dear. I think you're taking that too literally. It was just a joke, I'm sure." She shot me an apologetic look. "He asked about our conversation after the scene with Sherry, and I just happened to remember that I said the way to deal with nut . . . uh, people like Sherry, was to kill them with kindness and Rena said 'or just plain kill them.'"

Taffy had an almost surreal ability to remember snippets of conversation. It made it great fun to gossip with her, because she remembered every bit of dirt she heard in perfect detail, but at that precise moment her memory proved highly inconvenient.

She leaned across the table to snag Jack's attention. "But it was just a joke, I swear. I only mentioned it because I wanted to emphasize that we were already laughing about the incident."

"Uh-huh." Jack nodded. "Maybe. But I think it may be time for me to talk to Miss Hamilton."

CHAPTER
Six

Before we could fetch Rena from my third-floor apartment, someone rapped sharply on the glass door of the shop, the knocks like Morse code—two long, two short, one long.

My subconscious recognized the sound first, sending all the blood from my brain and leaving me lightheaded. I knew that knock.

I hopped up to go answer the door and saw a figure standing on the other side, the overhead porch light casting deep shadows over his face. Still, there was no mistaking that long, lanky physique, or the posture: a strange mix of nervous energy and casual attitude, hands shoved deep in the pockets of his parka, head down as though he were contemplating his shoelaces, whole body rocked up on the balls of his feet.

I paused with my hand on the doorknob, the door half open, and he raised his head to meet my gaze. Black coffee eyes beneath straight heavy brows; a wide, mobile mouth now bracketed by deep laugh lines; a mop of unruly dark curls.

Sean Tucker.

Sean Tucker had pledged his love for me the week before we graduated from Merryville High. And with that pledge, he killed the friendship we'd shared since he'd moved to Minnesota in the fourth grade.

I still remember every detail of that night. A sudden storm had blown through, dotting the sills of my open windows with droplets of water and leaving a scent of ozone in the cool damp air. I'd pulled my favorite pink and green quilt up to my chin and was trying to drift to sleep, visions of my perfect future with Casey Alter dancing in my head.

The soft *twang* of a pebble hitting my window screen jolted me alert. A second pebble hit the side of the house with a *thunk* that sent me scrambling out of bed.

"Hush," I called down, expecting to see Casey in my yard. In my girlish fantasy, he would be standing beneath the apple tree, a single rose in his hand, ready to serenade me softly.

But instead of Casey's head of wavy blond hair, I saw Sean's dark, rumpled curls. His ten-speed leaned against the apple tree, and the rainwater had plastered his T-shirt to his scrawny body. Even from the second floor I could count his ribs.

"Sean?"

"Izzy."

"What the heck are you doing here in the middle of the night?" I hissed.

"Izzy, I love you."

I glanced over my shoulder, as though he might be talking to someone else.

"No, you don't."

He flashed a smile, there and gone like a streak of lightning. "Yes. Yes, I do. And I think you love me, too."

My breath caught.

"No. No, I don't," I repeated more forcefully, letting my voice rise above a whisper. I looked over my shoulder again, this time worried that all our chitchat might attract my parents' attention. Or, worse, attract Lucy's attention. If my bratty baby sister heard even a bit of this conversation, she'd never let me live it down.

I dropped to my knees and rested my elbows on the damp windowsill.

"I mean, Sean, of course I love you. But like a friend, you know? I'm *in* love with Casey."

He braced his legs apart and clenched his fists at his sides, like he was itching for a fight. "You just think you love Casey. I know he's smart and handsome and all, but he doesn't treat you the way you deserve to be treated. He takes you for granted. You're like his sidekick, not his partner."

"No," I breathed, mortified that he would even suggest a crack in my rock-solid relationship. Though, to be honest, a tiny part of my brain immediately called up the image of Casey soliciting a drink refill by tapping an empty glass against my arm, not even looking at me or breaking the flow of his conversation. But that was just a comfortable relationship, I told that rebellious bit of gray matter, like we didn't even need words to communicate with each other. That wasn't him taking me for granted at all.

"I love Casey," I insisted. "Please don't ruin this for me."

Sean's head dropped forward, and I could see his shoulders lift and fall in a mighty sigh.

"I won't ruin anything, Izzy. But I won't stand back and watch you throw away your life on a user and a loser like Casey Alter. I'll respect your decision, but I can't support it."

He jerked his bike upright and began walking it off into the darkness. Another flash of distant lightning ripped open the sky, and I swear I could see the droplets of water clinging to the dark curls at his nape.

"Sean," I called softly.

I didn't know if he could hear me, but he didn't turn around, and I didn't know what I would have said if he had.

Instead, my mother's voice calling from downstairs, inquiring about the commotion, pulled me away from the window in a hurry. But not without one last glance at Sean's retreating form, his slumped shoulders and hangdog shuffle.

Of course I'd seen Sean over the years: at graduation, class reunions, occasional encounters at the Grateful Grape or across the brunch crowd at the Thistle and Ivy. But that night was the last night he spoke to me as a friend rather than an acquaintance.

"Izzy, I love you." How could four simple words cause such a rift?

And now, on this awful momentous night, here he was again. I could only imagine what earthshaking words he might utter this time.

He wasted no time. "Rena called me. Said y'all were having quite a night."

Sean's family had moved to Merryville from a little town right where Tennessee, Mississippi, and Alabama kiss, and he'd never quite shaken the hint of a drawl in his voice. My mom, who'd had Sean for eleventh-grade English and who continued to play canasta with Sean's mother, Hetty, told me he'd gone back south after graduation, first to Tulane and then to attend law school at Ole Miss. His stint south of the Mason-Dixon Line had clearly sunk his southern roots deeper into his vocal chords, rounding his vowels and resulting in the occasional dropped consonant.

"You could say that," I said, as I let him pass and closed the door. "Sherry Harper is dead."

"I know. I was with Carla and her mom at the Grateful Grape when the police arrived to notify them."

Even though Sean and I didn't move in the same circles anymore, I knew he'd been dating Carla Harper, Sherry's cousin, for over a year. My sources (namely, my mom and Aunt Dolly) suggested that wedding bells would be chiming soon. I was a little surprised that Sean had left Carla under the circumstances.

He was looking past me into the interior of the shop. "It looks real nice, Izzy," he said. "Sorry we couldn't make it for the grand opening. We had Carla's mom's birthday dinner at La Ming, and then we all went to the Grateful Grape to celebrate."

While Carla had been born to the family trust, her mother had grown up next door to Rena's dad, so far on the other side of the tracks that they couldn't even hear the train whistle. Virginia Larsen moved way, way up the socioeconomic ladder when she became Virginia Harper. She didn't inherit any of the family money directly, as she wasn't a blood relative of the paterfamilias, Grandpa Harper. Still, Carla had bought her mother the space to open the Grateful Grape, a wine bar that served small plates and fancy desserts.

While our grand opening had been an open house, Sean made it sound like he'd been issued a special invitation, and I wondered if maybe my mom or Rena had personally asked him to come. And then I wondered why they wouldn't have told me if they had. And then I decided I was being a crazy person, and pushed the whole matter out of my mind.

"Listen, I need to talk to Rena, if that's okay," he continued.

"Oh. Of course. Let me run get her."

But before I got halfway across the room, I heard Rena practically thundering down the stairs, her boots making an almighty racket as she pounded down the wooden treads, the clicking of Packer's toenails on the bare wood signaling that he was not far behind her. She tumbled into the room in a flurry of bony arms and legs.

"Sean!" She dashed across the room and threw herself into his arms. "Thank you for coming. Thank you so much."

He bent his tall frame to wrap her in an awkward hug. "Of course. You said it was an emergency."

She pulled him aside, to the counter by the cash register, and they put their heads together in a hushed and frantic conversation. He handed her a pen, then pulled a sheaf of papers from an inside jacket pocket and flipped through them one by one, pausing now and again for her to scribble something in the margins. Finally, she reached into her black cross-body purse, pulled out a crumpled bill, and handed it to him.

Sean stood up a little straighter, squaring his shoulders with an authority I didn't associate with my gawky teenage friend.

"Officer Collins, my name is Sean Tucker. I am an attorney and I represent Rena Hamilton. Any questions you have for her should be directed to me."

CHAPTER
Seven

Jack Collins left with very little information about Rena's relationship with Sherry Harper.

What little he got came from Sean's lips, not Rena's. Jack would ask a question, Rena would whisper in Sean's ear, and Sean would reply with either a terse answer or a simple "next."

My mom, Aunt Dolly, Ingrid, Taffy, and I traded anxious glances throughout the interview. I know we were all thinking the same thing: It was like watching a cop drama on TV, except it was happening right in front of us. The notion that Rena might need to speak through an attorney seemed positively surreal.

Finally, Jack asked about the text message Rena had received at the end of the party, inquiring whether he could perhaps just take a look at Rena's phone. This prompted a frantic exchange between Rena and Sean.

In the end, Rena folded her arms across her chest, mouth set in a mutinous pout, and Sean sighed.

"My client assures you that there is nothing on her phone related to Sherry Harper or her untimely death, but she declines to let you look through her phone records without a warrant. And I'd bet dollars to doughnuts you can't find a judge willing to sign off on a warrant based on nothing more than your powerful desire to get a look at that phone."

When Jack left, his shoulders slumped in defeat, we all pinned Rena with stern glares.

"What?" she challenged.

"Why not just give them your phone, Rena?" I asked. "It makes it look like you have something to hide."

"I'm not hiding anything. It's just private, that's all. I didn't get a text from Sherry, and beyond that, it just isn't anyone's business."

"All right, you and I can talk about this later," Sean said, "but right now I think it's time everyone got some sleep."

I glanced at the clock hanging on the back wall of the barkery. It was nearly three in the morning.

"Rena, dear, you've had a terrible evening," my mom chimed in. "Can we drive you home?"

"Thanks, Mrs. McHale. But if it's okay with Izzy, I'll crash here tonight." She shot me a questioning look.

"Of course you can stay. As long as I have a couch, you have a place to sleep."

During the round of goodbye hugs, I found myself facing Sean. I shifted from foot to foot, not really sure how to proceed.

"It was good to see you, Izzy," he said, breaking the awkward silence by extending a professional hand.

"Wish it had been under better circumstances." Before I could grasp his hand in return, Packer wiggled his way between us and began tapping his paw on Sean's shoe. Sean bent down to give Packer's flanks a brisk rubbing, sending my dog into a frenzy of joy. Sean stood again just as I was beginning to join them at floor level. As we shifted past each other, one of his curls brushed against my bare arm, a feather-soft caress. I jolted upright and took a step back.

He held out his hand again, and this time I took it. His palms were square, his fingers long—solid, strong hands. I shivered.

"Do you like animals?" I asked, instantly realizing how abrupt and weird the question must sound.

"I do," he said with a smile. "In fact, I have a basset hound named Blackstone. Why?"

"Oh, well, we're hosting a pet costume contest at this year's Halloween Howl. We'll have prizes, treats for the animals. I was wondering if you'd be interested in judging. It might be good publicity for your practice."

"I'm honored," he said, "but I'm sure to have clients who are entered. It might be awkward."

"Oh. Sure, that makes sense. Still, you should come." I suddenly realized I was still gripping his hand, so I dropped it. "With Carla, of course."

"Carla's not much of a pet person, but I bet we'll stop by. I think her mom mentioned that the Grateful Grape is involved this year."

"Right." Of course. I should have known Sean already had a reason to attend the party, and I felt silly for having invited him.

"Actually," he said, "Carla's mom has a corgi that she loves beyond reason, and I know Virginia would be thrilled to dress Sir Francis up for Halloween. Maybe you could ask her to be one of your judges. You're right that it would be good publicity, and the Grateful Grape could use it."

"That's a great idea," I said, trying to inject a little enthusiasm in my voice. I don't know why I was so disappointed that Sean had declined my invitation to judge the contest.

When everyone had gone, I marched Rena upstairs—leaving Ingrid at her own apartment door on the second floor—and loaned her a pair of yoga pants and one of Casey's old sweatshirts, which hung nearly to her knees.

Once we were both in comfy clothes and huddled together on my patchwork-covered couch, Packer hunkered down between us and Jinx sprawled over Rena's lap, I got down to brass tacks.

"I want to know what happened in Minneapolis."

Rena ignored my question. "I hadn't realized how much I missed spending time with you and Sean until I saw you two together tonight."

I shrugged. "No reason you can't hang out with Sean."

Rena chuckled. "Who says I haven't been hanging out with Sean? I see him all the time."

I drew back, stunned at this revelation. "Why didn't you ever mention it?"

She cocked a brow and tipped her head to one side, silently communicating a big "duh."

"You didn't talk about him; he didn't talk about you. . . . I decided to keep my head down and wait for you two to work it out. Never guessed it would take this long."

"Well if you've been seeing Sean all along, I'm not sure what there was for you to miss."

"What I meant is that I missed having the three of us together. I mean, you're my best friend, but Sean was always like the third leg in our relationship, balancing us out, making us even stronger."

I rested my hand on Packer's head, and ran my finger over the crease at the base of his ear. "I guess I've missed that, too. I just didn't realize it."

Rena was staring down at Jinx as she rhythmically stroked her soft fur. "I know why you and Sean stopped speaking," she said. "He told me."

"Oh."

"Yeah, you pretty much broke his heart. But like I said, I thought you two would get past it, eventually be friends again. I never imagined you would shut him out of your life entirely."

"What can I say? It was stupid. I was young. I waited for him to apologize to me, when I probably should have been the one apologizing."

"I don't think anyone needed to apologize," Rena said. "You just needed to get past that one little incident and move on. But I guess it was a big deal to both of you."

I'd never thought it had been a big deal to me, but after my reaction to seeing Sean on my doorstep that evening, I wasn't so sure. Now, though, it was my turn to ignore her question. "Come on, Rena. What happened between you and Sherry in Minneapolis?"

Rena cocked her purple head. "It was stupid. I was young," she said, echoing my own excuse back to me. "Can we just leave it at that?"

"No. Listen, I'm not going to judge you. I just need to know."

"After high school, I went a little wild. It sounds pathetic, but you and Sean were my only real friends, the only people who didn't act like I had some sort of disease. And you'd both just left me."

It felt like she'd smacked me in the head with a two-by-four. "I didn't leave you," I argued.

She waved her hand dismissively. "I know you didn't mean to ditch me, but that's effectively what happened. You were in Madison, Sean was in Louisiana, and I was stuck here. You guys were so busy, you hardly ever came home."

"You never came to see me, either," I said.

"Don't get defensive. You asked what happened, and I'm telling you. Besides, I couldn't come visit you. What would I have done? Hung out in your dorm room while you went to class? Gone to parties where I didn't know anyone? Please."

I opened my mouth to argue, but then snapped it shut. She was right. All those years, I'd never really questioned what Rena did while I was away. I'd call her to tell her about my new friends, about Casey, about classes and work, but she rarely offered anything about her own life . . . and I didn't ask. When I came home for the occasional holiday, I just assumed she'd be around, ready to go out and take up right where we'd left off. Like she was a doll, tucked away in its box, waiting for me to pick her up to play whenever the mood struck me.

I'd been selfish. A terrible friend.

"I'm sorry." The words didn't begin to cover it, but she smiled.

"Hey, we were *both* young, right?"

"And stupid," I agreed.

"Exactly. Anyway, I got a fake ID and started hanging out down at the Silent Woman a lot, and that's where I met Nick and Sherry. Nick was a quiet guy, but Sherry was a force. I couldn't help being drawn into her orbit."

A shadow of a smile kissed her lips, and her eyes took on a dreamy cast. Whatever had happened to sour her relationship with Sherry, Rena remembered those early days of raising hell fondly.

I felt a pang of jealousy.

"She was older, you know," Rena continued, picking mindlessly at the cuff of the sweatshirt, "and I thought it was cool how she was always angry about stuff. She talked about politics and corruption and the little guy getting what was his."

"Right. Like she's the little guy."

"Oh, I know. Her jeans were old, but they were from a vintage clothing boutique, not the Salvation Army. And that old Saab she drove probably cost more than my dad's house. But I didn't exactly examine her financial records. The words coming out of her mouth appealed to me."

"So how did you two end up in Minneapolis?"

She raised her hands to cover her face and blew out a big sigh before dropping them back in her lap. "Sherry was part of this antiglobalization group. We went down to Minneapolis to protest the government's response to Y2K."

"Y2K?"

"You remember . . . how everyone was scared that all the computers would crash on January first of 2000."

"Oh right," I said, "I remember now. Casey and I were on a ski trip for the holiday and he joked that we'd be stuck in the chalet like the Donner party . . . but with lots of cocoa and a huge collection of eighties movies on VHS."

"Right. Well, Sherry's group thought that the whole computer crashing thing was a massive international conspiracy that would allow governments to conveniently 'lose' information about all the corporate corruption and kickbacks that greased the wheels of widespread globalization."

"Really?"

Rena winced. "Yeah, it sounds crazy. Young and stupid, remember? Sherry sounded like she knew what she was talking about, and all these other activists from Duluth and Des Moines and even from Fargo met us in Minneapolis so we could march outside the Federal Reserve building there."

"What happened?"

"Things got out of hand. This woman from Duluth brought white spray paint, and a bunch of the protesters started writing all over the building." She made a wide, sweeping gesture, as though demonstrating the scope of the graffiti. " 'Whitewash.' One of the security guards tried to stop them, and someone sprayed him in the face. Pretty soon, the police arrived, and all hell broke loose.

"Sherry and I were pressed against the building, so there was nowhere to run. She was holding a can of paint, but when the cops started making their way toward us, she shoved it in my backpack."

"No," I gasped.

She smiled, a crooked little half smile. "Yes." She shrugged. "Later, she said that she wasn't trying to get me in trouble, just hide the paint can. But whatever she intended, the bottom line was that I was arrested and charged with criminal damage to property. Obviously, I couldn't make bail or hire a lawyer, so I waited in jail until I could meet with a public defender."

"How long?"

"The courts were pretty busy. Holiday rush, I guess. I was in jail for about three weeks, total."

"Rena, why didn't you call me? I can't believe you were in jail for three weeks and didn't call me."

"What could you have done for me? Hire me a lawyer? Break me out of jail? You were in Colorado with Casey, remember?" She fidgeted with a loose thread on her cuff. "Besides, I was mortified. I didn't want anyone to know what had happened. And you have to promise me you won't say anything to, like, your mom or anyone."

"Of course I won't."

Her shoulders sagged in relief. "Anyway, by the time the dust settled, I ended up pleading guilty. I was criminally responsible for all of the damage done to the building. Plus the security guard. Thank God he wasn't hurt, but he could have been, and that increased the seriousness of the charge. It was a felony."

"Oh, Rena."

"I was lucky, I guess, because the judge stayed the sentence, so I was released after the plea hearing. By then, Sherry had gone back to Merryville, so I ended up selling plasma to make the money for a bus ticket home."

I shook my head. "I can't believe she dragged you into something so crazy."

She shrugged and let her gaze drift away from mine. "Home was really bad. Dad had lost his job and gone completely off the rails. Somehow I'd decided to fight fire with drunken fire, so I was drinking a lot, too. I didn't have a job or any hope of a future. Sherry was like my anchor. She made me feel good about myself when everything else in my life was complete crap."

"Still. You were always such a good judge of character. I can't believe you didn't see what she was really like."

Rena didn't move, but there was a new and sudden tension in her posture. "Love is blind," she said, her lips barely moving to form the words.

"Love?" I blurted the question, the word sounding unnaturally loud and shrill.

She flinched, but didn't answer.

"What do you mean, 'love'?" My mouth was moving faster than my brain, and the instant the words were out I wanted to suck them back in.

"I loved her. Or I thought I did." She raised her head to look me in the eyes, her own pooled with unshed tears. "I'm gay."

"Oh."

She snorted a surprised laugh. " 'Oh'? That's the best you can do? I'm coming out to you after nearly thirty years of friendship, and I get an 'oh'?"

I rolled my eyes. "Cut me some slack. This is pretty big news."

Her impish smile faded. "Are you mad?"

"A little."

"Oh."

I reached out to grab her hand. She tried to snatch it back, but I held firm. "Dork. I'm not mad that you're gay. I'm mad that you're just now telling me."

"Guess we didn't share everything about our love lives," she said pointedly, a not so subtle reminder that she'd learned about Sean's declaration of love from Sean and not from me.

"Fair enough," I said. "But I'm entitled to a little surprise here. I mean, what about all those horrible boys you dated? Like Buster Knowlin. Why on earth would you go out with a sleazebag like Buster Knowlin if you didn't even like guys?"

She laughed abruptly. "God, I'd forgotten all about Third-Base Buster. I nearly broke his arm when he tried to put the moves on me."

"Third-Base Buster," I snorted.

"I wasn't really interested in any guys. I guess I figured if I sampled enough, eventually one would strike my fancy. But it never happened. I never felt that soul-deep tug until I met Sherry Harper."

She laughed again, only a hint of bitterness there. "And she pinned me with a felony and abandoned me miles from home. I can really pick 'em."

"She wasn't all bad," I said. "She sure did love that guinea pig of hers."

Rena and I fell silent, staring at each other in sudden horror.

"Dear heavens," I muttered. "Where's Gandhi?"

CHAPTER
Eight

Rena and I crawled around the alley on our hands and jammie-covered knees, dodging snowflakes the size of silver dollars and searching for that guinea pig for nearly an hour. While we inched across the bricks, Packer pranced and danced around the alley, snuffling his nose into the occasional crack or crevice, doing what dogs do in the crazy, scatterbrained way dogs do it. The snow falling was the heavy, wet kind that clung to your hair and eyelashes and then melted in icy trickles down your back. By morning it would be nothing but a layer of slush on the sidewalks, gone in the afternoon sun, but that night it was an absolute nuisance. To add to our misery, every few minutes the alleyway would suddenly go dark, and one of us would have to stand up and wave our arms to trip the motion sensors on the security lights.

All our crazy jumping up and down and searching did no good at all.

PAWS FOR MURDER 79

In the end, Packer found Gandhi's baby sling between a stack of pallets and the back wall of Xander's Spin Doctor, but the pig himself was in the wind.

My heart broke to think of poor little Gandhi trying to make his way in the fast-approaching Minnesota winter, trying to stand his ground against the occasional raccoon that made its way into town in search of food during the lean months. I only hoped his Andean ancestors had given him the genes to withstand the cold. Or the good sense to come out of hiding when the going got tough.

Rena, exhausted and totally depressed—and apparently not processing the significance of the sling itself—said good night and trudged back up to my apartment.

"I'll be right behind you," I said.

But before I followed her, I clambered over the pallets to carefully extricate the baby sling and bring it into the shop.

My rational mind knew I should hand the sling over to the police immediately, but my emotions were all a jumble. While we'd put most of the hurt behind us, I was still smarting a bit from the tiff I'd had with Rena earlier, still reeling at the notion there had been this part of her life that was closed to me, and still harboring a little annoyance that in her hour of need she'd called on Sean to help her. Granted, he was the one with the law degree, but still . . . I wanted to be the great friend who saved the day. Dizzy Izzy to the rescue!

If I'm being brutally honest, I was also afraid that Rena *had* gotten a text from Sherry that night, and I didn't want to be the one who turned damning evidence over to the authorities. If I handed them the sling containing Sherry's phone and Rena's number was on the call list, I'd feel like a traitor.

So despite that still, small voice saying, "Call nine-one-one," I carefully reached into the slightly funky baby sling and started pulling out its contents, laying them out on the red folk-art table in the barkery. There was the usual guinea pig detritus (chewed tissues, dried nubs of carrot, some commercial guinea pig bedding) and the usual person stuff (a few packets of soy sauce from La Ming's, three gnawed tubes of lip balm, and a scrap of cellophane-backed yellow paper with some Chinese characters picked out in a deep red). I guessed that the last was from a bag of that awful ginseng Sherry made me eat. Poor, poor Gandhi.

But there were also a few items that struck me as particularly interesting: one of the bright green paper plates we'd used to serve snacks at the grand opening event that evening; a crumpled receipt for two dinners at the Mission (a prix fixe locavore restaurant in nearby Lac du Chien); a dog-eared book that appeared to be about wetlands conservation; and a half-chewed napkin from the Silent Woman, the name of the bar and its trademark headless female form in silhouette against a stark white background.

What I didn't find was even more interesting. I didn't find Sherry's phone.

"Do you want the bad news or the worse news?" Rena asked as I poured us coffee to help fuel the postparty cleaning binge we were about to undertake on only three hours' sleep.

Packer, lying limp across his dog bed, opened his mouth in a huge and vocal yawn, followed by a wet little snort.

I jerked my thumb in his direction. "What he said." I huffed, something between a sigh and a laugh. "Seriously, after last night, I don't think I can take the worse news. Let's stick with plain old bad."

"Val seems to have picked some pockets. I found a necklace, an earring, and a wallet in her hammock."

"Dang it. I already returned one wallet last night. She's such a devious creature."

Rena shrugged. "She likes pretty things. Can you blame her?"

I handed Rena her mug of coffee, pale with cream and thick with sugar. Jinx, lured by the siren scent of dairy, leapt down from her spot on top of the armoire, rattling the glass front of the display cabinet when her impressive weight hit the oak floor. She insinuated herself into Rena's lap and nosed into her mug. Rena pushed away the coffee and twisted Jinx around so they were nose to nose. "Why can't you seem to remember that you're lactose intolerant? No dairy for you, big girl."

I sipped my own coffee—black as the midnight sky—and then took a look at the loot Rena handed over. The necklace was Taffy's, one her sister, Jolly, had made her for Christmas last year, and I knew she'd be missing it soon. Thankfully, the tea shop was just down the street, and I could return it to her the minute she opened for business.

The earring was actually mine, one I'd lost weeks ago during the renovation. I made a mental note to give

Val a bit of chicken jerky as a thank-you for finding it for me.

The wallet was black, a fine-grained leather trifold wallet like the kind my dad carried in the back pocket of his pants. I flipped it open, but it didn't have a special pocket for a driver's license, so I had no choice but to start digging through the bits of paper stuffed into the card holders.

I found the ID quickly, tucked behind a well-loved customer loyalty card for Harmon's Donuts, one of my favorite treats from my days in Madison. It appeared Hal Olson was only one punch away from a free dozen. Lucky guy.

"Holy cats," I muttered. "Of all the people Val could have picked on, it had to be one of the richest, most powerful men in town with one of the witchiest wives."

"Sorry," Rena said. "You want me to return it?"

I gave her a quick once-over. Her hair was standing straight up, and she was wearing a pair of my old overalls rolled up to the knees, one of Ingrid's plaid shirts, candy-striped knee socks, and her Doc Martens. She looked like an extra from an eighties music video. I couldn't see her getting into the Olson's gated community, much less past their front door.

"No, that's okay. I'll do it. And what's the worse news?"

Rena held up an envelope. "You got mail! A notice from the zoning board that there's been a complaint about the use of this location as a business. Apparently the neighborhood is zoned residential, and all the other businesses have zoning variances."

Originally, the area that is now downtown Merryville was nothing but houses—big summer retreats for Chicago and Minneapolis businessmen and their big Midwestern families—with a courthouse smack in the middle. Now, the giant houses on two long blocks of Oak and Maple had been turned into shops and offices. This new shopping district was bordered by Alder Street to the north, the courthouse (across Oak from the Spin Doctor and the Grateful Grape) to the east, Thornapple Avenue to the south, and Dakota Park (across Maple from Trendy Tails and Taffy's Happy Leaf Tea Shoppe) to the west.

"Are you kidding me? Ingrid ran the Gift Haus here for decades. No one ever complained about her needing a variance."

"Yeah, well, now someone's in a tizzy about it. And," she continued, "if I had to guess, I'd say that one"—she pointed in the general direction of the Greene Brigade, the rare book and military memorabilia store run by Richard Greene—"is the one who's stirring up trouble."

I sighed. I knew Richard was annoyed that there would be all manner of animals traipsing in and out of my store, and worried about the noise disturbing the dusty hush of his business, but to pick an actual legal battle? It was just too much.

Rena suddenly chuckled. "Good thing I now have a lawyer on retainer," she said. "I'll get Sean to look into it."

Normally I would have balked at the thought of turning to Sean for help, but under the circumstances I would take what I could get.

"Great. You call Sean, and I'll go return all of Val's ill-gotten booty."

Pris and Hal Olson lived in Quail Run, hands down the spendiest neighborhood in Merryville. The houses all dated to the mid-1980s, when sleepy Merryville transformed, seemingly overnight, from a getaway for hunters and suburban families with fifth-wheel campers into a weekend retreat for wealthy refugees from Chicago and Minneapolis . . . sort of the Hamptons of the Midwest.

The Olson house was a formal French Provincial mansion of peach-colored stucco with a steep hipped roof and hedges trimmed into tall spirals on either side of the towering front door. The overnight snowfall had clung to every bare branch of the majestic oaks in the front yard and limned the exquisite architectural details, giving the house the look of a fairy-tale castle.

As befitted a house of its grandeur, the doorbell chimed the opening chords of Beethoven's Fifth, the deep gonging resonating through the heavy oak door.

Hal answered the door in his work "uniform." As the owner of the largest RV park in all of Minnesota and the Dakotas, Hal Olson spent most days in a golf shirt (today, a manly hunter green) tucked into a pair of wrinkle-resistant khaki pants, with a pair of loafers that perfectly matched his belt and a leather bomber jacket for walking the lot in cold weather—business casual with the emphasis on the casual, the perfect look to appeal to sportsmen and retirees while still maintaining the upper hand with them.

His expression was frazzled, like he had someplace

he'd rather be, something he'd rather be doing, but he quickly manufactured a smile for me.

"Izzy! This is sure a surprise. Come on in."

I hesitated a beat, because really I just needed to hand Hal his wallet back, but part of me was curious to see the inside of the palatial house.

I stepped into the travertine-tiled foyer, careful to keep my slushy shoes from touching the spendy-looking Oriental carpet. The interior of Prissy's house was as cold and determinedly neutral as she herself was: a model home decor ranging from white to ecru to a muted beige with a few burgundy accent pieces all straight out of an interior design catalog.

The bottom steps of one side of the iron-railed double staircase were littered with yard signs and posters: OLSON FOR MAYOR, GOOD FOR GROWTH.

"I see the rumors are true," I said.

He looked startled for an instant, then laughed as he followed my line of sight. "Oh, yes indeed. I just filed the paperwork yesterday, so it's official: I'll be on the ballot next April. Hope I can count on your vote."

" 'Good for growth'?" I hedged.

"My platform's based on economic development. Over the years, the tourist industry has grown, but the town has been passive, just let it happen. We need to take charge, live up to our potential. We need to make the most of our assets."

"Which assets?" While the new business owner side of me liked the idea of bringing more people to Merryville, another part of me liked our sleepy little town just the way it was.

"We've got a booming business district, your own

little store included," Hal said with a patronizing smile. "We should capitalize on that. We need to host a festival of some sort, maybe work on bringing in events. And we need to make the most of our beautiful surroundings, including the lake."

"Hal? Who's there?" Prissy's voice drifted down from the second floor to fill the vaulted-ceilinged space.

"Izzy!" Hal boomed. "Izzy McHale."

I heard a faint gasp and the rustle of her scurrying through an unseen hall, but by the time she reached the landing above the foyer she was calm, even reserved. She wore a fine-gauge twin set of the palest lilac with perfectly pressed gray wool trousers, and her hair was upswept in a flawless French twist. Incongruously, she held a garden trowel in one hand. Once again, Kiki lay draped over her shoulder.

"Izzy dear, we read in this morning's *Gazette* that you had quite an eventful night last night."

"Yes," I muttered, feeling a little sick just thinking about it. "It was pretty horrible."

"Have they figured out how she died? I mean she was just so tragically young."

"No. It looked like maybe she had a seizure or a stroke or something. But I bet they won't know more for a while."

"Her family must be devastated," Pris said as she completed her descent to the foyer. "I'll have to call on Virginia later today."

"I didn't know you were friends with Virginia Harper." They seemed an unlikely pair, the pageant princess and the hippie-turned-businesswoman.

Pris gestured with her trowel. "Garden club. We're

meeting to plant bulbs outside the courthouse later this morning. We really should have done this a couple of weeks ago, so I'm not sure they'll take. But I doubt Virginia will join us under the circumstances."

Hal raised a finger as though he were going to interject, but just as Pris turned to face him, Kiki got a look at me.

The cat screamed.

Startled, Pris dropped the animal. I expected the cat to tear out of the room, to run and hide, but instead she stood her ground. She angled her body to the side, hunched up her back, and puffed up all her fur to make herself look bigger. With her ears flat against her head, she licked her lips and emitted this strange sound somewhere between a cluck and a meow, a sound that cycled up and down the register like a siren.

Pris looked from me to the cat and then back to me.

"Honestly, I've never seen her behave this way. She's usually just the sweetest cat."

I glanced at Hal and caught him rolling his eyes. His expression, the scratch on the back of his hand, and the bandage on his finger all suggested that Kiki wasn't "just the sweetest cat" around Hal, either.

"I'm so sorry, Pris. I usually get along just fine with animals." Other than that nightmare incident with my friend's peeing dog, I really did get along with animals. "Maybe Kiki smells Packer on my clothes?"

"That must be it," Hal said. "Pris is always saying we can't have a dog because it would upset Kiki's delicate constitution."

"Now, Hal . . ." Pris began.

A rhythmic *horp*ing sound cut her off. We all directed

our attention to Kiki, who had dropped into a crouch and was convulsing slowly as she tried to cough up something.

"Oh dear," Pris said.

"Not on the damn rug," Hal grumbled.

They both stepped toward the cat as though they might somehow intervene, but I'd witnessed enough cats upchucking to know that there was no way to halt the process once it had begun. With one final heave and a loud *whluck*, Kiki expelled a small mound of kibble and a red string.

"Oh dear." Pris sighed. "Where did Kiki get ahold of string? That could have killed her." She shot Hal an accusing glare.

It was true. Contrary to the popular image of a cat playing happily with a ball of yarn, yarn, string, and rubber bands are terrible toys for cats. They can swallow the long, narrow items with ease, but once inside their digestive tracts, the strings can wreak all sorts of havoc.

"Don't look at me," Hal huffed defensively. "You won't let me tie flies in the house because of that cat. Maybe she got into that needlepoint kit you bought and never finished."

"I honestly don't think . . ." Pris teared up as she hoisted her Kiki back into her arms. "Poor baby."

I felt singularly uncomfortable bearing witness to this little domestic spat.

"Um," I said, "I don't want to keep you two. I just wanted to return your wallet." I pulled Hal's wallet from my purse and handed it to him. "I'm afraid Rena's ferret, Val, is a bit of a kleptomaniac. We found this in her stash this morning."

"Oh jeez," he said, his tanned face turning a mottled red, "I thought I'd left this at the office. Even went back last night to look for it. Thought it must be gone for good. Thank you so much for returning it."

Pris's eyes narrowed as she studied her husband. "Yes," she said softly, turning her eyes on me with a look of frank speculation, "thank you."

CHAPTER
Nine

Even though the horror of finding Sherry was still fresh in my mind—and the pain of losing Sherry was still fresh for Rena—we had a fledgling business to attend to, and I had the Halloween Howl to plan. Rena was tucked behind our main display case, carefully arranging our selection of cat and dog collars by color, laying them flat and overlapping them, creating a gorgeous rainbow effect. I'd often wondered if Rena was just a tad OCD. Her ability to sit quietly and concentrate deeply on such a precise, detail-oriented task boggled my mind. After all, I tended to jump from one flight of fancy to the next.

While Rena labored, lost in her own thoughts, I was working on hand stitching ribbons to a handful of pumpkin stem hats made of batting and green felt, with wired ribbon leaves. The hats would complete the dozen pumpkin costumes I had stitched, two in each of six sizes, from teacup Chihuahua to standard poodle.

I looked up when the bell above our door rang. Of all people, it was Virginia Harper. A pink leash attached her to a lovely fawn and white corgi.

"Virginia," I said, laying aside my sewing supplies and getting up to greet her. "I wasn't expecting you."

Virginia wasn't born a Harper, but she acquired their cultured manners and champagne tastes the minute she married into the family. The proprietor of the Grateful Grape was a tall, broad-shouldered woman, who exuded a lush femininity. She wore a flowing black dress draped with an ombre scarf in shades from palest silver to deepest charcoal, and her long dark hair fell in a wild array of curls about her shoulders. She wore a heavy perfume, rich with the scents of jasmine and tuberose, which just barely concealed a hint of cigarette smoke.

By the look of her—bruiselike circles around her eyes, posture slumped—she hadn't gotten a wink of sleep, and the tragedy of last night clearly weighed heavy on her. Still, she mustered up a smile.

"Carla's been smothering me with kindness all morning, and we've already gotten enough hot dishes to keep us fed for a year. I needed to get away."

"And who is this?" I asked, dropping to my haunches to greet my four-legged visitor.

"This is Sir Francis." Even through her grief, her love for the dog shone through the tone of her voice.

"Sir Francis is very handsome," I said, rubbing my hand beneath the dog's chin.

From the back of the store, Jinx wandered over to check out the new faces. She did a little swish through the bottom of Virginia's skirt, then gave Sir Francis a detailed sniffing. Apparently approving of our guests, she strolled to the front of the store and found a stray sunbeam in which to bask.

"What a beautiful cat," Virginia said. "I don't think I've seen such a large cat. Not fat, but just large."

"Jinx is a pretty special cat," I replied.

It was true. About three years after Casey and I returned to Merryville, he brought home Packer to alleviate my loneliness. Packer did keep me hopping. He was a big dork and required a lot of attention. I never intended to get another animal.

But that Christmas I was at the mall to buy my dad a sweater, and there was a bustling pet adoption event going on in the food court. I'd just bought myself a cinnamon pretzel when I saw Jinx. She was the last cat left. She was enormous—her frame the size of a fox, large even for a Norwegian forest cat—but so skinny I could see her shoulder blades through her dreadlocked black-and-white fur. She had a notch in one tufted ear, and a jagged line of stitches stretching across a bald spot on her flank. In short, she was a mess.

But she sat there in the midst of the craziness, a picture of absolute dignity, her ragged tail wrapped neatly around her toes. She looked at me with her huge green eyes, flicked her tongue across her whisker biscuits, and she was mine.

She came with her name, and it turned out to be apt. In the first month she lived with us, she clawed a hole in the bottom of our box spring, completely unraveled an afghan I was crocheting, and peed all over a pair of Casey's shoes. (To be fair, after Casey dumped me, I treasured the memory of those ruined shoes, but at the time it was horrible.)

In short, Jinx is a bad, bad cat, and there's no question that she's the real head of our household, but I love her more than words can say.

I snapped myself out of my moment of nostalgia. "What can I do for you, Virginia?"

"Oh, nothing much. When Sean came back to the house last night, he mentioned that the store was lovely, and I thought I'd hide out here for a few minutes of peace." She sighed. "And I also want to thank you."

"Thank me?"

"I guess it's more of an apology. I loved Sherry as though she were my own, but I know she caused you quite a headache with her protest. I'd been trying to talk her out of it for weeks."

"Oh, Virginia. You don't owe me an apology. For heaven's sake, I hold no ill will toward Sherry, God rest her, and I certainly hold no ill will toward you."

I gave her an impulsive hug, and was enveloped in her motherly presence.

"In fact," I said as I pulled away, swiping tears from my eyes, "I have a proposition for you. I know the timing isn't very good, but I was wondering if you would be willing to be the judge for the pet costume contest at this year's Halloween Howl."

Virginia drew herself up. "Well, Izzy McHale, I would be honored. It will be the perfect thing to keep my mind occupied while the family works through this . . . this whole thing.

"Now," she said. "Show me some of these cute clothes you have."

Sean stopped by Trendy Tails that evening to bring the bad news.

Rena had just locked the door and quickly flipped it back open when she saw Sean bounding up the porch stairs, a wheezing basset hound in tow.

"Hope you don't mind that I brought Blackstone," he said as he stamped his feet and rubbed his hands briskly to warm himself. Blackstone, who was a bit zaftig, heaved over on his side, his tongue and ears all flopping in the same direction.

"Of course not," I said. "Blackstone is our target demographic."

Sean chuckled. Packer wandered over to give Blackstone a tentative snuffle and then, apparently deciding that the other dog had passed some sort of doggy test, flopped down next to his new friend.

Meanwhile, never one to be left out, Jinx had strolled in to see what the commotion was all about. Unafraid, she strutted up to Sean, sniffed his pant cuff, and began making figure eights around his legs.

"Oh dear. Sorry about that. She'll get fur all over you."

"Not a worry." Sean bent down and scooped Jinx up in his arms. She rubbed the top of her head against the underside of his chin while he made deep cooing sounds and stroked her fur.

For some reason, watching him cuddle with my cat made me feel jittery. I glanced over at Rena to find her watching me, a sly smile on her face.

Sean let Jinx hop out of his arms. "Let's get down to business," he said.

We clustered around the folk-art table with a pot of Taffy's famous calming herbal tea.

"They've completed the autopsy," he said. "They won't have an official cause of death until the toxicology results come back, and that could take several weeks. But a picture is starting to emerge, and it doesn't look good.

"When they found Sherry, there was a bag next to her and a bunch of stuff on the ground around her."

I vaguely remembered seeing the bag and the scattered bits of refuse, but the whole event had become a bit of a blur.

"Well, it looks like Sherry was holding the bag when she died, dropping it as she fell to the ground. There was still some sweet cereal mix—the kind Rena was serving to party guests that night—in the bag as well as all over the bricks. But there was other plant matter mixed in with the cereal. The forensics guys sent that over to the U of M Extension office and they identified it as dried water hemlock root."

"Water hemlock?" I asked. "That sounds positively Shakespearean, like something from a witch's cauldron."

"Apparently it's one of the most poisonous plants in North America. Even a small amount of it could have killed Sherry in fifteen minutes or less."

"Dear heavens," I muttered. "Where would someone get something like that?"

Rena was as pale as skim milk. "It grows wild all over the place," she said. "Lots of it down by Badger Lake."

"How do you know these things?" I wondered. Rena hadn't gone to college, but her brilliant brain was stuffed with all sorts of bits of arcane information.

Rena clicked her tongue against her teeth. "Didn't you pay any attention at all in camp? All those nature walks where they told us not to pick the flowers that looked like Queen Anne's lace?"

In truth, I'd been too busy mooning over Casey during all those idyllic walks to pay a whit of attention to the information about the local flora and fauna.

Rena reached a hand out to Sean. "Are they sure that's what killed her? It's a horrible way to die."

"They haven't completed toxicology studies, but the contents of Sherry's stomach are consistent with her eating both the cereal mix and several pieces of the dried hemlock shortly before she died."

"Could it have been an accident?" Rena asked.

"Highly unlikely," Sean said.

"And I can't imagine Sherry taking her own life in our alley," I added, "especially leaving Gandhi there to fend for himself."

"Exactly," Sean said. "The police suspect foul play. The working theory is that Rena spiked the cereal mix with the poisonous root and killed Sherry."

Sean placed a hand over Rena's. "It may not be official, but I think you're a murder suspect."

I knew Rena couldn't have killed Sherry, but that didn't mean the rest of Merryville wouldn't speculate. Rena hailed from a poor neighborhood called Frogtown, where the rickety houses seemed to sprout from the low-lying landscape like pale and crooked mushrooms. Her family had had more than its share of brushes with the law. Rena herself had a reputation as a small-time juvenile delinquent—though, to be fair, that reputation mostly arose from fights in which she'd been defending herself or her dad—and the incident in Minneapolis was sure to come to light. A few superstitious souls in Merryville even gossiped that Rena—with her skulls and studs and purple hair—dabbled in the occult . . . making her a prime candidate for serving up a sack of hemlock-laced treats.

Bottom line, if the police made their suspicions public, most of Merryville would be only too quick to believe them.

"So what's next?" Rena asked, spreading her hands, palm up, in the universal sign of surrender.

"Mostly we wait," Sean answered.

"No way am I just going to sit around waiting to be arrested. No way."

I didn't know if Sean was aware of Rena's unfortunate incarceration in Minneapolis yet—though eventually he would have to be—but I knew that Rena wasn't about to go down for someone else's crime again.

"I know what you're thinking. You're thinking of trying to find the killer," Sean said, echoing my own concerns precisely. "But that would be a mistake. If you're seen talking to potential witnesses, it may look like you're attempting to manipulate them. You'll look even more guilty."

Rena rested her elbows on the table and collapsed, her head in her hands.

"Don't worry," Sean said. "We'll take care of everything." Sean and I exchanged a brief look, but I couldn't read the expression in his eyes, leaving me to wonder whether the "we" meant he'd forgiven me for that long ago slight.

Sean turned his full attention to Rena. "Speaking of looking even more guilty, you want to tell me what that text message was about?"

Rena opened her mouth to answer, but Sean held up his hand. "Before you say a word, I want you to think about whether that text is really incriminating or not. Because what you say to me is protected by privilege, but what you say in front of Izzy may come back to haunt you."

"Wow," I said. "That's brutal."

"That's the law," he explained. He paused a beat, and then sighed. "Sorry. That did sound a little harsh, but that was my intent. This is deadly serious business, and I don't want Rena to do something that will hurt her case down the line.

"Is the text really safe?" he asked.

Rena nodded.

"Then let's have it."

Rena sighed. "I got a text from Nadya Haas."

"Nick's mom?" I asked.

"Yeah. Look, I really shouldn't tell you this, and I'm only doing so because, A, you won't ease up until I explain and, B, I trust you two to take this to your grave. Nadya and I go to the same Al-Anon meetings."

Of course that's how she knew Nick's mom—Al-Anon. I imagined Rena at those meetings, with Mrs.

Haas and all sorts of other people I didn't even know, eating cookies, drinking coffee, and sharing the sort of easy camaraderie that comes from common adversity. Once again, I was faced with a part of Rena's life that had been hidden from me, a part of her life I could never fully understand and share. Coming right on the heels of Sean's admonition to Rena to watch what she said around me, I'd never felt more alienated from this little pixie girl I loved so much.

"We take the 'anon' part pretty seriously. I don't want Nadya's text, reaching out to me for help, part of the public record."

"What did she text you about?" Sean asked.

"After Nick left Trendy Tails that night, he went on a bit of a bender. When he got home, he and his mom got into it."

"'Got into it'?"

"Most of the time, Nick's a gentle drunk, but he's got a hair trigger. We got a glimpse of that when he and Sherry got into that fight in front of the store. Later that night, Nadya made the mistake of asking him about Sherry, and he lost it."

"He hit her?" I asked.

"Yeah. I tried to get her to phone the police, but she wouldn't do it. I walked Packer as a pretense for booking it to her house to check on her. By the time I got there, Nick had gone someplace to cool off, so Nadya said there was no point involving the cops. She's really, really codependent."

I thought of Nick raising his fist to Sherry during their fight, the way her body winced away even as she faced him down. Had he hit her before, too? Had he been angry enough at her after their fight—and after his "bender"—to murder her?

"Do you think Nick could have hurt Sherry?" I asked.

Rena laughed, though there was no humor in it. "Oh, he did. And she hurt him right back. They had a volatile relationship. Most of the time, she bullied him around. And on those occasions he cracked and took a swing at her, she'd clock him one. She is—was—a lot bigger than he is, and she didn't scare easily."

"What about the night she was murdered?"

"Oh," Rena said, letting her head fall back and her eyes drift shut. "I see. You think Nick might be the killer."

Sean shook his head. "If she'd been assaulted, I might buy it. But she was poisoned. That requires forethought, careful planning. Nick's pickled half the time, and I can't imagine him stringing together such a well-thought-out plot."

Rena nodded her agreement. "Even when he's sober, Nick doesn't have the sense God gave a goose. My bet's on Ken West. It cost a pretty penny to open the Blue Atlantic, and while Ken had a few investors, I heard he sank every penny he owned into the venture. Lost it all, which is why he stayed here instead of moving back to Chicago."

"I don't know," I hedged. "He just didn't seem that upset when he saw Sherry the day before the opening. He clearly didn't like her, but he didn't seem emotional enough to kill her."

"But that's what I mean," Sean insisted. "Poisoning

is a deliberate way to kill someone. Cold and calculated. You don't have to be emotional or even angry, just determined. And Ken had access to the food that night. He had motive and opportunity."

"Rena, you said Nick had already left his mom's house when you got there?"

"Yes," she conceded. "He'd taken off into the night. God only knows where he went. But I don't think he came back to kill Sherry with water hemlock."

I had to admit they had a point.

"Okay, so we have a suspect and a half. Ken West and maybe, on an outside chance, Nick Haas."

"Guys," Rena said, rubbing her eyes with her fists, "I'm going to have to call it a night. I have to pick up groceries for my dad and me before I go home, and I'm beat."

"We're going to help her, right?" I asked Sean when Rena had gone. "Even if it means figuring out who killed Sherry ourselves?"

"Of course. Rena's our friend. That's what we do."

"Rena said you two kept in touch over the years." Until the night before, Rena hadn't mentioned Sean to me even once since we'd graduated high school. In retrospect, that seemed odd—that his name wouldn't come up at least in passing.

He shrugged. "Not as well as we should have— phone calls for birthdays, the occasional lunch when I came home for holidays. And once I moved back to Merryville, we've had a standing date for dinner at La Ming, first Friday of the month. But still, not as well as we should have. Not as well as you two have," he added.

It was my turn to shrug. "I'm not so sure I've kept up with her all that well. It seemed like we just fell back into the rhythm of our friendship when I moved back to Merryville, but I think I missed a lot. She went through some serious stuff while I was in Madison, and I didn't have the slightest clue."

He smiled, a wry twist of the lips. "No offense, Izzy, but you do miss a lot."

I blushed at that sideways reminder of his midnight confession, the fact that I'd never suspected the torch he carried for me.

"Are you happy?" I asked, suddenly desperate to know.

He laughed. "That's kind of a big question."

"I suppose so. But it seems like the answer should be simple."

"Well, it's not. Mostly, I'm happy. I'd planned to make a life in the big city—Atlanta, New Orleans, maybe Chicago—but when my dad died, I decided I should move back to be close to my mom. It wasn't my first choice, but it's turned out just fine. I hung out my shingle, and business is good."

"Your social life is good, too," I prodded.

"You mean Carla? Yes, that's good, too."

He clearly wasn't going to give me the information I was fishing for, details about how close they were and whether they were planning on marriage. To be honest, I wasn't really sure why I wanted to know or even *if* I wanted to know. It was like a loose thread I couldn't resist pulling.

"What about you?" he asked, turning the tables. "Are you happy?"

"You want the simple answer or the true answer?" I said, trying to keep my tone light. I knew the subtext of his question: He wondered whether I was at peace about Casey dumping me after all those years.

"The truth, the whole truth, and nothing but the truth," he quipped.

The truth was that we weren't close enough—anymore? yet?—for me to tell him how much Casey's defection had burned. The truth was I couldn't stand the "I told you so," whether he uttered the words out loud or not. The truth was it was late, and I was tired, and I needed to focus on my friend.

"I'm fine," I said. "Except for this thing with Rena."

"Fine is hardly an answer," Sean insisted.

I was saved from having to elaborate by a sharp rap on the front door.

I dashed to the door, expecting to find Rena had returned and simply forgotten her key, but I was surprised to find Richard Greene on my porch, looking like he was ready to storm the beach at Normandy.

"Miss McHale. Thanks to you, I have a rodent in my place of business, posing a serious threat to the precious books that are my stock-in-trade."

"Excuse me?" I'd never heard Richard Greene string together quite so many words at once. He must have been out of his mind, crazy angry.

"A rodent. Some sort of big furry tailless rat. Saw it dart behind a bookshelf just last night. I don't know how it got into my shop, but I know it came from your establishment. This is exactly the sort of nuisance I anticipated from the onset of your harebrained scheme."

"Mr. Greene, I'm sorry you have an infestation of

some sort, but I don't see how it's related to Trendy Tails. I'm certain none of my customers has left a pet of any sort behind, not even a rod—" I slammed to a halt midword.

"Holy cats," I breathed. "It's Gandhi."

My heart sang that the wee guinea pig might have survived the cold snap and made his way into the Greene Brigade, but at the same time I realized the peril Gandhi faced. Between Richard and Macarthur, the pig needed help.

"Mr. Greene. Richard. I'm pretty sure the animal you saw is a guinea pig that belonged to Sherry Harper. He went missing the night she died. He's completely harmless."

"He's a rodent. He's not harmless; he's a pest. I have precious maps, books, military uniforms, all of which might be chewed and destroyed by a rodent."

"I'll take care of it, Mr. Greene. I promise."

As if I didn't have enough on my plate: launching a new business, investigating a murder, and now wrangling a rogue guinea pig.

CHAPTER
Ten

The next morning, news of the poisoning—attributed to a high-placed source in the Merryville Police Department—appeared in the *Merryville Gazette*.

Sean stopped by around eleven, large cups of coffee from Joe Time nestled in a brown cardboard carrying case.

By silent agreement, Rena and I set aside our projects—Rena was adding rhinestones to a white and baby blue Elvis cape, and I was hand stitching the red satin lining for a feline Dracula costume—and gathered around the big red table.

Sean handed Rena a cup billowing with whipped cream and a drizzle of chocolate syrup over the top. "One large caramel mocha with extra whip, for you."

"Dear heavens, Rena, why don't you weigh a thousand pounds?"

Rena feigned a pout. "I use skim milk."

I shook my head in consternation. Rena could eat

like three lumberjacks and never gain an ounce. If I even took a sip of that coffee drink, I'd gain five pounds.

"And for you," Sean continued, passing me a steaming cup, "extra dark roast, black."

He'd remembered, I thought, my knees melting on cue. Or, some cynical part of my brain piped up, Rena told him. Either way, I told myself, it was a lovely gesture.

"You've seen the paper?" Sean asked, as he pulled his own coffee from the carton and took a sip.

"Yeah," I said. "So it really was poison?"

"It's not officially official, but it's sure looking that way."

Jinx made her way to Sean, somehow wrapped her whole body around his ankles, and settled in for a nap.

"Well, if it was poison, it was probably in something she ate," I said. "And the Extension service told the police that the water hemlock acted fast, so it must have been something she ate that night."

"And that's why a lot of suspicion will fall on you, Rena," Sean said. "The police have been holding off, waiting for a cause of death, but now they'll likely start homing in on you. Because they know she ate food prepared by you and delivered by you in the minutes before she died."

"What about Ken West?" Rena asked. "He sent a plate out for her, too."

"And he had a huge motive," I added. "She'd ruined his business."

"He's a viable suspect," Sean agreed, "but police tend to wear blinders when they investigate a crime. They identify a suspect, and it takes a lot to sway them from their path. You're the most obvious suspect, Rena. You fought with the victim right before her death, and people saw you taking the food out to her. Besides, you know how people are. Ken's clean-cut, dresses like a vacationing businessman, and you . . ."

"Right," Rena said with a sigh. "I look like I might sacrifice chickens in my spare time."

"I wouldn't go that far," Sean hedged, "but you're definitely not the norm in Merryville."

"So what do we do?"

Sean shrugged. "Nothing, really. I'm just keeping you in the loop." He fixed Rena with a piercing stare. "For now, your job is to keep your head down. No wackiness, no fights, no nothing. You're just Suzy Sunshine, okay?"

Rena plastered a brilliant smile on her face. "Aren't I always?"

Despite the gravity of the situation, it was impossible not to laugh at my fierce pixie friend striving for Stepford wife.

Before we could get back to business, Rena's phone rang. She pulled it out of her pocket and glanced at the screen. "Dang it," she muttered. "It's my dad," she announced more loudly. "I have to take this."

As she headed back to the kitchen, we overheard her side of the conversation.

"Hey, Dad. . . . No, I will not bring you a bottle of Canadian Mist. . . . Right, well, I've told you before . . ."

Poor Rena. She had this conversation with her dad at least once a day.

I turned to Sean. "So. What are we really going to do about this?"

Sean sighed. "We're going to have a little chat with our best suspect, Ken West."

Fortunately, we didn't have to wait long to talk to Ken West. The only person I knew who was close to Ken was my aunt Dolly—and that was using the term "close" pretty loosely. Still I gave her a call.

"Aunt Dolly?"

"Yes, dear?"

"I don't suppose you know how I could get in touch with Ken West, do you? I could call him, but I'd rather see him in person, and I don't even know where he lives."

"Well you can see him right now. I'm sitting right next to him."

"What?"

"We're having tea at Taffy's shop and talking about Ken's plans for a new restaurant right here in the historic district."

"Aunt Dolly! You're not thinking of investing in his restaurant are you? He ran the last one into the ground."

"Never you mind that. I'll ask Ken to stick around a few extra minutes. But do hurry. He's a busy young man, you know."

Dolly hung up, and I handed Sean his coat. "He's right down the street. Right now."

Deciding I could kill two birds with one stone, I leashed up Packer for the brief walk to Taffy's, and then we set off together.

The McHale girls are above average in the height department, but I had nothing on Sean. He looked to be about six-two, and his stride devoured the sidewalk. I had to bustle to keep up with him, and that meant pulling Packer along at a brisker pace than he was used to. Every few steps he'd sit down in protest, so it probably took us a good five minutes to walk the block to the Happy Leaf Tea Shoppe.

We found Dolly and Ken sitting at a beautiful tiger oak table, dainty cups of tea and a plate of finger sandwiches between them. They made an odd pair. My tiny aunt wore a pair of leggings, a long purple sequined tunic hanging nearly to her knees, and a pair of silver boots. She could have passed for a schoolgirl if it weren't for the ice white of her hair and the network of lines her perfect makeup couldn't quite hide. Ken, on the other hand, looked like he was ready to go pheasant hunting, and he absolutely dwarfed Dolly. The delicate teacup in his hand only served to emphasize his size and masculine vibe.

Taffy was behind the counter, polishing spoons. She gave us a wave, but gave us our space.

Sean and I pulled up chairs to join Dolly and Ken. While I greeted Dolly with a buss to her cheek, Sean reached out to shake hands with Ken. Packer made a circle around Ken's chair, whining as he went, then draped himself across Sean's feet and began snoring softly. Apparently Sean had already become part of Packer's pack.

"To what do I owe this pleasure?" Ken said, though the gleam in his eyes suggested he already knew the answer.

"Perhaps you saw the paper this morning?" Sean asked.

"Indeed I did."

"Then you know that anyone who fed Sherry is going to be a suspect now."

Dolly gasped. "Oh, Izzy. If I'd known you were going to come here to accuse Ken of something . . ."

Ken hushed her with a gentle motion of his hand. "It's fine, Dolly. I'm actually amused that Izzy and Sean here beat the police in contacting me. It's perfectly okay for them to ask their questions about Sherry."

"She did cause you a lot of trouble, didn't she?" I asked. "Maybe you decided it was time for a little payback. The police have been focusing on the fact that Rena had a big blowup with Sherry that night, but you've had the chance to stew in resentment for quite some time. And Rena wasn't the only one to give Sherry food that night. She took out a plate that you made up, too."

He laughed. "Oh, where to even begin with that? First, if I'd killed Sherry Harper, do you think I'd actually tell you?"

He had a point.

"Second, I sent out a plate, but I guarantee Sherry didn't eat anything on it. When Rena asked me to put something together for her, I placed a few chicken skewers, a beef pasty, and a little crab cake on the plate, wrapped it in foil, and sent it out for the vegetarian." He shrugged. "I suppose it was petty, but after she boycotted my restaurant and slandered my food, the last thing I wanted to do was feed her."

"But we found the plate empty."

"You found the plate empty in an alley filled with Dumpsters. If I had to guess, that's why Sherry was back there in the first place: so she could throw out that food, because God forbid she litter."

I wasn't sure I believed him, but there was really no way for me to prove or disprove his assertion.

"Let's say you didn't poison Sherry."

"Yes, let's," Ken deadpanned.

"You were back in the kitchen," I said. "Surely you heard or saw something that night?"

"Nothing useful. At one point I thought I heard someone out there, raised voices like maybe someone was arguing, but I was busy keeping the kitchen in order. When I finally did take a break, pop out the back door for a breath of fresh air, I didn't see a soul. If I had to guess, Sherry was already dead by then. I only stepped out onto the back stoop for a smoke, and I couldn't see around to the front of the Dumpster. Her body could have been there without me ever being the wiser."

"Am I just supposed to believe you?"

"Izzy, Izzy, Izzy. I can see you're not inclined to let this go, and I can't afford to have you spreading rumors about me, so I'm going to let you in on a little secret. I didn't like Sherry Harper very much, but she didn't ruin my life."

"But she cost you your business," Sean said.

"Her boycott of the Blue Atlantic didn't bring down the restaurant. I had other . . . issues."

"Issues?"

"Not that it's any of your business, but I've had an on-and-off love affair with blow."

Sean nodded, but Dolly and I stared at him blankly. He sighed. "Cocaine?"

"Oh," we said simultaneously.

"I've got it under control now, Dolly. I want our business dealings to be completely transparent. You should know I had this problem, but I've taken care of it. I go to NA meetings at least once a week.

"But when I was trying to get the Blue Atlantic off the ground, I was under a lot of stress. It's not easy being both the chef and manager of an upscale restaurant. I started taking the coke so I could squeeze more hours into the day, but I didn't make the best business decisions under those circumstances. The restaurant was hemorrhaging money, and I was burning up even more buying drugs. That's what put me under. Not Sherry."

"But you told me it was her fault," I said.

"I told everyone it was her fault. Better to let everyone think that the boycott was my downfall. I certainly didn't want them to know the truth. Ultimately, though, as much as I disliked her, I had no reason to kill Sherry. Heck, if we're being honest, my business actually picked up a bit when she first started her protest . . . people coming in to see what all the fuss was about."

Dolly reached out to pat Ken's hand. "That's very brave of you, telling us that."

Ken lifted a shoulder. "To be honest, I wasn't going to be able to hide my past indiscretions for long. Even if they have their sights fixed on Rena, they'll have to at least consider me as a suspect. Eventually, everyone will know about my old drug problem."

"Well," Dolly said, "you just know that I'll be rooting for you. We all make mistakes, and we shouldn't be judged solely by our lowest moments."

Good heavens. I was afraid Dolly was about to whip

out her checkbook and write Ken a fat check right there, right then.

Ken, thankfully, took that moment to bow out. "I have a busy afternoon," he said. "But I hope I settled some questions for you all."

When he'd left, Dolly took us to task. "I know Rena didn't kill that young woman, but neither did Ken."

"How can you be so sure, Aunt Dolly?" I asked.

"I just know. He's a little uptight, but he's a good boy. No killer could make a crab cake as tender and delicious as his."

"I don't think 'crab cake' is a legal defense to murder," Sean said, his mouth twisted in a wry smile.

"Oh, hush, young man. You know what I mean."

"Actually, I don't," Sean answered. "But for the moment, there's not much we can do to check out Ken's story. I think we'll have to take a different approach."

"What approach?" I asked, hoping Sean had a brilliant new tack to take.

"I think we need to talk to Nick Haas."

"But I thought we'd already decided that Nick was unlikely to be the killer."

"True. But no one knew Sherry better than Nick. If we're going to get any insight into who might have wanted Sherry dead, Nick's our best lead."

The next morning, we found Nick Haas where I imagine one could generally find Nick Haas: on a barstool at the Silent Woman. Never mind that it was 8:30 a.m. on a Tuesday.

He'd found a perch right next to the cut-through in the bar where the waitresses passed to deliver and pick up drink orders. It was prime real estate for chatting up the bar staff.

Merryville wasn't a dry town. You could order beer and wine at most of the nicer restaurants, the Thistle and Ivy styled itself as a genuine pub, and we even had two liquor stores (one high-end that sold imported beer and one more down-to-earth place where outdoor enthusiasts could pick up a twelve-pack before casting their lines in Badger Lake or holing up in a deer stand for the day).

The Silent Woman, though, drew a harder crowd. A lot of long-haul truckers played a game of pool and raised a few before sacking out in their sleeper cabs in the Woman's generous, edge-of-town parking lot. Herds of bikers on their way to Sturgis from points east would peel off the highway to have a cheap beer at the Woman every summer. And the local regulars were a far cry from the Chamber of Commerce and Lutheran Ladies set: all looking to raise hell and kill brain cells.

The bar itself looked like hundreds of others scattered across northern Minnesota: posters for Jaeger and St. Pauli Girl beer (the latter displayed more for the busty blond models than for the beer itself), a cement floor littered with used pull tabs, the faint acrid scent of ammonia and rotting bar fruit in the air.

It was dismal.

And it was where Rena's dad used to drink, before the stroke that rendered him homebound.

Most of the time, Rena had left her dad to his own devices, happy that he'd chosen to drink in a bar instead of in their home. But on exactly three occasions she'd begged me to come with her to the Silent Woman to find him: when Rena needed the checkbook to pay the gas bill before it got cut off in the dead of winter, when she decided to warn her dad that the cops were looking for him after he plowed his car through a line of mailboxes on his way to the bar, and when she had to find him to let him know his mother had died. Every single time, he'd been sitting exactly where Nick was sitting that morning.

"Sean!" Nick sat bolt upright on the scarred wooden stool. At first I thought he was sober. Sick, but sober. In the dim light from the shuttered window, I could see the yellow cast to his pallor. Without the bulk of his winter coat to pad him, I could make out the knobs of his spine through the thin fabric of his stained T-shirt. Yet, despite his skeletal physique, his face was round, puffy, eyes sunk in bruised-looking flesh.

"Hey, Nick," Sean said, resting a hand on his shoulder as he climbed onto the stool next to him. "How've you been, man?"

"Fan-effing-tastic. Love of my life just *died*, man; how do you think I am? I'm an effing wreck." He frowned. "Did win seven bucks playing pull tabs, but mostly I feel pretty shitty."

I suspected that Nick was a wreck long before Sherry died, but that didn't diminish the pain of her passing.

"I'm real sorry about Sherry," Sean offered. "I know that must be hard for you."

Nick sniffed, mollified. "Yeah, well, I just have to keep putting one foot in front of the other. Take it one day at a time."

Sean and I exchanged a look. The irony of Nick invoking that mantra of sobriety—one day at a time— was not lost on either of us.

"That's a good attitude, Nick. Haven't seen you in a while." On the drive over, Sean informed me that he had represented Nick in two DUI cases, so Nick not seeing Sean was really a positive step in Nick's life. "You been staying out of trouble?"

Nick giggled, the alcohol allowing his mood to turn on a dime. "Haven't been arrested, if that's what you mean."

The bartender, a beefy guy with a half-inch plug stretching each earlobe and a tattoo of a dragon coiled around his neck, leaned in. "No more DUIs for Nick because he sold me his car. Ain't that right, Nicky?"

On the one hand, I knew Merryville was a safer place because Nick Haas no longer had wheels. But it saddened me to think that was the only thing keeping him out of legal trouble.

Nick giggled again. "Got my very own limo service," he said. "Don't need a car."

Sean and I both looked at the bartender, who shrugged. "His mom."

Well, that was just dandy. Guy hits his mom when he's drunk, but she's willing to shuttle him to and from the bar. I was pretty sure that wasn't part of the Al-Anon playbook.

"Tell your mom 'hi' for me," Sean said. Given Nick's perpetual state of inebriation, I imagined that Sean had talked more with Mrs. Haas than with his actual client.

"Nick," I said, "we wanted to talk with you a bit about Sherry. Would that be okay?"

His lopsided grin melted away. "Aw, man. Effing-A. Girl broke my heart."

"How long did you two date?"

Nick reached out a hand, swiping it across the empty expanse of the bar, feeling for a glass that wasn't there. The bartender cocked a brow at Sean, who sighed but nodded.

The bartender pulled a beer, pale as lemonade, in a hazy pint glass. Nick grabbed it right out of the barman's hand and took a long swig.

He giggled. "Never drink anything other than American beer before noon."

I guessed everyone had to have standards, but this particular line in the sand didn't seem to be holding back Nick Haas's demise.

Nick threw back the glass again, downing over half the contents. He swayed a little on his stool before finding his balance. "Me and Sherry, we were together off and on since high school. It was weird not knowing what she was up to, you know? We shared everything, and I guess I thought we'd always be together. She got me, you know? No one else gets me."

"You loved her," I said.

"Effing-A." Nick finished off the beer with one last swallow.

Sean and I exchanged a pained glance over Nick's head. Poor Nick. He might have loved Sherry to the best of his ability, but I doubted he could love anything or anyone more than the booze.

Sean pulled the wrinkled and chewed bar napkin from his jeans pocket and laid it gently on the bar.

"Sherry had this with her when she died. Do you know why?"

I held my breath. There were a dozen completely innocuous reasons for Sherry to have had a Silent

Woman napkin with her that night, but I desperately wanted the napkin to be some sort of clue to her death.

Nick reached out a short, square-tipped finger and traced the edges of the napkin gently, as though he were tracing the lips of a lover.

"Gandhi got ahold of this, huh?" He smiled. "Cute little guy, but he chewed holes in all my good T-shirts."

"Nick, did you give Sherry this napkin?" The night of the grand opening, when Nick and Sherry were fighting in front of Trendy Tails, he'd said they'd been separated for a couple of months. If Nick gave Sherry the napkin, it would have had to be that night. The question was, did he give it to her before or after the fight?

He dropped his head and looked up at me through his lashes. With a lopsided smile quirking his lips and a "you got me" glint in his eyes, I could see the ghost of the boy he had been, impish and charismatic.

"Yeah. I know you told me to leave that night, and I did. Took Razor home and kenneled her. But I couldn't leave things with Sherry like that, so I walked back uptown."

The truth likely had more to do with his fight with his mother and needing a place to stay than any desire to make amends with Sherry, but I let Nick tell his story the way he wanted to.

"She was just giving up on her picketing when I got there, and I followed her around the side of the building to the alley."

"Why to the alley?" I asked.

"She had some trash to get rid of. A paper plate covered in foil. She went to the alley to use the Dumpster."

His account squared with what Ken had said. Sherry

hadn't eaten Ken's food; she'd thrown it away. Why she pitched the food but kept the plate, we'd probably never know.

"Did you fight again?" Sean asked.

Nick's head tilted to one side. "No. Not really. First, she said she was sorry for what she'd said that evening. She didn't really think I was a loser, and someday I'd understand why she needed her space. Then she told me to leave, and I swear I turned right around. But then she stopped me and asked me for a ride."

Stupid, considering Nick had been drunk as a sailor on leave that night.

"At first I thought that was weird, because she only lives a couple of blocks from your store, Izzy. Then I thought, 'well, maybe she wants an excuse to spend more time with me.' I told her I'd sold the car, but I'd walk her home if she wanted. But she waved me off, said that wouldn't work. Guess she was going someplace other than home."

"Did she say where?"

"No. I asked, but she just hemmed and hawed. Wouldn't give me a straight answer. She sneezed, and I handed her the napkin. Always have a few in my jacket pocket. She'd already pulled out a tissue, but she took the napkin anyway."

He seemed to take comfort in that fact—that she would accept his gesture of kindness. No matter what you might say about Nick's lifestyle choices, he clearly loved Sherry Harper beyond reason.

I thought of Gandhi's baby sling and all the odds and ends Sherry had tucked in there, maybe thinking they would come in handy, and I could picture the scene: Nick handing Sherry the crumpled napkin and her taking it, in case she needed another tissue later. But there was no later for Sherry, no chance to put all those napkins and strings and soy sauce packets and half-empty lip balms to good use.

"What happened then?" I asked.

He shrugged. "Nothing. I can take an effing hint. She didn't want me around, so I left. Called it a night. Hit the hay."

I didn't know Nick Haas well, but even I knew that taking an "effing hint" was not his strong suit. And something about the twitchy way he fiddled with his glass as he spoke told me we weren't getting the truth from Nick Haas. At least not the whole truth.

"You just left, huh?" I pressed.

"Yes." He pronounced the word with exaggerated care, and there was a hint of a threat in his tone.

I narrowed my gaze to study him, and he glared right back at me. He wavered on his barstool, but his stare was rock solid and turning meaner by the second.

"Tell me more about Sherry," Sean said, trying to defuse the sudden tension. "You two had split up before she died, right?"

"Not my choice, man. Girl broke my *heart*," he reiterated. "Said I didn't have ambition. But that was the whole point. She used to go on and on about how her family only cared about money and *stuff*, you know? How she loved me because I lived in the now. I'm still right here, in the now, but suddenly that wasn't what she wanted."

"You two had broken up before," Sean said.

Nick sighed, a dreamy smile ghosting his lips.

"Yeah, we fought a lot. After a big fight, Sherry would always walk out and swear it was the end. But she always came back to me."

I thought back to the night of the grand opening and the look of unleashed rage on Nick's face. Those must have been some wicked fights. I couldn't believe Sherry would keep going back for more of that.

"This time was different though," he said. "No fight. Just 'I need my space,' and then out the door. I begged and pleaded with her for months. Gave up booze and weed." He waggled his glass at the bartender, asking for a refill. "Well, mostly at least. But none of it mattered. She was always too busy to even see me. When I went to her apartment, she just yelled at me through the door. 'Go away.'"

He sniffed and then literally shook off his gloomy mood. "You know Sherry, always had irons in the fire."

I didn't bother to point out that ruining my business had been one of those irons. It didn't seem like the right time to mention it.

"But whatever she was up to the last few months, she said it was the most important thing she'd ever done. More important than me, I guess."

He dropped his head to his hands, and I was afraid he would start weeping. "Worst of all, she was seeing someone new, someone who had 'apser . . . aspirations' and 'connections.' Someone who could really help her out." Nick sneered while sketching quotes in the air with his fingers. He snorted. "I had an aspiration, too. Just one: to love Sherry. What's wrong with that?"

I could have delivered a dissertation about the dangers of living only to love someone else and having no personal goals beyond the circle of that love. But I held back for two reasons. First, Nick Haas was already so stinkin' drunk that I didn't imagine my words would be able to seep through the alcohol haze. Second, what? Sherry had someone new? Another guy?

Holy cats.

No one had mentioned a love interest for Sherry . . . other than poor, sad Nick, of course. Who was the mystery man? And, perhaps more importantly, why was he still a mystery? Why keep such a low profile?

"Nick, did Sherry say who she was dating?" I asked.

He waggled his head slowly. "Nah. I asked, but she said it was none of my business. Whoever it was, I bet he was the one who gave her that effing phone."

"What 'effing phone'?" I asked.

"That cell phone she was carrying."

Aha! I knew I'd seen Sherry with a cell phone the day she came in to Trendy Tails. It had a pink anarchy sticker on the back and the corners of the case had tiny tooth marks, evidence that Gandhi had shared some quality time with the phone.

"Why do you think her new boyfriend gave it to her?"

"Sherry knew all about cell phones, man. They give you brain cancer. Plus, they let the government listen to your conversations. Big Brother, man. No way Sherry would have bought a cell phone for herself."

I snagged Sean's attention. "If she had a phone, wouldn't the police have pulled her phone records? Maybe she called someone that night."

"I have a friend on the force. He said they pulled Sherry's home phone records but no cell records."

"Why wouldn't they have gotten the cell records?"

"Maybe they don't know about the phone. The phone wasn't on her when she died. It must have been a burner phone, like drug dealers use: a prepaid phone with prepaid minutes bought at some big box store. No contract to trace. I bet with the phone itself, the cops could trace it back to whoever purchased either the phone or the minutes, but right now, I don't think they even know it exists."

"How do you know this stuff?" The Sean I remembered knew about medieval history and classic rock. He didn't know about the standard operating procedures of drug dealers.

"Occupational hazard," he answered with a smile.

Sean leaned in across the bar. "Nick, you know the police think Rena killed Sherry, right?"

Nick sputtered in disgust. "Rena? No way, man. Not Rena. She's good people. Heart of gold."

"Do you know who might have wanted to hurt Sherry?" I asked. "Someone who was mad at her?"

He raised his glass in a solitary toast. "Sherry was an effing warrior. People don't know what to do with all that righteous power, you know? Half of Merryville wanted her out of the way because she held up a mirror, you know? Forced them to see themselves for who they really are."

"Any one more than the others?"

"I can't think of anyone. That Prissy woman acted like Sherry was gum on the bottom of her shoe, but she never threatened Sherry or anything. She just thought Sherry was a lowlife because she hung around with me."

I imagined Pris's contempt for Sherry had as much to do with Sherry's public displays of crazy as her choice of romantic partner. Still, disdain didn't seem a likely motive for murder, especially since Pris actually seemed to enjoy demeaning people. Why would she want to eliminate one of her favorite targets?

We'd hit another dead end.

If Sherry had been stabbed or shot, I might have looked closer at Nick. After all, he'd admitted to coming back after their fight and being in the alleyway where Sherry died, and we knew from his encounter with Sherry and from his mother that Nick was in a genuinely dangerous mood that night. But Sean was right. Sherry'd been poisoned. As angry as he was, I couldn't imagine Nick getting his act together enough to stage a poisoning—finding the water hemlock, drying it, somehow slipping it into her food. The guy didn't even have a car.

The only progress we'd made talking with Nick was that we now knew Sherry had a new boyfriend. It seemed to be a well-kept secret, so I wasn't sure how we could suss out his identity. And we knew she'd had a cell phone, but it was missing in action. Still, they were leads to follow.

"The police didn't find Sherry's cell phone," I said. "You don't happen to know where she kept it, do you?"

"Nah. Only saw her with it once. The night she died. She got a text, right as I was leaving the alley. Couldn't believe my Sherry was texting like some middle-class suburbanite."

Rena had gotten a text the night of Sherry's death, one that prompted her to take Packer out for a walk.

Was it possible that Rena and Sherry were in communication? I immediately put the thought out of my mind. Rena had said the text was from Nadya Haas, and I chose to believe her.

"I saw her stick the phone in Gandhi's sling," Nick said.

"But I found the sling, and it wasn't there."

Nick shrugged. "I don't know, man. What can I say?"

Someone else must have been in that alley between when Nick left and when I found Sherry's body. Someone who took the cell phone. Her killer, perhaps?

"Thanks for talking with us, Nick," Sean said. "We'd better get going. We'll see you round."

We were both sliding off our barstools when Nick shifted on his, hiking up his grungy Vikings T-shirt and rooting around in the pocket of his jeans.

"If you want to look around her place for that phone, you can borrow my key."

Both Sean and I froze.

"You have a key?" Sean asked.

"Sure," Nick said, as though having a key to his ex-girlfriend's apartment was the most natural thing in the world. "We had a deal that I wouldn't use it unless it was an emergency or Sherry said I could. I always respected Sherry's privacy like that, but I guess that don't matter much anymore."

Sean and I exchanged a glance. I could see the wheels turning behind his eyes. The phone couldn't possibly be in Sherry's apartment, as there hadn't been time for her to go home after seeing Nick and then make it back to the alley to die. Still, access to her apartment might yield a clue to the mystery man's identity.

"Hasn't her family cleaned the apartment out yet?" Sean asked.

"Doubt it," Nick answered, retrieving an unadorned key ring from his pants. "Sherry's rent was always paid up front, every three months, so the landlord won't be in any hurry to dump her stuff. Besides, she'd never let her family have keys to her place, and I'll be damned if I'll let them in. They'll have to go through the proper channels."

I didn't have the faintest clue what those proper channels would be, and I doubted Nick did either.

"Heck, I doubt her effing family will even bother. They always pooh-poohed Sherry, like she was no-account and a loser. They'll probably just let the landlord throw out her stuff. So, anyway, it should all still be there, and you can have a look around if you want."

"Don't we need to go through the proper channels, get permission to go into her house?" I asked.

Sean pulled out his phone. "I can ask Carla. I don't know why I didn't think to ask her to look around the apartment before. She must be next of kin—or at least know who is—and I'm sure they can arrange something with the landlord to get us in."

"Carla? Carla Harper?" Nick sneered. "Aren't you paying any attention to me? Sherry hated Carla. You don't need to ask that prissy bitch for anything." I shot Sean a worried glance. His lips tightened at the slight to his girlfriend, but he didn't take Nick's bait.

"I can give you permission. I'm on the lease," Nick added, a hint of pride in his voice.

"Why would Sherry have put your name on the lease? Don't you live with your mom?" There was a hint of contempt in Sean's tone, but Nick was too blotto to notice.

"Yeah, but last year Sherry and I had this big blowup and I went on a bender. My mom was getting all into this intervention bottom line crap, and she threw me out for a while. Sherry felt so bad about me spending a night down at the shelter at St. Stephens that she put me on the lease so I'd always have a home."

"Why not just give you the key?" Sean asked.

Nick dropped his chin and stared up at Sean as though Sean had just asked Nick why he liked liquor. "Because she didn't want anyone hassling me when I used the key. But, like I said, I wasn't supposed to use the key except for emergencies, but being homeless . . . that was an emergency. And I guess this is, too."

Nick sniffed. "That's how she was, you know? Effing heart of gold. Anyway, if you'll give me a lift, I'll let you in."

CHAPTER
Eleven

Sherry lived on the second floor of a Victorian mansion on Birch Lane, just across Dakota Park from Trendy Tails. Her apartment overlooked the park, with its picturesque band shell and dozens of oak and maple trees. As predicted, Saturday's snow had melted in the late-afternoon sun, leaving the trees bare of their white frosting, but the dark web of the limbs held its own beauty in the crisp morning light.

When we unlocked the door to her apartment, the scent of patchouli and jasmine wafted into the hallway like Sherry's ghost come to greet us. I shivered, even as Sean flipped the switch by the door and flooded the expansive space with light.

The walls of the apartment were painted a warm, buttery yellow with accents of deep moss, the floors and molding all darkly shining wood. A chandelier of patinated brass and milk glass hung from a plaster ceiling medallion that had been painted a dozen sunrise colors. Yet in the midst of that stately beauty, Sherry had accumulated a vast array of clutter.

Every surface of the apartment—from the Mission-style dining table to the battered brass daybed in the corner—was covered with stacks of paper. Empty margarine tubs, jelly jars, and whipped topping containers littered the small counter that separated the galley kitchen from the rest of the space.

Nick made a beeline for the daybed, picking up a red chenille throw draped over its side and burying his face in it. His shoulders jerked, and I realized he was crying.

Sean and I left him to his grief, taking a quick turn around the apartment. We were in search of a clue about Sherry's alleged lover, but I was trying to keep my mind open, in case any other potential clue jumped out at me.

Sherry's apartment was a beautiful space, with generous rooms, but it consisted only of the combined living and dining room, a single bedroom, and a bath. I stepped into the bathroom, which actually reminded me of my own: claw foot tub fitted with a shower and a circular curtain rod, the floor covered in white hexagonal tiles, the mirror on the medicine cabinet clouded with age. Sherry had painted the walls a deep azure that contrasted nicely with the white of the tile.

Even the bathroom was cluttered with stacks of towels and old magazines, but I couldn't help noticing that the tile, the sink, and the toilet were sparkling clean. I happened to glance at the paper holder and saw that the end of the roll had been folded into a neat triangle, like you see when you first check into a hotel room.

Sherry had a cleaning service.

I tried to imagine the workers shifting all the stacks of paper to scrub under them, the monumental effort of cleaning around so much *stuff*.

I wandered back to the living room to find Nick sprawled in an oversized armchair, the chenille throw tucked around his shoulders.

"Was Sherry packing or something?" I asked.

Nick opened one eye and gave me a bleary smile. "Because of all the stuff? Nah, Sherry was a conservationist, you know? Didn't want to waste anything."

More like a hoarder, I thought.

"But surely she could have recycled this stuff. The newspapers and such."

Nick shrugged. "I guess. But she always said 'I could use this,' or 'this might come in handy.'"

This explained why Sherry had held on to the paper plate Ken had sent out. She must have thrown away the food and kept the plate, the way she kept stacks of newspapers and old margarine tubs, figuring she'd find some use for it later.

"Her family had a lot of money," Nick continued, "but Sherry was thrifty."

"But she didn't have to be, right? I mean she could afford household help so she must not have been poor."

My mother would have had my hide for asking such a tacky question about the finances of a dead woman. But my mother wasn't present, and Nick didn't seem to mind.

"Oh, I guess she had money. I mean, she didn't have a job or anything, but she did okay. She said once that the family trust was split equally among all of Gene and Pearl's grandkids. Sherry got her piece of the pie when she turned thirty."

Gene had been the patriarch of the Harper family, careful steward of its fortune, for decades. He had the bad fortune to outlive all of his own children, so I guess all the money went straight to his grandchildren. Gene's eldest child was Sherry's dad, George, and Sherry was an only child. Gene's second son was Carla's dad, Kevin. Kevin and Virginia Harper had two kids, Carla and her teenage brother, Jeff. The baby of the family, William, had had twin boys. A total of five grandchildren. If Sherry had an equal share of the Harper family fortune, she must have been stinkin' rich.

"But Carla handled all that," Nick said with a dismissive wave of his hand. "I don't think Sherry even had a checkbook. Didn't trust banks. Didn't think too highly of the way the family had earned all that cash, raping the land and such. Carla gave Sherry cash when she needed it. Like I said, Sherry was thrifty."

I didn't bother to point out that Sherry's livelihood, no matter how thrifty she was, depended on all those trees her family had whacked down to make lumber and paper, just as surely as if Sherry herself had wielded the ax. Besides, I'd seen Sherry's clothes. It took a lot of money to look that disheveled. It sounded to me like Sherry was able to rationalize the source and size of her income by dealing solely with Carla and cash. She played at poor, but she was still a trust-fund baby through and through.

"Hey, Izzy?" Sean called from Sherry's bedroom. "Nick? Can y'all come back here?"

Nick followed me down the short hallway. Sherry's

room looked like a National Geographic had exploded onto the walls. Fabrics in every hue and texture, from silks to homespun cottons, covered the walls and the massive four-poster bed. Woven baskets overflowed with colorful scarves and strings of beads and Sherry's eclectic clothing was strewn about every surface.

Sean stood in the midst of that vibrant chaos with a stack of papers in his hands.

No, not papers, photographs.

"Nick," Sean said, "did Sherry take all these?"

"Yeah, man. She was always taking pictures. She used to have a dark room set up in her closet, but now she's strictly digital."

Sean waggled the stack of pictures. "Maybe she took a picture of her mystery man."

"Oh, dude, if she did, I don't want to know, okay? You all do what you gotta do, but I'm going to just hang in the living room." Nick ducked out and left us alone in Sherry's room.

"There are stacks and stacks of these prints," Sean said. "Why don't you start on that side of the room?"

I found a dozen or so eight-by-ten photos weighted down by a jade figure of the Buddha and began leafing through them. They were beautiful landscape shots, close-ups of flowers and reeds, some more panoramic shots of water and lush vegetation.

Another stack of photos, tucked between two hardbound books, yielded similar shots, though this time I recognized the location: They'd been taken down by the old Soaring Eagles Adventure Camp. I saw the familiar pale blue cabins and the zigzag pier jutting into Badger Lake.

Just about every kid in Merryville had gone through Soaring Eagles in one capacity or another. At the insistence of Grandpa Gene, all of the Harper children and grandchildren had been sent to the camp to experience "roughing it." Priscilla Olson—then Glines—had practiced her mean girl skills by terrifying an entire cabin of ten-year-olds into giving her their pin money. Even Nick Haas had gone to camp, his fees paid by some well-meaning anonymous donor. I remembered him sneaking off into the woods with the older counselors to smoke weed after curfew.

I'd spent nearly every summer in those rotting cabins, first as a camper and later as a counselor. Rena, Sean, and I had shared our deepest secrets on the end of that pier. Casey Alter and I had fallen in love and planned our lives in the clearing behind the longhouse. Heck, I'd even been kissed for the very first time right beneath the Soaring Eagles flagpole.

I'd heard that the Andersons, who owned the camp, had gone bankrupt. Kids had stopped wanting summer camps where they made lanyards and learned to tool leather and instead wanted summer camps where they learned to program computer games and practice being crime scene investigators. Soaring Eagles hadn't kept in step with the times and had paid the price. Last I heard, the city had seized the property because the Andersons hadn't been paying their taxes. Now the sky-blue cabins were sinking slowly back into the earth.

I flipped through the pictures slowly, feeling the deep pull of nostalgia. The last two pictures, aerial shots of the camp that Sherry simply could not have taken herself, were marked up with a Sharpie. The outlines of the camp were picked out by a quavering line, and a couple of spots on the campgrounds themselves had been circled.

Strange. Probably another one of Sherry's wacky conspiracy theories. Sites of alien abductions? Secret government nuclear testing ground? As Nick had said, she'd had a lot of irons in the fire.

"I can't stand it," Nick said. He'd returned to the doorway to Sherry's room. His feet remained in the hall, and he'd braced his hands on the lintel, letting his body curve into the room. "Did you find him?"

"No," I replied. "Just tons of pictures of Soaring Eagles."

"Aw, yeah, man. Sherry's family owns the property right next to the camp. They have a cabin"—he sketched quotes in the air with his fingers—"on the water. Place is big enough to house the whole Harper clan. Carla was always complaining about what an eyesore the camp had become, but Sherry liked it. She wandered all around there with her Aunt Virginia, taking pictures of the birds and stuff, picking wildflowers. All that nature stuff."

"What about you, Sean? Any sign of our mystery man?"

Sean looked up from a stack of photos he'd been thumbing through. "No. I got squirrels, a robin, a beaver, and three shots of Virginia's corgi, Sir Francis, but no mystery man." He looked back down at the photo in his hand. "Well, in this one it looks like there's another person."

He walked the photo over so both Nick and I could see what he was looking at. "See here," he said, pointing to a blurry splotch at the edge of the frame. "That looks like part of a person. Maybe a pair of chinos?"

"Great. A man in Minnesota who owns a pair of khakis. That doesn't exactly narrow it down."

"Besides," Nick said, "that's a woman."

"How can you tell?" I asked.

"That's the curve of a hip. Men aren't built like that. And up here"—he pointed to a spot just above the alleged pants—"that looks like the ruffle of a blouse to me. Something frilly with flowers on it."

I looked more closely at the photo and was startled to realize he was correct.

"Well, then, that gets us exactly nowhere."

It seemed our search of Sherry's apartment hadn't yielded a thing.

CHAPTER
Twelve

"Nothing," I reported to Rena. "Just some wildlife photos and the blurry edge of a woman. No mystery man."

"Why are you assuming it's a mystery *man*?" Rena asked. She was frosting a tray of banana pupcakes with peanut butter icing. "Sherry liked men and women. Did she specifically tell Nick she was seeing another man?"

I mentally kicked myself. "I never thought to ask."

"So maybe the woman in the photo is the mystery lover after all." She looked down. "Just another minute, buddy, I'll give you one when they're done."

Packer sat at Rena's feet, head cocked, ears up, licking his lips with anticipation, whining softly and shifting anxiously every time it looked like Rena might hand down one of her treats to him.

"We still didn't get a picture with a face, nothing to actually tell us who the woman would be."

"But if Sherry was involved with a woman, the number of possibilities is dramatically reduced," Rena pointed out as she put the finishing flourish on her tray of canine confections. She proffered one of the treats to Packer, who wolfed it down in a single joyous gulp.

"Also, if Sherry was involved with a woman, someone else must have known about it. The gay and lesbian community here is very small. You can't sneeze without the entire community saying 'God bless.'"

I finished folding a stack of dog sweaters and placed them on a display stand in front of the white molded plastic doggy mannequin. The sweaters were a red-and-green Argyle pattern, and I expected them to sell like gangbusters as we moved into the Christmas season. "Well, did *you* hear anything?"

"No. What with the store opening and all, I wasn't really keeping up with the latest. But I know who would know."

"Who?"

"Jolly Nielson."

"Taffy's sister? I didn't know she was gay."

"Dork. You didn't even know I was gay until a few days ago."

Rena was right. Heck, Nick Haas—whose brain was positively pickled with booze—had been more observant in studying those photographs than I had been. If I was going to figure out who killed Sherry Harper, I was going to have to step up my game.

"By the way," Rena said, "Sean's going to be stopping by in about half an hour. I don't know how much new information he has, but he's promised to make regular reports and keep me in the loop."

My hand jerked and I knocked the whole stack of sweaters onto the floor. I bent down with a sigh to pick them up and start folding them all over again. "That's fine," I responded.

"Are you sure?"

"Why wouldn't I be sure?"

"Well, thanks to this whole murder thing, you two have gone from twelve years of silence to near constant contact basically overnight."

"So?" I ran my hand briskly across a fold in the sweater I was holding, making sure it was neat and crisp.

"So, you're folding those dog sweaters like they're origami, and your left eye is twitching."

I reached up to touch my face. Sure enough, the corner of my left eye jerked in tiny spasms.

"Still don't see your point," I said, returning to my military-style sweater folding.

"Well, you were totally relaxed five minutes ago, and the minute I mentioned Sean, you wound yourself tight as a top." She walked to my side and laid a hand on mine, forcing me to stop my folding. "Look at me, Izzy."

I looked at her, but my lips were drawn tight. I was losing patience with this conversation.

"Don't you think it's even possible that you're a little shaken by Sean coming back into your life like this? I mean, you two didn't really resolve anything that night he came to your house. And all that business with Casey has left you pretty vulnerable."

Rena patted my hand softly. "I'm just worried about you."

I felt tears welling in my eyes. Rena was looking at a possible murder charge, and she was worried about my stupid feelings.

"Oh, I'm fine. I guess it's a little tough. That night, I felt sorta sorry for Sean. I had my life with Casey, and he wasn't even dating anyone. Now the tables are turned, with him practically engaged to Carla and me still looking all pitiful because Casey played me for a fool. For fourteen whole years. It's just a little embarrassing."

"Just a little embarrassing," Rena echoed. She sounded like she wasn't entirely convinced that my reaction to Sean was purely embarrassment. Heck, I wasn't sure it was purely embarrassment. But now wasn't the time to hash it out with Rena. My Sean issues would wait until she was in the clear, legally speaking.

"Okay," Rena said. "So Sean will be here soon. Maybe we can all go pay Jolly a visit."

Jolly Nielson had nearly a decade on her sister, and her hair was the blue-black of a crow's wing while Taffy's was the color of sun through honey. Still, the family resemblance was uncanny: warm amber eyes, soft curvy bodies, and sweetly rounded features.

Jolly's studio and store were on Oak, right between the Spin Doctor record shop and the Grateful Grape. Sean, Rena, and I found her polishing a tray of hammered silver bangles. Jolly made jewelry that echoed natural forms, often using simple elements to create beautiful and unusual pieces, like polishing river rocks instead of using gems or using a willow wand to create a mold for casting a segmented silver necklace. Her work was wildly popular with Merryville's upscale tourists.

She greeted us with hugs all around.

"I hope you don't mind that we brought Packer," I said, indicating the wheezing dog at my feet. "I'm always looking for opportunities for him to burn off a little energy, but I can take him for a turn around the block while you all talk."

"Nonsense," Jolly said. "He can't hurt anything here, and I love dogs. He's a welcome guest."

She dropped to one knee, and Packer pulled his leash from my hand as he bounded toward her, raining sloppy kisses all over her face.

"Packer!" I hissed, mortified by his bad manners.

"Really, I don't mind. Love is love, in all its forms."

Jolly stood again, and Packer dropped onto his haunches at her feet, staring up at her with frank adoration.

"Well, look at this! The three musketeers back together again," Jolly laughed. "You three used to be thick as thieves. It takes me back to see you all in one place again. Back to summer camp and twilight games of capture the flag. Those were good times."

Although Jolly was a little older than we were, and significantly older than her sister, she'd stuck close with Taffy during their summers in Merryville. They were always on the outside, of course, just seasonal friends, but she was right that those carefree summer days were some of the best memories I had.

"What can I do for you?"

"This is a little awkward," Rena said, "but we were

wondering if you'd heard anything about Sherry Harper being in a romantic relationship with a woman."

"Ah, taking advantage of my position as queen bee, I see. What makes you think Sherry was dating a woman?"

Now it was Rena's turn to blush. She opened her mouth to speak, and I thought she might spill the beans about her long-ago fling with Sherry, but Sean cut her off.

"We don't know that she was. We just know that she was involved with someone other than her long-time boyfriend, Nick Haas, and we haven't ruled out the possibility that the someone else was a woman."

"Maybe this will help," Sean said, handing Jolly the picture with the half-shadowed human figure it. "We found this in Sherry's apartment."

Jolly raised an eyebrow. "Snooping in her house? You guys are pretty serious about this, aren't you?" She clucked her tongue but took the picture and studied it.

"Well," she said, "I hate to break it to you, but this isn't Sherry's mystery date. This is her aunt Virginia."

"How can you tell?" Rena asked.

Jolly set the photo on a table covered with glittering silver on luscious black velvet. We gathered around to see. "Look here," she said, pointing at the blur of the woman's right arm. "You see that little flash?"

Just at the edge of the blurry figure, there was a white spot in the photo, a flash of light off metal.

"Right beneath that flash, you can see one of the charms on a bracelet. It's pretty small, but it's distinct. A bunch of grapes with tendrils of grapevines. I made that charm for Virginia myself."

My heart sank. One step forward, two steps back.

"Sorry," Jolly said. "And as far as her love life went, I can't help you. Sherry dated a couple of girls in her younger days, but I think she was just experimenting. Lately, I haven't heard any scuttlebutt about Sherry at all." She smiled sadly.

"Well, that's not entirely true. I mean, I do have an ear for gossip, and not just of the same-sex variety, and there's always gossip about Sherry."

"Heard anything lately?" Sean asked.

Jolly hummed softly, staring at the ceiling as she thought. "The other morning, I was at Joe Time getting a peppermint mocha latte." She stopped suddenly, eyes wide. "Oh dear, you girls can't tell Taffy I was there. She made me swear off coffee a year ago, tried to get me hooked on this detoxing herbal tea. She'd be crushed if she knew I was cheating on my promise."

"Your secret is safe with us," Rena said. She cast a sidelong glance in my direction. "Turns out we're pretty good at keeping secrets. Now, what did you hear at the coffee shop?"

"It was probably nothing. Lois Owens from First National was talking to Diane Jenkins about Sherry. Appears she'd set up camp outside the bank manager's office for a whole day, refusing to budge until he met with her. When he did, Lois said all the tellers could hear Sherry screaming away in his office. Once Sherry left, the manager told his assistant he wouldn't take any more calls or appointments for the day." Jolly chuckled. "Lois said the guy keeps a bottle of whiskey in his desk drawer, and all the tellers were going to take up a collection to buy him another one after that kerfuffle."

"Any idea what kind of bee Sherry had in her bonnet?" I asked.

Jolly shrugged. "No. Probably one of her harebrained protest plans."

That made sense. Nick had said that Sherry didn't trust banks, only dealt in cash. I couldn't imagine what would have drawn her to First National other than a chance to raise heck.

"I don't think it means anything," Jolly added. "That girl might have been on the side of the angels, but she did have a knack for rubbing folks the wrong way."

"Did you have a run-in with Sherry, too?" I asked.

"Just once, and only indirectly. Only a few days before she died, actually."

My ears perked up. "What happened?"

"She got mad at her aunt because Virginia let me onto the Harper's lakefront property to pick some flowers and gather some rocks for my work. Nothing valuable or endangered, but Sherry still threw a fit. I think it had less to do with me taking the rocks and twigs and more to do with Virginia being the one to let me onto the property."

"Why do you say that?" Sean asked.

"Well, she didn't even look at what I had in my bag—two dead tree limbs, about six rocks, and three pine cones. If she'd looked she'd have realized that I wasn't harming anything. Instead, she yelled that Virginia didn't own the property and she needed to remember that she wasn't a real Harper."

"That doesn't sound like Sherry," Rena said.

I had to agree. For all her faults, everything pointed

to Sherry being generous with her worldly belongings. She gave Nick a key to her apartment so he'd never be homeless, and she even gave me the last of her ginseng . . . despite thinking I was a terrible person for opening up a pet boutique. She may have used the Harper money to get by, but I'd never heard of her lording it over other people that she came from such a distinguished family . . . especially not her aunt Virginia, with whom she'd always been close. The whole incident really did seem out of character.

"In any event," Jolly said, "I haven't heard a peep about Sherry involved with anyone—male or female—other than poor old Nick. I can't speak for the straight population, but if she were seeing a woman, I would know. Unless it was someone from out of town."

Out of town. Of course!

After we bid Jolly goodbye and bundled out of her store, I floated my theory to Sean and Rena.

"When I was going through Gandhi's sling, I found a receipt for dinner for two at the Mission in Lac du Chien. Maybe she was meeting a significant other there. Could be someone from out of town. Rena, you said she was part of a whole network of activists, so maybe she met someone from Minneapolis or Madison."

"It's possible," Sean conceded. "It might even be someone local who was willing to drive a few miles to keep his affair with Sherry a secret."

"Only one way to find out," I said. "We go to the Mission and see if anyone remembers Sherry and her dining companion."

"Don't look at me," Rena said. She pointed at her

hair. "I'm not really the Mission's usual clientele. They wouldn't tell me anything."

"That just leaves us," I said, giving Sean a hopeful look.

He dropped his head. "Carla's going to kill me, you know. We haven't spent an evening together since Sherry died."

I struggled to keep my expression neutral and to quell the pang I felt in the pit of my stomach. Jealousy? Surely not.

"You don't have to come with me," I said. "I could drag along my aunt Dolly, or even Ingrid."

He laughed. "Somehow I can't imagine you making much headway with either one of them as your side-kick." He sighed, but a trace of a smile still lingered. "All right," he said. "It's a date. I'll call for a reservation. Tomorrow at eight?"

I couldn't tell if he was happy to go with me or whether obligation drove him to say yes. The boy who wore his heart on his sleeve had become a cipher, and I couldn't help thinking I was partly to blame for that.

CHAPTER
Thirteen

Late the next afternoon, I was adding silver studs to a shearling-lined leather motorcycle jacket—cut for a golden retriever—to match the studded leather boots I'd made for him the night before. As I punched in the final stud, I was startled to see Jack Collins from the Merryville PD bounding up the steps outside Trendy Tails. For a moment, I lost all sensation in my body. He was coming to arrest Rena. I had to signal her somehow, keep her from leaving the kitchen, hide her in the pantry.

Then my brain processed the fact that he wasn't in uniform and that he was holding an amazingly fat beagle in his arms.

The brass bells above my door tinkled as he pushed open the door, sending a rush of bitter cold air swirling through the shop. I shivered before I mustered a smile for him.

"Hey, Jack. What can I do for you?"

He wheezed as he lowered the beagle to the floor where it immediately flopped on its stomach and let out a little doggy groan.

Jack pointed down at the dog. "This is Pearl, my mom's dog. She doesn't like the snow. Had to carry her from the dang car." He paused to glare down at the offending animal. "My mom can't carry her, especially in the snow and ice, and I'm tired of having to drive by twice a day to shovel a little clear spot in the yard and heave Pearl to it so she can do her business."

"Ah. I can help." I ducked out from behind the counter and led Jack over to the selection of snow booties. "Sometimes it can be a little tricky getting these on the dogs, but I don't think Pearl's going to put up much of a fight." As if to prove my point, Pearl let out a very unladylike belch and rolled onto her back.

"Since her, um, tummy is so close to the ground"—in a way no beagle's should be—"you might want to consider one of these fleece jackets, too. They button at the front of the neck and down the dog's back, so they're really easy to get on."

"Huh." Jack studied all of the fleece items carefully. He picked up a pair of lavender booties and matching jacket. His face reddened and he cleared his throat. "It's my mother's favorite color."

"She'll love them," I said. "And so will Pearl. But, uh, you might go up a size or two in the jacket."

Jack looked over at Pearl and heaved a sigh. "Yeah. I keep telling my mother she shouldn't feed the dog chips and dip. But apparently Pearl likes French onion, and my mom can't say no."

I died a little inside at the notion of Jack's mom feeding her dog that crap. But it was my job to sell clothes for pets, not to judge their owners.

As I rang up Jack's purchase, he cleared his throat again. I glanced up to find his face and throat consumed in another furious blush. For an instant I saw grade-school Jack, a clunky fireplug of a kid who stuttered when the teacher called on him in class and who took numerous beatings on the playground just because his mom had told him he wasn't allowed to hit kids smaller than he was . . . and every kid was smaller than Jack.

"Uh, Izzy?"

"Yes?" I started wrapping Pearl's new outdoor gear in tissue, sealing it with one of our bright purple paw print stickers.

"I stopped by Joe Time this morning. Ran into Jolly Nielson. And Ken West."

I paused a moment, but then continued slipping his purchase into a silver paper bag.

"Jolly said you'd been asking her about Sherry," he continued.

There was no sense lying. "Yep."

"Look, I know Rena's your friend, and you must feel pretty bad that Sherry died during your party and all, but you should be careful poking around in police business."

I looked him straight in the eye. "Am I doing anything wrong? Breaking any law?"

A flash of hurt lit his hazel eyes. "Well, no. I know Sean's got to ask questions for his client, and you're not doing anything wrong, per se. I'm just worried about you. I know the police in this town, we seem like a bunch of donut-eating doofuses, but sometimes this job is really dangerous. I don't want to see you get hurt."

My heart melted a little. It was true, I'd always taken Jack for a bit of a doofus, but his concern seemed genuine.

"I'll be careful," I said with a smile.

I waited until Jack had hefted Pearl back into his arms before I handed him his bag, and then I held the door for him so he could balance Pearl and the package.

Before I could push the door closed against the icy wind or Jack could get down the steps, Richard Greene materialized at the foot of the stairs, blocking Jack's way.

"Officer Collins," Richard barked. "You should issue this woman a citation."

"For what?" I asked.

"For public nuisance. You can do that right?"

Jack cocked his head. "Well, yeah, but is she? I mean is she causing a public nuisance?"

Richard crossed his arms across his chest, heels dug in for battle.

"Not directly," Richard said, "but she's the instigator."

I rubbed my arms briskly, trying to stay warm without my coat. "I don't think I've instigated anything."

"Yes, ma'am, you certainly have. It is because of you that I have a rodent in my store, destroying my belongings."

This again. I sighed.

"Richard, I've told you that the guinea pig is not mine. It was Sherry's. I'm happy to help you try to trap him, but you really can't blame me for his presence in your store."

Jack shifted Pearl in his arms. "Sir, I don't think this is a police matter. Perhaps you and Izzy could work something out?"

Richard opened his mouth to argue.

I cut him off. "Tell you what, Richard, I'll come over right now to help you track down Gandhi. Let me just tell Rena to mind the store."

He nodded brusquely. I could tell the solution didn't sit well with him, but he wasn't in a position to argue.

I ducked back into the store, glancing down at my watch as I called for Rena. Gandhi better surface quickly, because I had a datelike investigation to get ready for.

CHAPTER
Fourteen

"There, in the map." Richard Greene pointed at a wall unit packed with rolled maps, his finger gnarled by age and arthritis, but his tone and determination harkening back to his days in the military. It was that tone that brought me running to save Gandhi when Richard stuck his head inside Trendy Tails to inform us he was calling an exterminator.

I followed his gesture. Sure enough, two button eyes peered out at us from a map tunnel.

I clicked my tongue softly against my teeth and extended a hand with a piece of carrot. "Come on, little guy. Come get some delicious carrot."

Gandhi's nose twitched in his tiny auburn face.

I kept up a steady mental monologue, silently willing Gandhi to take my bait: *Yummy, yummy carrot. You need to come out now, little friend, or Mr. Greene might fry you up for his supper. And wage a private war against Trendy Tails to boot. Come on. Yummy, yummy carrot.*

The nose twitched again, and I was sure the pig was about to cave, when suddenly he bolted.

Quick like a bunny, I dashed to the wall unit, hoping to catch sight of Gandhi before he disappeared again, but no luck.

I glanced at my watch. I only had twenty minutes before Sean would be picking me up for our trip to the Mission, and Gandhi was nowhere to be seen.

"Mr. Greene, I don't think this is working."

"Your powers of observation are stunning, Miss McHale," he snapped bitterly. "How do you propose to remedy this problem?"

"I'll get you some humane traps, help you set them with some greens and carrot to try to lure him out. We'll get him, Mr. Greene. I promise."

"You better be right. I've been an upstanding member of this community for sixty-nine years. I believe I can call in a few favors and get that planning and zoning board meeting moved up a bit. One way or another, this animal nuisance will be eliminated."

I dressed in a rush, spritzing on a little perfume to cover the scent of moldering paper that clung to my skin and slapping some mascara on my eyelashes so I'd look a bit less frazzled. Jinx sat on my dresser, tail flicking occasionally, but otherwise unmoved by my antics. I sometimes wondered if that cat thought I was just a big monkey, dancing around for her amusement. Packer, on the other hand, leapt frantically around the room, trying to help but managing only to get underfoot as I tugged on a pair of reasonably dressy boots. A quick barrette to hold back my hair, as I'd worked up a bit of a sweat hunting guinea pig and my wavy hair had worked its way into Medusa-like curls.

I dashed down the stairs to find Rena, Ingrid, and Aunt Dolly each holding a spoon, a quart of ice cream between them on the shiny red table.

"Great dinner," I chided.

"Hey, you get to eat at one of the nicest restaurants in outstate Minnesota tonight," Rena said. "I think we're entitled to a little mocha almond fudge."

Ingrid, her long white hair woven into girlish pigtails, her rhinestone glasses glittering in the light—and all of it incongruous with her Carhartt overalls and fisherman's sweater—waved her spoon in my direction. "Don't know about these gals, but I'm old. I can eat whatever I want whenever I want it. I guarantee, fifty years from now, you'll feel exactly the same way.

"I'd give up this ice cream in a heartbeat if I could have dinner at the Mission," Dolly said. While Ingrid was tall and raw-boned, Dolly was a tiny, girly little thing. That night, she had a wide pink satin ribbon wrapped around her head and tied in a perfect bow. The ribbon perfectly matched the flowers on her velour tracksuit . . . though I think when the target market is a woman of Dolly's age, they stop calling them "tracksuits" and start calling them "cruise wear."

While she looked like some weird hybrid of little old lady and tween girl, Dolly had developed sophisticated tastes during the years she was married to my uncle Ned. She was the closest thing our family had to a genuine foodie, and she frequently waxed poetic about the culinary delights of various restaurants in the area.

"It's a pity you can't indulge in the grass-fed beef medallions in red wine reduction, but the winter vegetable pot pie is wonderful, too." She sighed. "And you get to go with a handsome man on your arm. Are you sure we can't trade places for tonight?"

"No way. After the day I've had, I deserve a night on the town, even if it's all in the name of investigating Sherry's death."

Rena waggled her spoon. "I was just filling Dolly and Ingrid in on Richard's latest threats and the plight of the purloined pig."

"I like the alliteration, but Gandhi wasn't purloined. Just lost and resisting being found. And it's the straw that broke the camel's back as far as Richard is concerned. I'm terrified he'll make good on his threats and get us shut down before we even have a chance."

Dolly waved her hand dismissively. "Let me handle that old coot," she said. "I know Richard Greene from way back when. He's always been a stick in the mud. But he had a crush on me once upon a time, and this old girl's still got a little pepper in her shaker."

Ingrid and Rena both burst out laughing.

"Dolly, I've lived next to Richard Greene for nearly thirty years. It's going to take more than a little pepper to get through to him."

"Trust me, Ingrid, you haven't seen me in action in a while. I've got some moves."

"Aunt Dolly, you will not use your feminine wiles on that old man."

"Be careful who you're calling 'old,' missy. And why shouldn't I use my best assets to help you out? I'd be protecting my own investment, after all. You just leave this to me. Now go have a wonderful time and find a killer."

Sean drove, giving me a chance to study him on the sly. He'd grown up well. He'd put on just enough muscle through his chest and shoulders to save his lean frame from awkwardness. His jaw had hardened since high school, and his green eyes were bracketed by fine lines, but his broad, mobile mouth and unruly curls—the color of dark chocolate—lent him a boyish quality.

I finally decided to tackle the elephant in the Honda: that long ago spring night, when Sean and I parted ways.

I cleared my throat. "It's been good to see you again." I reached back and twisted a curl of my hair around my index finger. "You know, after all this time."

Out of the corner of my eye, I could see Sean clench the wheel tighter.

After a few seconds, he responded. "Yes."

I wasn't sure what he meant, so I waited for him to continue.

"I'm sorry for that night. Sorry for what it did to our friendship."

Impulsively, I reached over to lay my hand on his, just briefly. "And I'm sorry for how that evening played out."

He let forth a short bark of laughter. "I'm not. God, I was so young and stupid. What if you'd decided to dump Casey for me? Where would that have gotten us?"

I swallowed the pain of his words, struggled to keep the hurt and bitterness out of my own. "Ah. So you didn't love me after all."

His mouth curled into that sleepy smile I knew so well. "I didn't say that, Izzy."

"Oh."

"I meant exactly what I said. What would we have done? You were already packing for Madison, I was on my way to New Orleans, and we were both eighteen. I think you'll agree with me when I say that we didn't have a realistic view of what the future would hold when we were eighteen."

Now it was my turn to laugh. I was the poster child for unrealistic expectations.

"No matter how I felt at the time, I acted rashly. And I'm glad you didn't listen to me then."

"Well. Good."

I struggled with his response. On the one hand, we'd cleared the air. On the other hand, he'd basically said he dodged a bullet. And the bullet was me.

It was a lot for a girl to take in.

After that, we rode in relative silence, broken only by his offer to turn on the radio and my own occasional sneezing fit. The cold I'd been fighting off for days was gaining traction.

As we turned off Thornapple Avenue onto Route 34, I saw the sign for the Sprigs organic market. On a whim, I asked Sean to pull in.

I occasionally shopped at Sprigs, splurging on exotic fruits or high-end pasta sauce, but I usually stuck with the regular grocery store for my food and I'd never ventured into the corner of Sprigs that housed homeopathic remedies, herbs, and organic skin care products.

I was perusing the shelves while Sean stood back, tapping his foot impatiently.

"Ginseng? Really?"

"Sherry swore this stuff would keep my cold away."

"And it makes perfect sense to take medical advice from Sherry Harper. I don't mean to speak ill of the dead, but the woman was a raisin or two shy of a fruitcake."

I turned to look him in the eye. "'Don't mean to speak ill of the dead'? That was absolutely speaking ill of the dead."

Sean shoved his hands in his pockets and looked at the floor, the toe of one shoe sketching little arcs across the laminate flooring.

"All I meant was that she wasn't exactly a doctor."

I gave him a playful shove. "I'm just teasing. Look, it can't hurt, right? And I really can't afford to be knocked out with a cold right now."

"Fair enough. But let's hurry."

"Can I help you?"

I looked up to find a young man in jeans and a green Sprigs apron. His dark brown hair brushed his collar, and rectangular tortoiseshell glasses rested on a long, narrow nose.

"I'm looking for dried ginseng. Someone told me it would keep a cold from setting in."

"Your friend is right. And the ginseng is over here by the echinacea and zinc and grapefruit seed extract . . . all of those things would help you out with your cold."

I followed him to the rack he pointed out.

"Here," I said, grabbing a cellophane packet with a yellow paper label. It was filled with bits of fibrous grayish brown plant matter. "I think this is the type Sherry used."

"Sherry?" the man asked. "Sherry Harper?"

"Yeah, you know her?"

"Of course. Sherry came in all the time. She had really bad seasonal allergies." He shook his head. "But that's not the ginseng she used. That brand is imported, and Sherry only used locally grown ginseng. Most U.S. ginseng is grown there in Wisconsin, you know. No sense using an import."

"I did *not* know that," I replied. "But are you sure Sherry didn't buy this? Maybe if you were out of her brand?"

"No way. She would have bought the tea or one of these herbal blends before she bought an import."

Come to think of it, when Sherry offered me the ginseng that day in Trendy Tails, the package had been red. But the bit of label I found in Gandhi's sling was yellow, like the package on the shelf.

Huh.

I studied the nubbins of dried root in the cellophane packet.

"Sean?"

"Yes, Izzy?" he intoned with mock formality as he sidled up to me.

"Look at this stuff." I shook the bag in front of his face.

"It looks vile."

"Mmm. Yes," I agreed. "But what about this? Sherry was poisoned with dried water hemlock root. How different could that look from this stuff?"

"Good question." Sean pulled out his smartphone and fired it up. "This," he said, holding the phone out to me, "is ginseng root. And"—he took the phone back, manipulated the screen, studied it a moment, and passed it back—"is water hemlock root."

"They look very similar to me," I said.

"Me, too. At least on this tiny screen. I'll double-check tonight. The police aren't the only ones with a pipeline to the U of M Extension. I've got a friend there, and I'll send him these pictures, see what he has to say."

"Let's assume they're pretty similar. So we know that Sherry was fighting a cold the day before she died, and she was out of her favorite ginseng because she gave the last of it to me. She'd said that Sprigs was out of her brand. That kid," I pointed to the young man who had helped me, who was now straightening a row of jars on a nearby shelf, "said Sherry would never buy the ginseng with the yellow wrapper, but I found a bit of that yellow wrapper in Gandhi's sling."

"I see where you're heading," Sean said with a nod.

"Exactly. We've all been assuming that the hemlock was mixed into Sherry's food somehow. But what if she ate it by itself, thinking it was ginseng? What if someone gave her a package of poison and she ate it without a care in the world?"

"But didn't the guy say that Sherry would never use the imported stuff?"

"Yeah, she never would have bought it. But if someone offered it to her—"

"—she might have taken it. But that means someone could have given her that package of fake ginseng anytime between when you saw her in Trendy Tails the day before the grand opening and when she died," Sean said. "We're going to have to track her movements for that entire time."

"No," I said, "I don't think so. I think her killer was in the alley that night."

"Why?"

"Because of what was missing. I found that corner of a wrapper in Gandhi's sling—little guy must have grabbed hold of it—but the rest of the package was gone. And the cell phone, too. Someone took the evidence of the crime from the scene.

"No," I said, shaking my head. "There's no question in my mind. Sherry's killer was standing right next to her as she died."

CHAPTER
Fifteen

The Mission nestled in a grove of quaking aspens, its low-slung architecture harkening to the movement that inspired its name.

Inside, stark white walls and plain oak plank tables lined up in neat rows lent the space an almost monastic feel that was broken only by a handful of canvases by local artists.

"I brought the picture of Sherry," Sean announced as soon as we were seated. He slid the photo over to me.

He'd borrowed the snapshot from Carla, and it showed Sherry at a Harper family gathering. She wore a jumper of patchwork calico over a white turtleneck and her hair was in long braids. She stood in a cluster of preppy Harper kin. While everyone else in the picture posed with ramrod stiffness, Sherry looked to be in motion, slightly blurred at the edges as though someone had taken an eraser to her and smudged her ever so slightly. Her brow was furrowed, as though she were annoyed about something, and her mouth was open, caught in midword.

"It's not a great shot," Sean said.

"I think it captures Sherry perfectly."

He smiled. "I guess it does, but it's a little hard to make out her features. Still, it was the best I could do. She never sat still for the camera."

"It should do the trick."

We decided to dine first, and then hit up the waitstaff for information after the evening rush subsided.

Dolly was half right about my evening. The winter vegetable pot pie was delicious—tender pastry covering a filling of parsnips, potatoes, onions, and mushrooms in a rich mushroom-and-red-wine gravy seasoned with thyme and a hint of rosemary—and Sean raved about his beef medallions.

But Dolly got the whole "on the arm of a handsome man" bit dead wrong. Don't get me wrong. Sean looked especially handsome that night, even if one sable curl kept falling in his eyes. And he smelled even better than the scrumptious dinner: of soap and juniper and crisp wintery mint. Still, I was not exactly on his arm. Rather, we mostly sat across from each other eating, our silence broken only by occasional bits of awkward small talk. The conversation in the car cast a pall over the whole dinner.

Finally, over two slices of apple tarte tatin a la mode, Sean broke the silence and, intentionally or not, went for the jugular.

"Have you heard from Casey?" he asked, just as I took a bite of caramelized apple and melting ice cream.

I took my time chewing and swallowing my dessert while I tried to get past my panic of talking about Casey with Sean. "Uh, yeah, a few times. We had years of life together to untangle. A joint credit card, bills. That sort of thing."

"So all business."

I chuckled. "Not entirely. In the first months after he left, there was a heated discussion about what would happen with the animals. We'd always thought of Jinx as my cat and Packer as Casey's dog, but he didn't take Packer when he left. I confess I was pretty brutal in my condemnation of that fact, calling him heartless and a deadbeat. But then he said 'fine, send Packer to me,' and I backpedaled big-time and said it was too late, Packer was staying with me."

"Ouch. I've handled a few divorces, and I swear couples fight more over custody of the family dog than they do over custody of the children."

"With kids, you can get visitation, but with a pet? Custody is the end. Thing was, he was right. Casey picked out Packer, named him—because you *know* I wouldn't have named him after that Wisconsin team, and when he got home at night, Casey was happier to see Packer than he was to see me."

"That might have been a hint of what was to come."

I chuckled, grateful that I'd reached a place where I could chuckle about those dark days. "Probably. In any event, I suppose I should have given him the dog. But I was hurt. I'd literally come home one day to find half the apartment cleaned out. I wasn't really mad that he'd abandoned Packer—after all, I didn't want to give up the little guy—but I was mad that he'd abandoned *me*, and it was just easier to talk about the dog." I shrugged. "After a few months, though, the sting wore off. I guess I could see why Casey had left."

"And why is that?"

"We lived totally different lives. You know we had this plan . . ."

"A plan?"

I waved my fork. "Yeah, a plan. We would go to college together, ride out Casey's residency at home, and then move to New York for our big, exciting lives. But by the time Casey left, all we had was the plan. You know?"

"No, I don't know."

"Well, I was just waiting for New York, I wasn't doing anything with the life I was living right then. I was so focused on the future that I wasn't appreciating the now. I never even stopped to think about whether we were still happy; I just kept thinking about how great it would be when the plan finally came to fruition."

"And when you *did* stop to think about whether you were still happy, what was the answer?"

"Clearly Casey wasn't happy, or he wouldn't have taken up with that skinny little diet girl. But, really, I don't think I was happy, either. Every move I'd made, I'd made for Casey, and that was starting to rub me the wrong way."

"So you were tired of being a sidekick?"

"Ah. I was waiting for your 'I told you so' moment, and I guess this is it."

He raised his water glass in a silent toast, his lopsided smile taking the burn out of the gesture.

I took another bite of my tarte. It was really too good for me to let it go to waste.

We'd dissected my failed love life, and I decided it was my turn to put him under a microscope.

"What about you and Carla? Things serious?"

He shrugged. "We've only been dating a while."

"A year," I blurted, both setting the record straight and tipping my hand that I'd been asking about him.

He raised an eyebrow at my quick correction. "I mean, that's what my mom said," I said, trying to sound nonchalant. "When Rena asked." I was trying to make myself seem uninterested and failing miserably.

A bemused smile twisted the corners of his mouth. "I guess maybe it has been a year. We're the only two lawyers in town under the age of sixty, so it was inevitable we'd be thrown together at bar functions and the like. I couldn't even pinpoint when 'dinner with a colleague' turned into dating."

"So romantic."

"I've tried romantic, and it didn't really work out so well," he drawled.

"Touché."

I saw a flash in his eyes that reminded me of summer lightning and the cool scent of apple blossoms in the rain. But, like lightning, it was gone in the space of a heartbeat.

I studied my plate, using my fork to pick apart the layers of pastry. "There are rumors of wedding bells."

Sean laughed. "There are rumors that Ingrid Whitfield and Richard Greene have been having an affair for twenty years. It's a small town. There are a lot of rumors."

"So you're not that serious."

"I'm going to plead the Fifth here. Let's just say, I haven't bought a ring."

"Fair enough."

"Now if you're done demolishing that tarte, let's see if any of the waitstaff can tell us something about Sherry and her mystery man."

It didn't take us long to get an answer.

CHAPTER
Sixteen

Our waiter didn't recognize Sherry, but he signaled to his manager, a compact man in impeccable gray slacks and a navy sport coat.

"We were wondering if you recognized the woman in this picture," Sean said.

Before Sean could lay the picture down on the table, the manager spread his hands in a halting gesture. "I'm sorry, but we value our guests' privacy. I wouldn't feel comfortable . . ."

His voice trailed off as he happened to glance down at the picture.

"Oh, *her*," he snapped. "Yes, how could I forget this one?"

"Her name's Sherry Harper."

"I know. She told me about fifteen times, all while she made an almighty racket about our duck."

"What, she didn't like it?" Sean asked innocently.

"She didn't even order it! She questioned the waiter

about how the duck had been raised, whether it was free range or not. The poor man did not know, and that woman started quite a ruckus."

"Free range ducks," I said. "I didn't even know that was a thing."

"Well, yes, of course," the manager huffed. "Any fowl can be raised outside a pen, and in fact we source our ducks, chicken, and geese from free range farmers, but that is not the point. The point is that she started yelling at my waiter because he couldn't answer her question."

"Oh dear."

"'Oh dear,' indeed. When I intervened, she began grilling me about everything on the menu. Were the potatoes organic, were the beets genetically modified, had the apples been picked by workers with fair labor conditions? Yes, no, and yes, by the way. I assure you that the food we serve is of the highest quality, from ethical and sustainable sources. But she would not be satisfied by anything I had to say. At least her companion had the good grace to try to calm her down."

Sean interrupted the manager's tirade. "It's actually her companion we were interested in. Did you recognize him? Or her?"

"It was a man," the manager said, "but I don't know who he was. Nothing really stood out about him. White, middle-aged, average build . . . maybe a little portly, like one of those former athletes who's starting to show signs of age. I do remember thinking he looked familiar, but I couldn't place him."

I sighed. We'd hit a dead end.

"You might ask Ken," the manager said. "As soon as

that Sherry woman saw him coming out of the kitchen, she had a fit. I'm quite certain he recognized them both."

"Ken?" Sean said.

"Yes, Ken West."

"What was he doing here?" I asked.

The manager narrowed his eyes. "You're not like this one, are you?" He stabbed his finger at Sherry's face in the photo. "You're trying to find some scandal so you can ruin my business like this one"—he stabbed at Sherry's face again—"ruined Ken's."

I raised my hands in a placating gesture. "No, no. I didn't mean that to sound like an accusation. I just know Ken—personally, I mean—and I was wondering why he would have been out here."

Despite my protestations that I didn't have any ulterior motive for my question, the manager had decided to tar me with Sherry's brush. He answered, but his words were measured and his tone wary. "He does a little cooking for us. Strictly as an independent contractor. You have a problem with Ken, you take it up with him, you hear?"

Honestly, I didn't have a problem with Ken—other than the possibility that he might be Sherry's killer—but I was hoping he might be able to shed some light on Sherry's mystery man.

Despite the looming threat of a murder indictment and the chaos of our new business venture, Rena insisted we invite Sean and Carla Harper over for dinner.

"His time is valuable," she said, "and he's insisting on representing me pro bono. If he's going to be my lawyer for free, the least I can do is make him a lasagna."

"Mmmm."

"Look, I know you're probably not dying to spend an evening with Sean and Carla, but you're going to encounter the two of them together eventually. Might as well control the situation, prepare for it."

We invited them to my house because Rena's house was perpetually occupied by her father, who was perpetually fifty percent drunk and one hundred percent mean. As a result, I got my first opportunity to really meet Carla Harper on my home turf.

The Harpers were northern Minnesota's answer to the Kennedys: a family dynasty of money and power dating back to the industrial revolution. They started coming to Merryville to spend summers at their rambling lodge on Badger Lake, but by the early 1960s the family's center of gravity had shifted away from the business hub of Minneapolis and the political hub of Saint Paul to the leisure hub of Merryville. There was no need to stay close to the Twin Cities because, by the 1960s, the family business was simply letting their old money accumulate new money like a chunk of ice accretes snow as it rolls down a hill.

I had a case of the nerves at the idea of both this daughter of privilege and my old, estranged friend seeing my apartment. The space itself—the third floor of 801 Maple—had charm: dormered ceilings, window alcoves, gleaming wood floors. But Casey and I had furnished the apartment during the lean years of his residency. I'd handmade the curtains out of discount calico. I'd hand painted the dining table and the mismatched chairs (the table was a twin to the red one in Trendy Tails, only painted a sunshine yellow). And the couch. Oh, the couch. We'd scavenged it from Casey's parents' basement, where it had been clawed by generations of cats and stained by generations of Alter children. I'd made it over by hand stitching pieces of calico, including scraps from the curtains, in a crazy patchwork pattern. I thought the effect was both practical and charming, but it was a far cry from what my guests—both young lawyers—were probably used to.

Sean and Carla arrived promptly at eight, after we'd locked up Trendy Tails for the day, and just as Rena pulled her spinach lasagna from my oven and set it on a trivet to rest. Their knock sent Packer into a frenzy of barking and lunging and leaping.

"It's so lovely to meet you both," Carla said, her voice all crisp consonants and perfectly formed vowels, without even a hint of the nasal, upper Midwestern accent in it. She carried a miniature rose bush in a terra cotta pot adorned by a bright blue satin bow.

"Likewise. You two make yourselves at home," I said, taking their coats and the hostess gift and waving them toward the heart of my apartment with its patchwork sofa and high-backed velveteen chairs. "Can I get you something to drink?"

"Wine would be wonderful, if you have it," Carla said.

"Ditto," said Sean.

While they settled together on the sofa, Sean's arm draped across its back to rest casually behind Carla's shoulders, I slipped into the kitchenette and studied her while I opened a bottle of Merlot. When I peeked through the pass through I saw Jinx trying to insinuate herself between Sean and Carla.

Jinx is what I call an aggressive snuggler. With the exception of Rena and me, Jinx will not tolerate anyone initiating snuggling with her. Snuggling must be on her terms. But when she decides she likes you and she wants to sit on your lap, she will not be deterred. Once there, she will make sure you pet her exactly as she wants to be petted (in fact, she prefers if you keep your hand still and let her move her head and body around beneath it). And every time you so much as glance away, she manages to wiggle a little closer to your face.

Sean didn't seem to mind Jinx's heavy-handed hints and her increasing violation of his personal space, but Carla was left swatting away Jinx's tail as it swished in her face. I caught her wiping her hand on the arm of the sofa after touching Jinx's tail. Apparently not a cat person.

I pulled my eyes away from Jinx's shenanigans to get a really good look at Carla.

I'd technically met Carla back in the mid-1990s, when I was a counselor at the Soaring Eagles Adventure Camp and Carla had been a counselor in training. But nothing about that tween girl—with the outline of her training bra vivid beneath her T-shirt, her retainer lending her an insipid lisp, her hair a nest of flame-colored knots, and more elbows than sense—prepared me for the stunning woman who walked through my front door.

Unlike her statuesque mother, Carla was trim and petite. I had several inches on her, but somehow she held herself with such poise that she seemed taller. She wore tailored black pants—which would undoubtedly attract every cat hair in my apartment—and a crisp white blouse, the collar popped around a luxurious length of floral-patterned silk that formed a luscious arabesque about her long, pale neck.

I suddenly felt frumpy in my jeans and my fisherman's sweater. Frumpy and a little plain.

Don't get me wrong; the McHale girls are no slouches in the looks department, but if she were half a foot taller, Carla Harper could have been a model. She had eyes as wide and blue as a prairie sky, long auburn hair tamed to fall in sinuous waves about her shoulders, and one of those full, pouty mouths that make men think simultaneously of bedrooms and bridal parties.

I shared a glance with Rena. "Hot," she mouthed.

No kidding.

I squared my shoulders and headed back to the den.

"So, Carla," I said, handing her a glass of wine, "I understand you're an attorney, too."

She took a sip of the merlot and for a second it seemed her lips tightened. She was probably used to much finer wines than what I had to offer. But she didn't make a fuss. Instead, she smiled sweetly.

"Delicious," she murmured. "Yes, I practiced for a couple of years in Chicago, but when Grandpa Gene died and I took over the management of the trust, I moved back to Merryville. That was, heavens, five years ago now."

"It must be interesting work," I said, taking a seat in one of the oversized arm chairs that flanked the sofa.

"Sometimes. I spend so much time managing the

trust, I don't take on many clients and most of my work is transactional."

I had no idea what that meant, but since she sounded disappointed I nodded in commiseration.

Sean must have sensed my befuddlement because he came to the rescue. "Carla did a lot of litigation, courtroom work, in Chicago. Now it's mostly drafting contracts and getting signatures. Important work, but maybe not as exciting as strutting her stuff in front of a jury."

"Ah."

"Come on, folks. Dinner is served," Rena called from the kitchen.

We adjourned to the dining area, and for a few minutes, we were consumed with dishing up Rena's ooeygooey delicious spinach lasagna, a lightly dressed salad, and golden garlic bread.

"What about you?" Carla asked. "Tell me how you started designing clothes for animals."

I cleared my throat. "Well, it's silly really. I studied fashion design at Wisconsin, and then when I moved back here, I didn't really have anyone to design for. I made my aunt Dolly a dress for a wedding once, and my sister Lucy a formal for one of her sorority functions. But for the most part, my fashion degree was simply gathering dust.

"Then one day, I was taking Packer for a walk, and it was raining. He didn't want to go, and kept tugging the leash to go back home. Every time he'd step in the grass, he'd do this little high-stepping move, like he didn't want to get his feet wet. I knew I could buy him little booties online, but I figured I could make them myself for about the same price, and I could make them fit his personality."

"His personality?" Carla asked.

"Yeah, Packer's a bit of a dork, but he's always trying to pal around with the bigger dogs at the dog park. I decided he needed some bad-ass boots to make him look a little tougher. So I used a black duck cloth and tricked out the tops with tiny silver studs. Then I decided that the whole look really needed a coat. And then a hat. By the time I was done, Packer looked like he was ready to ride off to Sturgis with the Hell's Angels."

"Which, by the way," Rena interjected, "doesn't fit his personality at all. That dog is about as tough as a newborn kitten." She pointed at Packer, sitting on the threshold of the kitchen, staring at us mournfully. He made pitiful whining noises when he realized we were talking about him.

Hate to break it to you, buddy, I thought, *but cheese and dogs don't go together. You'll have to settle for a couple of dog treats later.*

Sean laughed. "He could be a tough guy if he wanted to. Look at those choppers."

At that moment, Packer's whole body rocked with a violent sneeze and he buried his head under his paws. Tough guy, indeed.

"But that's the thing with fashion," I said. "People dress for who they want to be, not who they are. I imagine if Packer had his choice, he'd be a tough guy. So I dressed him like one."

Carla was watching me with a polite smile on her face, but Sean seemed genuinely amused.

"I like that. 'People dress for who they want to be, not who they are.'"

"Right," I said, momentarily letting my mouth get ahead of my brain, "like Sherry. Dressing to be a rebel peacenik instead of a trust-fund baby."

For a second, there was dead silence at the table. You could have heard a rat tinkle it was so quiet.

"Oh dear. Carla, I'm so sorry. I didn't think." The words tumbled out of my mouth in a mad rush of mortified apology. "There's a reason they call me Dizzy Izzy."

Carla dabbed at her lips with her napkin. "It's really okay," she said. "You're absolutely correct. Sherry did work hard to distance herself from the rest of the Harper clan. Which is why we weren't especially close. At least, not since we were little girls spending our summers out at the lake house."

"It sounds idyllic," Rena said wistfully. Thanks to the charity of local church groups, she'd been able to attend summer camp, but there were certainly no lake houses in Rena's childhood.

"It was. When we were little," Carla said. "Now the cousins are scattered across the country, and most of my parents' generation has moved to Arizona or died, so hardly anyone uses the place. It just sits there, empty. A waste, really."

She looked around the table as though she suddenly realized she was baring her soul to virtual strangers.

"If the Harpers weren't such a sentimental bunch, we'd probably sell off the land."

From what I'd seen of the Harper clan, "sentimental" was not a word I'd use to describe them . . . at least any of them other than Sherry.

"The bottom line," Carla said, "is that time has a way of changing everything, from real estate to relationships."

That comment brought the conversation to a screeching halt. After that philosophical bombshell, it was hard to figure out where to go.

Sean stepped into the breach. "So, Izzy, tell me more about your work. Is designing for animals the same as designing for people?"

"Actually," I said, grasping hold of his conversational lifeline, "cutting clothes for a dog or cat is a lot different than cutting clothes for people. Let me show you."

I pushed away from the table to stand, and indicated that Sean should do the same. "You'll be my model."

"I have been called a dog a time or two," he drawled. Then he laughed, just a low rumble in his chest. I wondered how old he was when his laugh started sounding like that, like the faint harbinger of a coming summer storm. His laugh struck me like a tuning fork, eliciting a harmonic vibration in my sternum.

I shook myself, disturbed by my inappropriate reaction. "Very funny, mister. So, first, with dogs and cats, the angle of the head relative to the body is totally different. Here, tip your head back." Sean complied and I studied him with narrowed eyes. "Just a bit more. There, that's about right. Feel how the collar of your shirt cuts into the back of your neck? I have to adjust for that.

"And the forelegs. They're not just like arms. See, raise your arms to shoulder height."

He spread his arms out to either side.

"No, not in a Jesus way. In a zombie way."

Sean and Rena laughed. Carla's lips tightened, and I worried that I'd offended her by making a joke about Jesus. "Sorry," I mumbled with a nod in her direction.

Sean put his arms out straight in front of him.

"What do you feel?" I asked.

"Well, my jacket is stretched across my back."

"Exactly. And in the front, there's extra fabric bunching up at the joint. And finally, there's the gravity problem."

"I've never thought of gravity as a problem," Sean quipped.

"In general, it's not. But when you wear a shirt, gravity works in your favor. It pulls the hem down so it lays flat around your waist."

I reached out to demonstrate by running my hands around his waist, but caught myself just in time. I glanced Carla's way, and saw she was glaring daggers at me.

I cleared my throat. "Well, for animals, gravity is not good for the lines of an outfit. Gravity pulls the front of the garment toward the ground.

"When I design for animals, I have to take all of these things into account. I don't just cut down the patterns, I have to alter their fit around the neck and arms, and I have to find some way to keep the lower end of the garment from dragging in the dirt."

Sean smiled and nodded appreciatively. "You know your stuff."

"Yes," Carla chimed in, her voice as cold and sharp as an icicle shattering on cement. "If someone's going to make clothes for animals, it's important to do it right."

I swear Rena actually leaned forward as though she might go for Carla's throat. I grabbed her gently by the sleeve and pulled her back. I glanced at Sean out of the corner of my eyes. His head was cocked, and he was studying Carla like he'd never seen her before.

I plastered my most gracious smile on my face. "You're absolutely right," I said breezily. "I'm not exactly curing cancer, here, but it makes people happy, and I like to have standards."

For some reason, my comment must have touched a nerve, because Carla's fair skin colored like a late-spring strawberry.

Stilted small talk and Rena's chocolate raspberry tart filled the next hour, until Sean finally suggested he and Carla should hit the road. Carla extended one pale, bony hand to both me and Rena. Sean, much to Carla's obvious annoyance, pulled us both into big hugs.

"Thanks for the grub, ducks," he said to Rena.

He wrapped his arms around me, enveloping me in his warmth. I'd known him most of my life, and seen him dozens of times in the last few weeks. I'd alternately loved him, scorned him, shied away from him, and grown to find him both charming and intriguing. Still, until that moment, he'd been as much an idea as a person, a symbol of a path not chosen rather than a flesh-and-blood human. But that hug made me suddenly aware of him as a man, a man with strength and gentleness, with broad shoulders and just a hint of softness at his waist. And I had a sudden desire to know about every experience that had changed him from the boy beneath my apple tree to the man standing in my living room.

As he gave me a tight squeeze, he mumbled into my hair. "Glad to have you back, Izzy."

CHAPTER
Seventeen

The next night, Rena, Lucy, Dru, and I took Xander out for his birthday. Since Rena still seemed to be under suspicion, we kept it low-key. Dru and Lucy punched out of their day jobs; Rena, Xander, and I locked up our stores, and we met at the Grateful Grape.

Virginia Harper had turned a Victorian row house into a quaint little nook for sipping wine and noshing on tasty treats. The Grape didn't serve dinner, but provided a "build your own" cheese board and delectable desserts.

Our table settled in with a board of French bread, a truffle-laced cheese, good old-fashioned Wisconsin cheddar, brine-cured olives, and a zesty horseradish-and-goat-cheese dip. With a couple bottles of merlot—far finer than what I'd served at dinner the night before—we were ready to toast the birthday boy.

"How old are you now, Xander?" Dru asked.

It was hard to tell. While we counted him among our

circle of close friends, Xander had managed to maintain an air of mystery.

Xander Stephens had moved to Merryville five years before from Milwaukee. His grandmother had passed away, leaving him enough money to live out his dream of opening a record store, and for some reason he'd settled on northern Minnesota as the place to do it. The Spin Doctor relied on the wealthy tourists who passed through Merryville and a thriving online business to sell everything from vintage vinyl LPs to concert T-shirts to books on the history of rock and roll. In a day when record stores were giving way to digital downloadable music, Xander had carved out a niche for himself that kept him solvent.

Merryville isn't an easy town to crack socially, but since Xander had opened the Spin Doctor in the building immediately behind mine—what was then Ingrid's Merryville Gift Haus—and Rena was Xander's first employee, he had an entrée into our little circle, and we were happy to dote upon him. A six foot three long-distance runner with a pale complexion and a military-short haircut, he perpetually looked like he needed to be fed, and the McHale sisters were prone to taking in strays.

By silent agreement, the topic of Sherry Harper's murder was off limits, but all other manner of gossip flowed about the small group.

We discussed, for instance, Hal Olson's run for mayor.

"The development platform will serve him well," I said.

"Maybe for some voters," Xander replied. "But I

moved here to get away from cookie-cutter suburbs and urban sprawl."

"Development doesn't have to mean sprawl," Dru countered. "Still, he's going to have to be a lot more specific about what he has in mind before he wins my vote." My older sister hated change with a flaming purple passion. Her accountant brain may have favored economic growth, but her heart wanted her hometown to remain untouched.

"I don't care about his politics," Rena said. "Man skeeves me out. He's just too . . . I don't know . . . too something."

"Too smarmy," Lucy offered. The two exchanged a high five across the table. "Yeah, at Izzy's party last week he told me I looked tense and asked if I wanted a back rub. A, we were in the middle of a party, B, his wife was right across the room, and C, when have I *ever* looked tense?"

Everyone at the table laughed . . . except Xander, whose brow wrinkled above his big, dove-gray eyes. I had a niggling suspicion Xander was sweet on Lucy, and the thought of any man hitting on her would give him fits, especially one so age-inappropriate and decidedly married.

I nudged Xander in the ribs. "Lucy's a big girl," I murmured. "She can take care of herself."

Lucy must have heard me, because she lowered her head and looked coyly through her lashes at her would-be Galahad. "Would you have saved me from pervy Hal?"

Xander blushed, a wildfire licking from his neck right up to his hairline.

While Xander had a crush on Lucy, Lucy seemed to be clueless. My sister could trade barbs with the best of them, but she was rarely deliberately cruel. Besides, I figured one of the reasons Lucy teased Xander so often was that she, too, was infatuated. Apparently, her tactics had not developed much since the grade school playground. If she realized how much her teasing hurt Xander, she would stop it. And if she realized how much Xander was into her, she'd have asked him out long ago.

Lucy laughed. "I'll take that as a yes."

Rena punched Lucy in the arm. "Why don't you put this boy out of his misery and ask him out, already?"

The corners of Lucy's lips curled up in a knowing little smile.

"Xander's a big boy," she said, echoing my own comment. "If he wants to go out with me, all he has to do is ask."

Xander crossed his arms and ducked his head. As shy as he was, actually asking Lucy out would require a heroic effort.

All the girls laughed. But I began thinking I might be wrong about how oblivious Lucy was. How much of the teasing was really teasing? I wondered if Lucy was actually putting her line in the water hoping to catch Xander . . . and whether Xander might actually take her bait.

"Sounds like you all are having a good time."

Virginia Harper had wandered up to our table as we laughed. She laid one hand on Rena's shoulder and the other on Xander's.

"How is everything tonight?" she asked.

"Wonderful," I answered. "This is the perfect place to celebrate Xander's birthday."

I didn't know it was possible for Xander's blush to deepen, but he flushed scarlet at the attention when Virginia turned a thousand-watt smile on him. "Birthday? I'll have to have the kitchen put together a pastry sampler for you all. On the house."

A chorus of demurs rose from our crew, who wouldn't dream of accepting such a generous gift from a fellow small-business owner.

"Oh, really—"

"We couldn't—"

"Thank you. That would be lovely," said Lucy, her casual acceptance of Virginia's largesse drowning out the rest of us. Leave it to Lucky Lucy to take such a show of generosity as her due.

Virginia laughed. "It's really my pleasure. I have a new pastry supplier, and I think you'll be impressed."

I watched as she walked down the back hallway, sticking her head in the kitchen for a minute, and then disappearing out through the rear fire door.

"Where's she going?" I wondered aloud.

Xander glanced over his shoulder to follow my line of sight.

"Probably out for a smoke. She's got a terrible habit."

"Why go outside in this frigid weather? After all, she owns the place."

"State law. No smoking in restaurants and bars."

"Really? How long has that been in effect?" I had strong memories of coming home from a night on the town smelling like an ashtray.

"Only about five years," Xander said, showing an uncharacteristic streak of humor.

"Huh. Shows you what kind of social life I've had."

Diane Jenkins, the Grape's bartender and general town busybody, delivered a plate of pastries to our table: a small stone fruit tart, a wedge of chocolate cake, and a perfect, golden flan. "Compliments of Virginia," she said as she set it down with a flourish.

Lucy leaned in to talk to Diane in a conspiratorial—though not particularly quiet—whisper. "It's quiet tonight," she said. Indeed, there was only one other couple in the bar.

Diane rolled her eyes. "Quiet every night.

"I love Virginia. She's the best boss I've ever had. Why, after she went and celebrated her birthday with her family, she came back here to celebrate with us. After Carla and Sean had left, she still hung out with us. Waited until closing time, then treated us all to a couple of bottles of our most expensive vintage."

"That was generous of her," I said.

"Sure was. If anyone could make a go out of this business, it's Virginia. She's such a great hostess. But I just don't think Merryville is a wine bar type of town. When the tourists come in, most of them are looking to let their hair down, drink some beer and do some shots. Sure, we get a few of the hoity-toity people from the big cities, the ones who rent lakeside homes for the whole summer." She dropped her voice. "Honestly, though, I don't think our selection of wine meets their standards, you know. Basically, there are two markets in this town, and Virginia's managed to fall smack between them. If things don't pick up, I'm going to have to look for another job. I can't make enough in tips to support myself." She suddenly colored and raised her hands as though to stop us from jumping to conclusions. "Not that you need to . . . I mean, I wasn't trying . . ."

Lucy cut her off. "Don't worry. I know you weren't fishing for a tip. But rest assured, most of us have waited tables at one point or another. We know where you're coming from. And we won't say anything to Virginia."

"Thank you," Diane breathed. "Sometimes my filter just turns off and I say the most inappropriate things."

I was pretty sure Diane didn't even have a filter. She could be counted on for the most no-holds-barred gossip in town.

With one last thankful smile, she made her way to the other couple in the hopes of peddling another cheese platter.

"If things are as bad as Diane says, I wonder how Virginia stays in business," I whispered.

"She's not just staying in business," Xander said. "She's been making all sorts of improvements. One of my buddies just installed a new furnace here, and this artist friend of mine is going to paint a mural on that wall. She's paying him really well for the job."

"Not to mention the new pastry person," Lucy said, forking up another bite of flan. "This stuff is killer."

She was right. My bite of tart had been sinfully delicious: just the right crispness to the crust, a filling of crème Anglaise perfumed with vanilla, and a perfectly balanced glaze coating the apricots and peaches that formed mesmerizing swirls across the tart's top.

I put down my fork and pushed the tray of dessert

in Xander's general direction. "No more of this for me. Between that meal at the Mission and tonight, I'll be lucky to button my pants tomorrow."

I excused myself to use the restroom.

A few minutes later, as I emerged from the ladies room, I caught sight of a familiar face heading into the kitchen.

Ken West.

CHAPTER
Eighteen

"Ken," I called.

He stopped, looking over his shoulder sheepishly. When he saw it was me, he relaxed a bit, but I could still tell he was itching to get away.

"I didn't know you were working here," I said.

"I'm not."

"But you . . ." I waved in the direction of the kitchen door, clearly labeled STAFF ONLY.

He sighed. "If you must know, I'm an independent contractor."

That's what the manager at the Mission had called Ken: an independent contractor.

"What exactly does that entail in the restaurant business?"

"If you must know," Ken said, "I've been reduced to working as a pastry chef."

"Wait. The desserts are yours? They're wonderful!"

"Well, of course."

"But you sound like you're ashamed of them."

"I'm not ashamed of the quality of my product, I'm ashamed that my product is dessert. There's a distinct pecking order in the culinary world, and pastry chefs are far below chefs de cuisine. It's paying the bills, but I'd rather not become known for pastry."

"That's what you were doing at the Mission, wasn't it? Delivering pastry?"

"My, my, my. Have you been spying on me, Izzy?"

"Actually, no." I wasn't quite sure how to play this, but decided to go for up front and honest. "I was tracking Sherry Harper's movements. We knew she'd had dinner there, and we went to ask the staff if they remembered her."

"Ah, and I assume they did. Sherry Harper's rage was sharper than a serpent's tooth."

"Yeah, they said she was already pretty worked up when she saw you, and then all heck broke loose."

He winced. "I suppose I should have been flattered to provoke such strong passions in anyone. But I had to do some fancy talking to keep the manager from sending me and my profiteroles packing after she made such a scene."

"You realize that gives you yet another reason to want Sherry dead, right? She knew your secret life as a pastry chef and she almost cost you your contract with the Mission."

He sighed. "We've been over this already, haven't we? Even if I wanted Sherry dead, I didn't have the opportunity to poison her." I started to interrupt, but he held up a hand to stop me. "And if I *had* had an opportunity to poison her, you can bet I wouldn't use something like hemlock. I'm not a locavore chef like those guys at the Mission. I don't know about all the local flora and fauna. If I wanted to poison Sherry, I would have used something a bit more classic and a bit more reliable, like arsenic or cyanide."

I wasn't sure I trusted him—especially since it seemed like he'd given the whole matter some serious thought—but I had little choice but to let the matter go.

"Listen, what we were really interested in at the Mission was the identity of Sherry's dining companion. The manager seemed to think you recognized him."

Ken narrowed his eyes and studied me for a second. "No. What with all the commotion, I didn't even see him."

I still wasn't sure I trusted Ken when he said he had nothing to do with Sherry's death. That night, though, I had no niggling doubts: For some reason, Ken West was lying to me. He knew who Sherry's lover was, but he wasn't going to tell me.

The next day, I found myself back at the Grateful Grape, meeting Virginia Harper to discuss her role in the upcoming Halloween Howl.

We sat at a table near the front of the bistro, mid-morning sunlight pooling on the distressed oak of the table and bringing out the warm tones in Virginia's skin and hair. She wore one of her signature flowing dresses, this one in a shade of deepest amethyst, which brought out the violet tint in her hooded blue eyes.

"Thank you for meeting me," I said as we sat down.

"Think nothing of it," she said, waving her hand dismissively.

"Oh dear, what happened to your finger?" I pointed to her index finger, wrapped in a giant Band-Aid. "I didn't notice that last night."

She moved quickly to tuck her hands under the table, as though she was embarrassed by them. But she stopped herself short and brought them back to the tabletop.

"It's nothing," she said. "Almost healed, actually. I cut myself on the blade of my wine key. Happens all the time." She held up both hands, palms out, as though to demonstrate how nicked and scarred her hands were.

"Well, I'm glad it's nothing serious. I'm such a klutz, the last time I tried to peel an avocado I nearly sliced off my thumb." She laughed. "The pageant should be fairly straightforward. We'll collect the entry forms by the band shell and give out numbers to each animal in the pageant. At nine o'clock, we'll have the animals parade past the band shell, and you can make note of the numbers of the winners."

"Do you think the turnout will be very big?" she asked.

I nodded. "Pris has been keeping count of the actual preregistrations, and that woman holds on to information like Scrooge held on to his gold. But she's indicated that things are going well. And if the number of people coming in to Trendy Tails to buy costumes is any indication, the event will be a huge success."

"So, are there categories or something?"

"Yes. You'll choose one winner from among the dogs, one from the cats, and one from the other pets— assuming we have some. Each winner will get a twenty-five dollar gift certificate to Prissy's Pretty Pets and one to Trendy Tails."

"I don't suppose Sir Francis can enter the contest."

"No, I don't think that would be fair. But by all means bring him out for the festivities, get him a costume, and have him join you on the stage. He can be our Canine of Ceremonies."

"Oh, perfect. Sir Francis loves to be the center of attention."

"Thank you for agreeing to judge for us," I said. "You're already doing so much by providing the beverages for the event, and this is such a terrible time for your family."

"Honestly, it will be good to do something to get my mind off of Sherry's death," Virginia said, her voice cracking with emotion.

"You two were close, huh?" I asked. Sherry had been the black sheep of the Harper family, but with Sherry living just a couple of blocks from Virginia's business and Virginia herself being a bit of an outlier in the Harper clan, it seemed they might have forged a bond . . . two earth mothers among the patrician Harper kin.

"We used to be. When the girls were young, we used to spend nearly every weekend at the family house out on Badger Lake. Carla, my brilliant little scholar, always had her nose in a book, but Sherry would go for long walks with me. It seemed like there was no limit to her energy. Sometimes we'd walk all the way to Soaring Eagles, just looking for plants and birds."

She gazed out the window, perhaps seeing a young Sherry dashing down a wooded path with a handful of wildflowers.

"Then, of course, she grew up and visits to the lake house grew less and less frequent as we all seemed to get busier. The rift between her and the rest of the family made it difficult to remain close. But she'd stop by here some mornings. I'd brew us some coffee and she'd tell me what she was up to."

"Jolly Nielson mentioned that you took her out to the lake house and ran into Sherry there."

Virginia looked momentarily startled, but then waved her hand in a dismissive gesture. "It was just a misunderstanding. Sherry was very protective of the lake house property."

"So I've heard," I said. But silently I wondered why Sherry would perceive Virginia as a threat to the property. After all, they both loved it dearly.

She looked me in the eyes, her own pooled with unshed tears. "No matter what anyone says about her crazy causes, you have to know it came from a good place. She was Dona Quixote, tilting at windmills."

Other than Nick Haas, Virginia was the first person I'd heard speak fondly of Sherry Harper. Those long walks must have been special, indeed.

Virginia inhaled deeply and sat up a little straighter. "Enough of this maudlin talk. How are you doing with your new business?"

I shrugged. "So far, so good. We've had a steady stream of customers, but I know some of that is just the novelty of a new business, and it will wear off. I'm counting on the Halloween Howl to keep people's interest and maybe get some of my Halloween customers back in for Christmas shopping, maybe even lure in a few new faces . . . and then it's a question of luring in tourists."

"Merryville is becoming such a pet-friendly place, I bet that won't be a problem. The Dogwood Cabins down by the Mississippi allow pets, and I heard that the new manager of the Birchwood Inn has changed their policy to allow pets with a deposit. And heaven knows there are enough dog- and cat-mad people living here in town, myself included." She uncrossed and recrossed her legs. "I'm sorry I didn't make it to your grand opening."

"Oh, that's okay. Sean said it was your birthday. Happy belated birthday, by the way."

She smiled, but the light didn't reach her eyes. "Thank you, dear. In all seriousness, I promise to be a regular patron. When I was there the other day, I saw half a dozen things I want to get for Sir Francis. Besides, I know what it's like to start a new business, so I want to show a little solidarity, too."

"Well, thank you. I confess I'm nervous about how we'll do. So many people are counting on me. Ingrid's leaving me in charge of her building for the next six months, and I have to make sure to pay her rent on time. Rena's invested her whole life in the barkery. And my aunt Dolly has invested a sizable chunk of cash. I don't want to let any of them down."

"It's a big weight to carry, feeling like you owe your friends and family." She reached across the table to grasp my hand tightly. "I know it motivates you, spurs you to work harder than you thought possible. But that pressure can consume you, too. Don't let that happen, dear. Promise me."

CHAPTER
Nineteen

With the autopsy finally complete and the toxicity reports finally generated, the city released Sherry to her family. The town of Merryville laid Sherry Harper to rest on a bitterly cold Monday as storm clouds gathered on the horizon, heralding the first hard snow of the season.

Aunt Dolly accompanied Rena and me to the service. Dolly and I flanked Rena, ready to catch her if her slight frame collapsed beneath the combined weight of her ankle-length black wool coat and her grief. Yet by the time we reached the church, it was clear she wouldn't need our support. She stood just inside the massive nave of Trinity Lutheran, shaking her head at the young man offering cups of hot chocolate, her hands thrust in her pockets and boot-clad feet braced apart. With her bright purple hair standing at attention and the brooding look on her gamine features, she looked like an anime hero ready to do battle.

"I can't believe I let you talk me into this," she muttered.

"You need to grieve."

"Not surrounded by hundreds of people."

"Why not?" I questioned. "People need people. That's why we have funerals in the first place. So we can share our grief with each other and start to heal."

She glared up at me through her dark, spiky lashes. "'People need people'? You drag me here into this crowd of people, most of whom wouldn't spit on me if I were on fire, and you tell me that 'people need people.' That's about as helpful as 'hang in there, baby!'"

I tamped down my annoyance. "Clichés become cliché for a reason. People really do need the company of other people on occasion. Especially when they're grieving."

"And what makes you think I'm grieving?"

"That sulk you've been wearing since Sherry died. That, and the fact that I've known you for thirty years. You have a good soul, Rena Hamilton, and Sherry was important to you at a critical time in your life. The fact that she died before you had the chance to right what was wrong between you, that's got to be eating at you. You need this chance to say goodbye."

She shrugged her shoulders and looked like she was hunkering in for a good fight when I was distracted by a strange wriggle around her midsection. At first I thought I was seeing things, but then her coat shimmied again.

"Rena, you didn't," I gasped.

"What?" she asked, all innocence.

"What?" Dolly asked, an edge of worry in her voice.

"Did you bring Val with you?"

"Well, yeah."

"No!" Dolly and I moaned in unison.

"She won't hurt anything. And I think Sherry would have approved."

Rena had a point there. Sherry didn't go anywhere without poor Gandhi, who was still missing in action, lost somewhere in the Greene Brigade. She would have been tickled to have Val attend her funeral.

We made our way to the pews, where Rena insisted we sit toward the back.

Just as we got ourselves settled, Nick Haas walked in with his mother, Nadya. She was a tiny husk of a woman, her square teeth and her square black-framed spectacles both too large for her long, narrow face. The heavy powder on her cheek barely concealed a bruise the faint purple of a twilight sky spreading across her jawline.

They paused in the aisle, both blinking owlishly, looking around as though they were surprised to find themselves in the middle of a church.

"*Pssst.*" Rena snagged Nadya's attention, and the two slid into the pew next to us. Nadya grabbed Rena's hand and gave it a sturdy squeeze. Even with two people separating us, I could smell the insipidly sweet scent of whiskey wafting from Nick's pores. He cleared his throat with a phlegmy hack and shifted uneasily in his seat.

As the organist plodded out the notes of some dirge-like hymn, I studied the people filing in. You can learn a lot about people by watching them at a funeral. Grief tends to tear down our inhibitions as surely as alcohol, and bring our true feelings into razor-sharp focus.

Richard Greene arrived in a neatly pressed single-button black suit, a skinny black tie, and a stark white dress shirt, so somber and unassuming he could have passed for the undertaker. He moved without a word to a pew halfway down the aisle where he sat ramrod straight, staring directly ahead. Even by Richard Greene standards, his comportment was rigid. I suspected the military bearing hid a deep well of emotion. He may have had little use for Sherry, but out of respect for her father, who had been a good friend, he'd shown up to give his respects in the best way he knew how. I wouldn't have been surprised if he saluted before the funeral ended.

Beside me, Rena wriggled out of her heavy wool coat, and I felt Val shimmy down into the armhole, finding a warm, safe spot to ride out the funeral.

I sighed.

At that moment, the family filed into the church, a parade of pale, freckled people with patrician features and hair in varying shades of red, from sunny strawberry to the deepest black cherry. I recognized the last two Harper cousins, Teal and Tarleton, twin ginger-haired young men who had attended nearby Soaring Eagles Adventure Camp when I was a counselor there. The two had stolen Jenny Steiner's training bra and run it up the flagpole one morning. I did not remember them fondly.

It seemed we'd all made our way through Soaring Eagles in one capacity or another. Such an ordinary place, one we all took for granted, but it united all the children of Merryville. It had been the great equalizer, bringing Rena Hamilton and Carla Harper, Nick Haas and Sean Tucker, all into the same orbit before the gravity of social status drove them apart again. The fact that it had been derelict for years now, sinking into the landscape, leaving hardly a trace of its existence, struck me as particularly sad.

As soon as the family settled, the service began. It seemed to last only a few fleeting minutes. The minister read the requisite biblical verses and made quiet noises about death being but a passage. Beside me, Rena shook with muffled sobs. I wrapped an arm around her shoulders and looked down to see Nadya Haas wrap Rena's delicate hand in her own knotty grip. Then suddenly it was over . . . no eulogy, nothing personal at all.

The congregation began shifting as they realized that the deed was done, softly rustling as though rousing after a short nap. Mourners gathered scarves and hats, drew coats closer against anticipated cold. The family got up first and formed a sort of receiving line by the door so they could thank people for attending and the attendees could offer a few words of condolence.

"Oh crap," Rena muttered.

"What?"

"Val. She's gone."

"What?" I hissed. "How did you not notice her crawling out of your coat?"

"I was grieving," she snapped.

"She's almost as big as a newborn baby," I pointed out.

"I felt her wriggling around," she conceded, "but it never occurred to me that she would bolt. I thought she was just trying to get comfortable."

As if Gandhi the Rogue Guinea Pig weren't enough, now we had to track down a ferret somewhere in the middle of a crowd of mourners.

Like salmon swimming upstream against the current, we began moving toward the front of the church, away from the crowd, looking under every pew and in every hymnal holder.

I was on my hands and knees, butt in the air, when I heard Pris Olson's sweeter-than-sugar voice behind me. "Izzy, dear, did you lose something?"

I sat up, blowing a lock of hair out of my face. Pris smiled down on me, her flawless ivory face framed by the portrait collar on her deep navy suit.

"Um, yes. Well, Rena did." She lost her ferret and her mind, not necessarily in that order. "Uh, her cell phone. It must have fallen out of her pocket during the service."

"Well then, wouldn't it be under the pew where you were sitting?"

"You'd think so." Unless you knew we were really looking for a critter with four legs and a mind of its own. "But it's not there. We thought maybe it got kicked around somewhere under here.

"Where's Hal?" I asked, trying to get the attention off our misadventure.

"Oh, he wanted to be here so much. He's been close to the Harper family for years, you know."

Whether he'd been friends with the Harpers in the past or not, if Hal was making a run for mayor he would need the family's goodwill and to be seen at events like this.

"Unfortunately," Pris continued, "there was an emergency out at the RV dealership. One of the new sales guys messed up the financing paperwork for a very important customer. Hal felt he needed to address the problem himself."

"Running Olson's Odyssey RV must take a tremendous amount of Hal's time."

Pris lifted one elegant shoulder. "Actually, as the business has grown, Hal's gotten more of his life back. When we first got married, he worked fourteen hour days. Now, he's got a huge staff to handle the actual sales, and so much of the paperwork is really computer work now. He still goes out to the lot every day and takes care of these sorts of snafus himself, but he's got time for other pursuits now."

"Like running for office."

"Among other things," Pris said, her lips tilting in the faintest smile, her tone a bit on the dry side.

"Listen," she said, "I've been meaning to talk to you about the Halloween Howl. I've been thinking that Hal should be one of the judges of the costume contest. He's got a lot of clout in this community."

She was right, but that didn't stop me from seeing her request for what it was: a media opportunity for Hal and his mayoral campaign. Besides, we'd already secured the panel of judges, and it included Paul Tinker, the current mayor and Hal's opponent in the spring election.

"I don't think that's a good idea, Pris. The Howl is less than a week away, and if we added Hal to the roster of judges we'd have an even number. I don't know how we could find yet another person to make it odd again in such a short amount of time."

Pris opened her mouth to argue, but just then Rena clattered up the aisle to our side.

"Hey, Pris. Izzy, we can go now."

"So you found it?" Pris asked.

Rena's brow furrowed, but she kept her cool. "Yes, I found . . . it."

"That's good," I improvised. "I don't know what you'd do without your cell phone."

The light dawned in Rena's eyes. "Right. Wouldn't want to lose my phone."

Pris looked back and forth between the two of us, clearly trying to suss out the subtext of our stilted conversation. "Well," she said finally, "I'll be off. But do consider my suggestion, Izzy."

As soon as Pris had gone a reasonable distance, Rena opened her coat like a flasher to reveal Val nestled in an inside pocket of the giant overcoat, nothing but her sleek chestnut-colored head showing above.

"Where was she?" I asked.

Rena smiled with apparent pride. "She'd managed to make it all the way to the altar. She was hiding behind the banner hanging from the lectern."

Rena helped me to my feet, and I bundled into my own outerwear.

"Nice cover with Pris."

"I couldn't very well tell her what we were really looking for, and a cell phone was the first thing that popped into my mind."

"Speaking of cell phones," Rena said, sotto voce,

reaching into a front pocket of her coat, "I think Val picked another pocket, because I found her with this."

She held out a black flip phone with a pink anarchy sticker on the back and tiny tooth marks on the corners.

It was the sticker that gave it away. Val had found Sherry Harper's missing cell phone.

CHAPTER
Twenty

Rena, Sean, and I sat around the dining table in my apartment, watching the phone in the middle of the table as though it might jump up and start dancing at any moment. Instead, it sat quietly and charged.

Packer and Jinx must have picked up on the tension in the room. Jinx sat on the oak floor, regal as ever, but made no move to snuggle anyone. Packer, too, was more reserved than usual. He found my feet under the table and draped himself across them. He didn't make a sound, but I could occasionally feel him shift his weight.

When Rena had shown me the phone, my first temptation had been to flip it open and scroll through the contacts, but its battery had been dead. Rena used her own phone to summon Sean while I made a pit stop at an electronics store out near the highway to find a charger that was compatible with the device.

And then we gathered around my kitchen table and waited.

"Would anyone like a cup of tea?" I offered.

They glared at me in response.

Finally, after a good five minutes, Sean picked up the phone and flipped it open. He began keying buttons.

"Nothing in the contacts. She must have never bothered programming anyone in," he muttered. "And all the calls in and out are to the same number."

Then, "Aha."

"What?" Rena asked, her voice tight with the same anxiety and anticipation I was feeling.

"Text messages. Not many, but"—he counted softly to himself—"seven. Seven text messages all from the same number, the number in the call log."

"What do they say?"

"Um, let's see . . ." He whistled softly. "That is not exactly PG-13. Wow. These are definitely from a, um, boyfriend."

Whatever the texts said, it must have been mighty racy, because Sean actually blushed as he read them.

"Okay," I said, "that's not getting us anywhere. What about outgoing texts."

"Just two," he said. "I'd want to double-check, but I think this first one is Carla's number, from about a week before Sherry died. It says 'This is Sherry, I need the money.'" He looked up from the phone. "That makes sense. Carla handled all of Sherry's finances, so if Sherry needed additional cash, she'd contact Carla."

He made a humming sound in the back of his throat. "Now this second one is a bit more interesting. It's addressed to the mystery man's number, and it's dated the night she died, eleven oh nine at night . . . so after she gave up her protest."

"What does it say?" I asked.

" 'Come get me.' "

We sat in stunned silence for a second.

"So whoever her mystery man was," I said, "she asked him to come get her the night she died. That means she definitely had the phone that night. And the phone, the one thing connecting the mystery man to Sherry, went missing between the time she texted him and the time I found her dead."

"That's how it looks," Sean said. "She asked him to come pick her up, he met her in the alleyway, he gave her the poison and then took the phone and left. It all makes sense."

"But who's the mystery man?" Rena asked.

"Only one way to find out," Sean said. "Call the number."

"Let's do this thing," Rena said.

"What do we say when he answers?" I asked. " 'Hey there, did you kill your girlfriend?' "

Sean shrugged. "Whoever this guy is, he doesn't know we have the phone. When he sees this number on the incoming call, he'll either answer—in which case we'll hang up—or, more likely, he'll freak out and reject the call, in which case it will roll over to voice mail and we'll have our answer."

Suddenly, Rena laughed. "I feel like we're eleven and about to prank call the principal."

I knew what she meant. My heart was beating faster than a bunny's and I had the insane urge to giggle.

Sean smiled grimly. "This is the least funny prank call ever."

He placed the phone in the middle of the table, put it on speaker, and dialed the number.

The phone rang once. Then again. And then we heard the subtle click as we were transferred to a voice-mail system.

"Hi there. This is Hal Olson from Olson's Odyssey RV Emporium, the largest RV dealership in the quad state area. I can't . . ."

Sean hit the button to disconnect the call.

"I guess we have our answer. Hal Olson."

"So what now?" I said.

"You and I go have a talk with Hal."

Olson's Odyssey RV Emporium occupied acres of land just off the interstate, right outside of Merryville. They offered everything from full-sized recreational vehicles that could comfortably house a family of four to pop-up campers and camping gear.

Hal Olson had grown the business from his parents' mom-and-pop sporting goods store, which had mostly catered to local folks looking for camping gear and the fishermen attracted to Badger Lake, the mighty Mississippi, and its tamer tributary, the Perry River. Now, for some, Olson's Odyssey had become a destination of its own. Families would take day trips from Minneapolis, Milwaukee, Duluth, Cedar Rapids, and even as far away as Chicago in order to treat themselves to one of the best selections of camping and RV equipment in the country.

Hal spent much of his days wandering the lot, shaking hands with customers, grinning like the politician he hoped to become. As a result, it was not quite so surprising that his office was as modest as it was: no window, just a battered metal desk and a couple of filing cabinets. The only high-end touch was the ergonomic chair parked behind the desk.

He showed us in, gesturing that we should sit in the wooden armchairs in front of the desk. He indicated his own chair as he sat. "Gift from Pris. Between the golfing, walking the lot, and an old football injury, my lower back gives me fits without the proper lumbar support."

He said it as though it were two words: lum bar. There was always a touch of good ol' boy in his speech, even though he'd gotten an MBA from the University of Minnesota. I guessed folksy went over better with the RV-buying crowd. Or maybe he was getting a head start on the election. After all, everyone turned into a good ol' boy when they ran for office.

"So," he said, "what can I do for you two? One of you looking for a camper?"

"Actually," Sean said, "we called earlier." He pulled Sherry's phone from his pocket and flashed it to Hal.

All the blood drained from Hal's face, leaving his sun-scorched face a sort of dusky orange.

"Oh dear God," he muttered. "Where did you find that? Have you gone to the police?"

"Not yet," Sean said. "But we will."

"Please, in the name of all that's holy, don't give that thing to the cops. It'll leak to the media for sure, and . . . did she save her text messages?"

"A few of them," Sean answered. "Enough to make the, uh, tenor of your relationship quite clear."

Hal groaned and tipped his head back as though he needed to confer with the Almighty before he continued.

"Look, you gotta understand, it was nothing serious. She came to me to ask me about my position on local development, pick my brain about business matters, and one thing led to another."

That didn't sound like a probable scenario. What did Sherry care about local development, let alone business?

"Your position on local development? Did she know you were running for office?"

"No, I was playing that close to the vest. She wanted to know . . ."

He trailed off, narrowing his eyes at us. "Let's just say it was a business matter. Had nothing to do with my political ambitions. But this"—he waved at the phone—"this could ruin me. If you take the phone to the cops, those texts will leak to the media, and then it's sayonara mayor's office."

I found it interesting that he was more concerned with the press getting their hands on his illicit texts than he was with his wife finding out about his affair. He hadn't brought up Pris even once.

"I'll be good for this town, help it grow just like I helped this business grow. For the sake of Merryville, don't give that phone to the police. Just let me have it back."

"I have to say," Sean said, "your ego is mighty impressive. But this isn't just about your reputation; this is about Sherry's murder."

"What? You can't think I had anything to do with that! Why would I kill the girl?"

"You had a lot to hide, and Sherry wasn't exactly discreet," I chimed in.

"Oh, no. She wasn't about to tell anyone about our little fling. I'm telling you, it was just sex for both of us. She even joked about how her reputation would be ruined if people knew she was running around with someone as square as I am."

I was ninety-nine percent certain Sherry hadn't used the word "square" to describe Hal Olson. I imagined a more colorful description of his uptight, establishment-loving self. But still, I *could* believe that Sherry might have been almost as motivated to keep quiet about the affair as Hal had been.

On the other hand . . .

"She sent you a text the night she died, asked you to come pick her up."

"But I didn't. I got her text that night. It wasn't like her to give me marching orders like that."

Sherry must have been a welcome change from Pris, I thought.

"I told Pris about missing my wallet—which was true, you know—and then drove into town to find Sherry. I drove around your block about six times, but I didn't see her."

He sighed. "I should have gotten out to look for her. Maybe if I had I would have found her before she died, been able to get her some help. You know, drop her off at the ER or something."

Because heaven forbid anyone actually see him with

Sherry. He would have just dumped her at the door and sped off into the night.

"That's why I couldn't bring myself to go to her funeral," he added. "It would have been a good political move to go, but I just felt too guilty."

Oh dear. I hadn't put it together until that moment. Hal hadn't been at the funeral, but that's where Val found the phone. If our assumption that the killer took the phone was correct, then Hal must be telling the truth.

We'd found our mystery man, but he didn't solve our mystery.

CHAPTER
Twenty-one

"Merciful heavens, Aunt Dolly, what are you wearing?"

She tottered across the floor in four-inch platform sandals, a skintight black pencil skirt, and what appeared to be a rainbow sequined vest. With nothing underneath it.

Behind her, Rena clasped her hands over her mouth and bounced up and down in barely concealed glee, and Ingrid Whitfield looked like she was about to lay an egg. Packer danced around in excitement over all the motion and commotion, and I was sure he'd get under Dolly's impractical footwear and make her fall. God, maybe she'd break a hip.

Dolly shot me an arch look. "It all came out of *your* closet, missy."

"I was in a really dark place when I bought those sandals, and I designed the vest for a magician's assistant in Madison who never coughed up the money for it. I'm not even sure why I kept it. But I sure never expected to see my sixty-six-year-old aunt wearing it." I sighed. "With nothing underneath it."

She squeezed her arms close to her sides to plump up her cleavage and then did a little rollicking dance to illustrate just how bodacious her tatas looked in the vest. "This granny's got it going on!" she hooted.

"Okay," Ingrid chimed in, "so a better question: *Why* are you dressed up like a two-bit hooker?"

"Oh, you're just jealous," Dolly scoffed. "I got dressed up for Richard."

As if on cue, the door to Trendy Tails swung open and Richard Greene stomped in on a gust of ice-crusted air. He paused to shake the slush from his boots before stripping off his parka and venturing onto my lovely hardwood floors.

"So where's this leak that needs fixing?" he asked without preamble. "Can't have an ice slick building up in that alley. Even bigger nuisance than the damn rodent."

"Richard," Dolly gushed. "You're our hero!" She sashayed to his side and leaned in close, resting one hand gently on his forearm. "I can't believe you came out in all this weather to help us."

His tufted brows knit together in confusion. "I just live next door, Dorothy. And it's just barely snowing."

Dorothy? No one ever called my aunt Dolly "Dorothy."

She threw back her head, her free hand pressed against the skin above her cleavage, and laughed like a giddy schoolgirl.

I wanted to squinch my eyes closed, slap my hands

over my ears, and start singing at the top of my lungs . . . anything to block out this scene of my beloved aunt tarting it up for Richard Greene. But at the same time, I just couldn't seem to look away.

"The leak is just outside the kitchen door. The spigot next to the back steps." Aunt Dolly ushered Richard into the old kitchen.

"What is she doing?" I asked Rena. "Did she have a stroke or something? I mean, what's up with those clothes?"

"Like she said, she found them in *your* closet. She's hoping to woo Richard Greene so he'll drop the planning and zoning complaint against Trendy Tails."

"And she thinks putting her bosoms on display is going to do the trick?"

Rena shrugged. "I don't see the harm in her flaunting her, uh, assets? Isn't that what she called them?"

Within minutes, Richard and Dolly were back in the store. "Not really a leak," Richard groused. "Just didn't tighten the tap enough." He shot a look at Ingrid. "Thought you mighta known that." Ingrid threw up her hands, unwilling to get involved in this particular situation.

Dolly batted her eyes like a practiced coquette. "That's why we need a big strong man like you around," she purred. Merciful heavens, she was laying it on way too thick.

"Nah," Richard scoffed. "Just get one of these strong young things"—he pointed at me—"preferably the big one there, to do it for you next time. Shouldn't be a problem."

The big one? True, the McHale girls weren't exactly

petite—Lucy was the shortest of us at five-seven—but I bristled at being dubbed "the big one."

When he left, I turned to Aunt Dolly and stared at her expectantly.

"Okay. So my plan is not working quite the way I'd hoped." She plopped down in a chair by the big red table. "I've stopped by the Greene Brigade three times, even brought him cookies once. He just complained that the crumbs would attract that 'varmint' that's been living in his shop."

While I couldn't entirely approve of my aunt's tactics, she looked so dejected sitting there in her completely inappropriate outfit.

"Maybe the blush is off the rose. Have I lost my feminine mystique?"

"He just doesn't recognize a good thing when he sees it," I said, walking over to rest a hand on her shoulder.

Ingrid shook her head. "Gonna take a lot more than a little glitz and glamour to turn that old coot's head," she said.

The sequined vest definitely constituted glitz, but I wasn't so sure about the glamour part.

"No," Ingrid continued, "you want to catch a man's attention, you have to play hard to get. Make him jealous. Nothing more powerful than the green-eyed monster."

"Is that how you snagged Harvey?" Rena asked.

Ingrid smiled a smug little smile. "Partly. Mostly he just couldn't resist me. But when we talked or chatted online, I may have thrown in a few comments about my ruggedly handsome neighbor."

"You sly boots," Rena said through her laughter. "So if you used Richard to make Harvey jealous, maybe Dolly could use Harvey to make Richard jealous."

The smile disappeared from Ingrid's face. "No way. No one's even pretending that Harvey is anything but mine."

Talk about the green-eyed monster, I thought. And then it hit me.

Ever since Sean and I had returned from our visit with Hal, I'd been trying to pin down a thought drifting around in my brain, and Ingrid's mention of jealousy made it all come together.

"Rena, what about Pris? What if Pris knew that Hal was catting around with Sherry? Could she have been jealous enough to bump off Sherry?"

Rena hopped up to sit on the table, tailor-style, warming to the idea instantly.

"Sure. While Hal wasn't at the funeral, Pris was. Pris could have stolen Sherry's phone the night of the murder and then Val could have stolen Sherry's cell phone from Pris's purse."

Ingrid tutted softly. "Girls, this is all just a lot of 'who shot John.' I'm not saying Pris is innocent, but you have no proof at all."

Rena looked deflated, but I held my ground. "The morning after Sherry died, I went over to the Olson house, and Kiki coughed up this red string. I swear I saw Sherry wearing a red string around her wrist."

"Sure," Rena said. "That was her Kabbalah bracelet. It's supposed to ward off the evil eye."

"Didn't do the poor girl much good, did it?" Dolly commented.

"No, it sure didn't."

"Why on earth would Priscilla Olson have been creeping around our alley in the middle of the night?" Ingrid asked.

Rena cocked her head. "Maybe she was out looking for Sherry. If she knew about the affair, she might have been biding her time until she got Sherry alone, and she knew that Sherry had been lurking around Trendy Tails. Or maybe she just followed Hal that night and did the one thing he didn't: get out of the car and go searching for Sherry."

"Weak sauce, girls," Ingrid insisted. "First, you're assuming that Pris knew Sherry was Hal's mistress. If I were Pris and suspected my husband was having an affair, my suspicions wouldn't likely land on Sherry as the other woman. Second, you have to assume that she would think to look down the dang alleyway to find her. And, finally, you have to assume Sherry would have taken something from Pris and eaten it."

"Okay, it's a little problematic. But if she did know that Sherry was the other woman, it would be logical for her to come back to Trendy Tails to look for her. And she didn't have to find Sherry in the alley . . . maybe she found her on the sidewalk and lured her into the alley."

I could see Ingrid was ready to argue the logic, and I admitted it was a bit of a stretch, but I held up a hand.

"Let's assume for the sake of argument that Pris was in the alley that night. If she was jealous and wanted to cover up the affair, she would have wanted the phone. She would have struggled with Sherry to get the phone that she kept in Gandhi's sling. In the process, the Kabbalah bracelet comes off and somehow ends up in Pris's bag. When Pris gets home, Kiki eats the string and then barfs it up the next morning."

"I'm telling you, that's not enough," Ingrid insisted. "Red string? That could have come from anything. Kiki was here the night Sherry died." She gestured around the showroom. "That cat could have found a stray piece of yarn or string in here, for all you know."

"You're right," I replied. "It's not like I could go to the cops with this theory. But it's the only theory we have at the moment. At a minimum, I think it warrants a little talk with the other Olson."

CHAPTER
Twenty-two

I invited Pris to Trendy Tails on the pretext of discussing the Halloween Howl and our pet costume parade.

She breezed in the door, ten minutes late, shaking snow from her luxurious red wool cape as she swept it from her body with dramatic flair. After hearing the bell, Packer had come bounding out of the kitchen to greet the guest, but the sudden gust of snow sent him scurrying away again.

While I hung up her cape, Pris wandered around the store, looking at my merchandise with a practiced eye.

"Are these Jolly's work?" she asked, peering into a glass case that held collar dangles made of semiprecious stones set in sterling.

"Yes. Beautiful, aren't they?"

"Mmmm," she hummed noncommittally. "You have quite a selection. Surely you haven't made the rest of this stuff."

"Oh, no. Some of the items I've purchased wholesale, and some from local artisans. But most of the clothing and bedding are my work. I had a lot of the stock on hand before the grand opening, but between running the store and sewing, I hardly have time to breathe."

Pris laughed. "Yet you seem to be finding time to poke around about Sherry Harper's murder."

"You've heard?" I asked carefully.

"Word gets around," she said. "I ran into Ken West yesterday, and he mentioned that you were grilling him about the night Sherry died. He didn't take too kindly to being treated like a common criminal."

"I didn't know you and Ken were friends."

"We're not, really. I asked him to cater an event for the garden club, and he's somehow convinced Hal to invest in his new restaurant."

I suspected I knew how Ken had pried open Hal's pockets: He knew that Hal and Sherry were having an affair and he blackmailed Hal into backing his restaurant. That's why he wouldn't fess up about who he saw Sherry with at the Mission.

"To be honest," Pris continued, dropping her voice to a conspiratorial whisper, "I find him a bit off-putting. A little too aggressive. But his food is divine, so . . ."

It was ironic, really, that she found Ken's personality too aggressive when Ken didn't even come close to the bulldozer-style of Hal Olson.

"You should really be a bit more discreet in your inquiries, dear, if you don't want to get people to talk."

"Well," I said, taking a deep breath, "discretion has never really been my strong suit."

She laughed again. "I'm beginning to gather that.

Inviting me here today, for example. Our business could have easily been conducted by phone, yet you brought me out in the freezing cold for some reason. And I think I know what it is."

I swallowed hard. Rena was in the kitchen, and if anything went wrong I knew I only had to call to her, but the thought of confronting a potential murderer alone was still way outside my comfort zone.

"So I guess there's no point in me mincing words," I said.

"No. By all means, let's get to the good part."

"We know you killed Sherry."

The smile melted from Pris's face. "Excuse me?"

"We know."

"Who's this 'we,' and what do you think you know?" Pris snapped.

"Rena and I figured it out. Your husband left the house after you got home that night, so you could have come back downtown yourself. You're a member of the gardening club, so you'd be familiar with native plants, including the water hemlock that killed Sherry. Your cat horped up Sherry's Kabbalah bracelet the morning after her death. And you certainly had the motive."

"First, my cat did not 'horp up' a bracelet, as you so delicately put it. She got into my embroidery floss, just like Hal said. I found all the skeins in a complete tangle later that morning. Second, I'm one of many members of the gardening club, so that's hardly evidence of anything.

"And what, pray tell, would be my motive for killing Sherry? She was picketing my competitor's establishment. Seems I should have been baking her cookies, not killing her."

"What about her affair with Hal?" I challenged.

"Her *what* with *who*?" Pris gasped.

She seemed genuinely surprised. Oh dear.

"You mean you didn't know?"

"That my husband was having an affair with that horrible hippie? No, I did not." She began to laugh . . . not a dry chuckle or a polite ripple of laughter, but full-on, losing-it hysterics. "Oh," she wheezed, "oh dear. That's astonishing. I can't imagine how I missed the stink of patchouli on him. Are you sure?"

"Unless he had another reason for taking her out to dinner at the Mission or for buying her a disposable cell phone, I'm pretty sure they were having an affair. But where did you think he went the night Sherry died? You knew he wasn't really looking for his wallet at the office because you knew he had the wallet at the grand opening . . . you ordered him to take it out to show me the pictures of Kiki."

"Oh, I knew he wasn't going to look for his wallet, and I was hoping he was meeting a little piece on the side, but I thought it was you."

"Me? Seriously?"

"Of course. He had the wallet at the party, he goes out on the pretense of having lost it, and you bring it by the next morning. If you were a deeply suspicious wife, wouldn't you have suspected that the woman dropping off her husband's wallet was really his lover?"

She had an excellent point.

"I actually thought that's what today was about,"

Pris continued. "I thought you were going to confess all. Maybe pledge your undying love and demand that I let Hal go or something equally déclassé."

"But if you thought I was running around with your husband, why have you been so polite to me? You actually seemed happy to see me this morning."

"Oh, Izzy. Don't you get it? I'm *dying* for Hal to have an affair. Hal Olson is about as exciting as unbuttered toast. I want out of this marriage so badly, while I'm still young enough to have a little fun. But 'our' money is really his money, and I signed a prenup. The only way I get half is if he commits adultery. I've been looking for the dirt on him for years."

The hysteria bubbled up again, and she wiped tears of mirth from her eyes. "You thought I killed Sherry out of jealousy, but her death is most inconvenient for me. If she were still alive, I could sic a private investigator on her and get proof of the affair, break the prenup. As it stands, the information is probably good for nothing but a good laugh. Unless, of course, I can get Hal to confess."

She sobered suddenly and cocked her head. "I was tickled pink this morning, thinking you were going to pour out your heart to me and make my life so much easier."

She reached into her handbag and withdrew a silver box about the size of a pack of gum. "I even brought a digital recorder so I could get the evidence I needed to get out of my marriage with my bank account intact."

"Really? You were that certain I was having an affair with Hal?"

She shrugged. "Actually, I carry this with me at all

times. You never know when someone will say something incriminating. And when you have a philandering husband to nab, well, it's a handy tool. But that's not the point.

"Don't you see? I'm the last person who would want Sherry dead."

CHAPTER
Twenty-three

That evening, Sean, Rena, and I held another strategy meeting in the Trendy Tails barkery. Rena was just finishing putting the peanut butter filling in another batch of carrot pupcakes. She dipped her finger through the peanut butter cream and licked it clean, then held out the spoon in offering to Sean or to me. We both declined, and she shrugged.

"Don't know what you're missing," she muttered.

"I know your food is great, Rena. But I just can't get past the fact that you're making this stuff for a dog."

"Whatever," she grumbled, as she took a seat at the table. "Let's talk about the bigger issue of whether or not I'm going to the hoosegow for murder."

"It feels like we're treading water," I said. "I keep getting glimpses of land, but we're not making any real progress."

Sean nodded. "This pursuit of the mystery man got us nowhere fast."

"Great," Rena said, folding her arms on the table and letting her head fall on them with a soft *thunk*. "My future is looking brighter and brighter."

"We have to look at this with new eyes," Sean insisted. "Presumably Sherry's death had nothing to do with her love life."

"You're right," I agreed. "At the beginning, we assumed it was an enemy who killed her, not a lover. Sherry had lots of enemies. We've been too focused on one possibility to the exclusion of others."

"So what do you think we ought to do?" Rena asked, raising her head to look back and forth between us.

"We use our best asset: our ability to get into Sherry's apartment. We search it again, this time with an open mind about what we might find."

"Am I still benched?" Rena asked.

"Yes, ma'am," Sean said. "In your current predicament, we can't risk you being anywhere near Sherry's home. You're just going to have to sit this out."

"Good thing I trust you two," Rena said with a half-hearted smile.

It broke my heart to see my feisty friend so dejected, and it filled me with fear to think I might not be up to the task of saving her. Never in my life had I been more scared of living up to my nickname: Dizzy Izzy.

Sean and I headed to the Silent Woman to fetch Nick and ask him to let us back into Sherry's apartment.

"Why?"

"Because we're still trying to figure out who killed her," I said.

"That's what cops are for, right? Maybe if they're

busy solving murders, they can lay off guys like me who are just minding their own business," he grumbled.

The bartender leaned over the bar. "Nick here got picked up for public intoxication a couple of days ago. Passed out on a bench in Dakota Park."

"I wasn't hurting anyone. Just resting."

"Listen, Nick," I said, "the cops are focusing on Rena. You like Rena, right?"

"Rena's good people," he agreed, repeating that familiar mantra.

"Then help us help her. We thought we were onto something, but we're back to square one, and we're hoping that something in the apartment will give us a lead."

Nick squirmed on his barstool. "I have to tell you something first. I've been staying at Sherry's place."

"Not at your mom's?"

"Nah, she effing evicted me."

I silently cheered Nadya's decision to kick her abusive baby bird out of the nest and make him fly on his own.

"I figured, my name's on the lease and the rent is paid up through the end of the year. It's what Sherry would've wanted. But I know the stuff inside is Sherry's, and I haven't sold anything. I swear."

Which meant, of course, that he *had* sold some of Sherry's belongings. But that was Carla's problem, not mine. As long as he hadn't inadvertently sold something that held a clue to Sherry's murder, I didn't care if he'd gutted the place.

Sean patted him on the back.

"It's okay, Nick. We don't care if you've been crashing at Sherry's. We just want to look around. For Rena."

"Okay. For Rena."

The apartment was every bit as cluttered as I remembered. But there was a faint whiff of bleach in the air, and the stacks of paper looked marginally straighter. If clutter could be tidy, this was it.

"Nick, have the cleaning people been here?"

"I s'pose so. They came every week, and they were paid up front, just like the rent." He sniffed loudly. "Yep, they've been here. They have their own key, come and go like ghosts. Only way you know for certain they've been here is the smell and the tiny triangle on the toilet paper."

Nick kicked off his shoes, made his way to the brass daybed, and curled up in a bony little ball there. He cocooned himself in the red chenille throw and inhaled deeply. It must have smelled of Sherry.

On the floor next to the daybed were three pizza boxes, an empty plastic bottle of cheap vodka, and dozens of crumpled tissues. It looked like Nick hadn't so much been living in Sherry's apartment as nesting there.

The first time we'd been to Sherry's apartment, we'd been looking for something very specific: the identity of her mystery man. This time, we were casting a broader net.

I started in the bedroom, while Sean took the living room.

Sherry's closet was bursting at the seams with long, flowing dresses, patchwork jumpers, and those chunky, brightly colored sweaters that are hand knit in Central America . . . but I found nothing besides clothes. Her dresser and a bookcase were littered with scarves, bangles, and piles of her photographs, but nothing new.

I joined Sean in the living room. "Any luck?" I asked.

"Maybe," he said. "I think I found her calendar."

I rushed to his side. "Did she actually keep a calendar? Like actually have appointments and stuff?"

He flipped through the pages, looking at the notations in the small squares, but before he could answer me, Nick piped up.

" 'Course she kept a calendar. I told you, the woman had effing irons in the fire. She belonged to a couple of big organizations that met in Minneapolis, one to save the environment and one to ban nuclear power plants, so she had to keep track of their meetings. And her protests."

Sean pointed at the date for the Trendy Tails grand opening. Sure enough, she'd scrawled "TT Open" in the box.

"Is there anything unusual in the days before her death?" I asked.

"Nothing I can make out. But look at this." He pointed at the square for tomorrow, Wednesday, October 30. "It's starred and circled, so it must have been important."

I leaned in for a better look, and my arm brushed Sean's. We both pulled back quickly, as though the point of contact had burned.

"Excuse me," I mumbled, silently cursing myself for reacting like a love-struck teenager with Sean of all people: a man I'd put squarely in the friend box many years ago and who was now quite involved with another woman.

I turned my attention back to the starred date on the calendar. "Courthouse, eight a.m.," I read aloud.

"Another protest?" Sean questioned.

"Maybe. Jolly said that Sherry had been hanging around the bank, making a pest of herself, and you know how much she loved a good conspiracy theory. A protest at the courthouse could be part of a grander plan. It seems the most likely theory. But it's so specific. Why eight a.m.? Maybe she was meeting someone there. Or was there some specific event she was protesting?"

"I suppose it's something," Sean said. "But whatever she was planning to do at eight a.m. at the courthouse, she'll never get the chance."

We continued our search through the detritus of Sherry's life, while Nick quietly snored away on the daybed, for another thirty minutes. That's when something caught my eye.

"Sean," I called. "Check this out."

I held up a stack of papers I'd found nestled between two mounds of old newspapers on the big oak dining table.

When he reached my side, I started leafing through them, turning over one after the next.

"Bank statements?"

"Yeah. And tax returns." I raised my voice. "Hey, Nick, I thought you said Sherry didn't have a checking account."

"Nah, man. I said she didn't have a checkbook. 'Course she had an account. But Carla handled all the money stuff. She just brought by a stack of checks every month and had Carla sign them. Then Carla gave Sherry her cash, and they went their separate ways."

"What about her taxes?"

"Same deal. Sherry didn't like paying her blood money to Uncle Sam and didn't want to waste a minute of her life on them. Carla brought the papers, Sherry signed, and boom, they were done."

Beside me, Sean continued flipping the pages.

He was going too slowly for my taste, so I gently knocked his hand away. For an instant, we both glanced up and our gazes met.

I cleared my throat. "This looks like five years' worth of bank statements and tax returns for the same time-frame."

"What's so strange about that?" he said. "Your sister is an accountant. Surely she has told you that you should always have five years of your financial documents on hand in case of an audit."

Indeed. And thanks to her relentless indoctrination, I kept five years' worth of tax returns and all the supporting documentation in a pretty blue flowered box beneath my bed.

"If it were anyone else, there wouldn't be anything strange about it at all. But every single person we've talked to has emphasized that Sherry didn't handle her own finances. Nick just said she didn't even have a checkbook, didn't bother reviewing her tax forms before she signed them. She let Carla handle everything. Can you imagine her being worried about an audit?"

Something was niggling in the back of my mind. Five years. It wasn't just the standard record-keeping period. There was something else.

"Nick," I called, trying to rouse him again from that state between awake and passed out. "How old was Sherry?" I knew she was a few years older than I was, but not exactly how much older.

"Thirty-five," he replied, a hint of annoyance creeping into his voice. "Her birthday was last month. I remembered. Even got her a card, but she sent it back."

Thirty-five. So the statements and returns dated back to when she turned thirty.

"These documents go back to when Sherry started drawing money from the Harper trust," I said to Sean.

"Well, that explains it. Five years ago was when Carla moved back from Minneapolis and started managing the trust. I'm sure Carla cracked down on Sherry, Maybe Carla is like Dru and made Sherry keep her statements."

I gestured around the apartment. "You think Carla would trust Sherry to keep important documents in this chaos? No, I would lay odds that Carla does Sherry's taxes, pays all her bills, handles her banking, and keeps the records herself."

"Then what is Sherry doing with these?"

"Excellent question." I flipped through the stack until I found what I was looking for. "Here. Take a look at this. See all these notes in the margins of the tax returns? Question marks. Like something didn't add up. Same with the bank statements. It looks like Sherry was going through all her deposits and withdrawals, and something struck her as off."

Sean laughed. "Are you suggesting the bank made an error, and *Sherry* of all people was able to spot it? Besides, Carla's a wiz. She started law school when she was nineteen, and got her job at the white-shoe law firm in Minneapolis when she was only twenty-two. She's brilliant. If the bank had made an error, she would have caught it. We can just call her and ask. Unless you're suggesting Carla's the one who made the error."

I realized I was on thin ice here, implicating Sean's girlfriend of any sort of wrongdoing, no matter how unintentional. Who would he trust: Dizzy Izzy or Carla the prodigy? It wasn't even close. But Rena's life was on the line, and that mattered more to me than Sean's relationship with Carla . . . or my relationship with Sean.

"I'm not suggesting anything," I said, though my pause had surely telegraphed my true feelings on the matter. "I just think it's strange that Sherry was going through her own bank statements and tax returns.

"Let's show them to my sister Dru first. If she can't find anything, then we'll talk to Carla."

I could see the emotions playing across Sean's face. Going to Dru first or to Carla first . . . his decision would reflect how deeply he trusted Carla to give us the straight story. It was an implicit test of his relationship.

He sighed. "Fine. We'll let Dru have the first crack at them."

I didn't realize I'd been holding my breath until it left my body in a rush of relief. And a tiny part of my brain wondered whether all that relief was for Rena's benefit.

CHAPTER
Twenty-four

Sean, Rena, and I approached Dru that very night with our questions about Sherry's bank statements in the most civilized of all settings: an emergency dinner with my family.

My parents had moved into their split-level home three weeks before I was born. My mother had often regaled us with the story of her hugely pregnant self trying to keep my sister Dru—then just learning to walk—from tumbling down the steps, while sweet-talking the movers into rearranging the living room six times despite the sweltering late-July heat.

A year after the move, my parents got Lucy and air conditioning.

Though I hadn't lived there in over a decade, I still thought of the tidy house, tucked amid a stand of elm trees in a middle-class neighborhood just a mile from Merryville's historic downtown, as home. In fact, my sisters and I had all moved into places of our own, leaving my parents with an empty nest, but my mom's elaborate Sunday dinners brought all of the chicks back to the nest. We even brought the occasional cuckoo into the nest: Rena, Xander, Taffy, and Lucy's bestie, Bethany, were regular features at the table. And while Sunday was the official day of feasting, my mom could always be called on in a pinch to whip together a homey meal. Given our current predicament, Mom was willing to offer a midweek version of her weekend spread.

Although she had technically worked as a high school English teacher, mom had also filled in as the home ec teacher. Out of necessity, she'd learned to cook like a champ. That evening, the house was redolent of fresh-baked bread and simmering gravy, a hint of cinnamon promising apple pie for dessert.

"Lucy, it's your turn to set the table," my mom directed. "Use the china."

"First, it's Dru's turn to set the table," Lucy said, "and, second, what's the occasion?"

"First, it is most definitely *your* turn," Mom said, "and, second, why do we need a special occasion to enjoy the beautiful china? It may be fancy, but it's still meant to be used. Besides, we have guests."

"Sean and Rena are hardly guests," Lucy grumbled. "They basically lived here for nine years."

"Still, we use the china. Now hurry up, Sean and Rena will be here any minute."

My grandparents—my mom and aunt Dolly's parents—had hoarded away all their nice things, insisting they were too good to use. When they passed, we found years of Christmas and birthday gifts, everything from nightgowns to silicone bakeware, tucked away in cupboards and drawers. My mom had sworn she would not deprive herself of the pleasure of her possessions. Still, eating on my parents' wedding china was a rare event.

"What's going on, Mom?" I asked.

She finished rinsing out a mixing bowl and wiped her hands on her apron.

"I don't know. I guess this thing with the Harper girl has me thinking even more about how short and uncertain life can be. 'Out, out, brief candle,' and all that."

I fished the silverware from the drawer, carefully counting out the spoons. "Is that all?"

Mom clucked softly. "Oh, I don't know. I guess I'm just happy to have all my chicks back in the nest. I've missed having Sean and Rena around."

"Rena's probably been to more of your Sunday dinners in the last decade than I have."

"But not Sean. You two were so close. I just don't understand why your friendship didn't last through college."

I felt heat licking my cheeks. I'd never confided in my mom or anyone in my family about the night of Sean's proclamation.

"It's complicated," I muttered.

Lucy set out the plates as I followed behind with the silver.

"Liar, liar, pants on fire," Lucy whispered. "The reason Sean's been MIA isn't complicated at all."

"What do you mean?" I asked.

"Sean and Izzy, sittin' in a tree . . ." she sang softly.

"How do you . . ." I cut myself off before I could say anything more incriminating.

"Are you kidding me? You two made such a racket that night, I can't believe the whole neighborhood doesn't know." Lucy shrugged one shoulder. "I'd been, uh, out that night myself and happened to be making my way in through the backyard—"

"Sneaking in, you mean."

"Well if you want to split hairs, yes. I was sneaking in through the backyard and heard it all."

"Why didn't you say something?"

"I always meant to. I was saving it up for some time when I really needed some leverage against you. But that time never came."

I stopped in my tracks, my hands still full of salad forks. "Lucy McHale. I knew you were devious, but I had no idea. How could you have kept such a juicy secret for so long? And, good heavens, what else do you know? What else can you use to blackmail me in the future?"

She smiled, her expression remarkably like Jinx's after she hides one of Packer's toys.

"That's for me to know and you to find out," she said.

Dealing with my sister was like dealing with a very smart, very worldly six-year-old girl. I couldn't decide whether to laugh or give her a noogie.

"What are you two whispering about?" Mom called.

"Nothing, Mom," Lucy said in her sweetest, most innocent, singsong tone. She dropped her voice again. "For what it's worth, I think he was right."

"Who?"

"Sean. When he said that you just thought you were in love with Casey."

I was flummoxed. Floored. Flabbergasted.

"But you were right, too, when you sent him on his way that night. High school romances almost never last. If you'd had a fling with Sean that summer, it would have burned hot and fast but then it would have fizzled, and you wouldn't be getting this second chance now."

"Second chance?"

"Oh, come on," she said. "I see the way you two look at each other. The chemistry's still there."

"Nonsense," I huffed. "He's got a girlfriend."

Lucy laughed. "Yeah, so? He's been dating her for a year and still hasn't put a ring on her finger."

True enough. And Sean had been pretty cavalier when he talked about his relationship with Carla, as though it was fairly casual even after all that time.

"Sister, I may be the youngest, but you know I've always been the wisest. At least when it comes to boys."

"Is it wise to torture poor Xander the way you do?"

She chuckled. "Ever hear of a long con? Biding your time? Trust me; I know what I'm doing with Xander. And you should also trust me on this one. Sean's not over you."

I was saved from having to respond by Sean and Rena's arrival. They'd been laughing together, and they all but tumbled through the door, red-cheeked and smiling, blowing into their cupped hands and stamping their feet to drive off the chill.

"I think we'll get our first hard freeze tonight," Sean said.

We gathered around my parents' table, gorging on mashed potatoes, mushroom gravy, roasted Brussels sprouts, and pot roast for the omnivores. We kept the conversation light—the Packers and the Vikings, the best snow tires, a few casual "remember whens"—and carefully steered clear of any talk of murder until after the dishes had been cleared and my parents retired to the kitchen to hand wash the fine china.

At that point, we pulled out Sherry's tax forms and bank statements and handed them to Dru.

"Anything seem out of place? Unusual?" I asked.

While we looked on, Dru pored through the stack of papers. Every now and then, she'd mutter something under her breath or tuck a stray lock of hair behind her ear, but the rest of us sat in absolute silence.

Finally, she rapped the papers on the table to straighten their edges and looked up.

"Well. This is intriguing."

"In what way?" I asked.

She flipped through the stack of papers until she found what she was looking for, turning it so we could all see.

"Sherry is getting large monthly checks from the Harper trust. See here, these deposits? But her overall balance is pretty low. I know she had a reasonably nice apartment, and she spent money on clothes and stuff, but compared to what she was bringing in, I don't see how Sherry could be going through money that fast."

"She didn't live entirely on the cheap," I said. "She had a cleaning service, and she must have had some camera equipment. And she had a really nice computer setup on that desk in the corner. Besides, those hippie clothes she wore cost a pretty penny."

"But," Rena said, "she didn't take lavish vacations, didn't even own a car. She might have been spending more than you or I could afford, but nothing even approaching her income. I mean, did you see the luxury cars Teal and Tarleton Harper drove to the funeral? They were worth more than the GDP of several small countries, and you know Teal and Tarleton have never worked a lick in their lives. Sherry didn't live as lavishly as she could have."

"Rena's right," Dru said. "The income from the trust must have gone straight into this bank account, because the deposits are huge. But so are some of the withdrawals. Most of the big withdrawals are here." Dru pointed to a number of check withdrawals that were too big to be rent or utilities, even if Sherry was paying those things a year at a time. Ten thousand, fifty thousand, even one hundred thousand dollar checks. Looking back to the earlier statements, there were only a few per year, but they'd become increasingly frequent, and in the past few months, they'd taken a sizable chunk out of the account's bottom line. "I mean, she's not broke by any means, but her balance isn't consistent with her income."

"Investments?" Sean asked.

"Maybe," Dru said, her tone skeptical. "But the checks themselves are not regular, you know? It's not like she was paying a certain amount per month into a retirement account. And if she was working with an actual investment banker—which sounds decidedly un-Sherry-like—we'd probably see larger withdrawals. Or electronic transfers. And"—she paused to pull out the most recent tax return—"we'd probably see her paying at least some capital gains tax. But she hasn't paid a dime in capital gains taxes."

"Maybe donations to nonprofits," I said. "Sherry was involved in so many causes. Maybe she was supporting some of those groups with large donations."

Dru shrugged. "Again, it's possible. But then we would expect to see deductions for charitable gifts on her taxes. And again, not a single deduction."

"But if she was making the donations in cash," Sean argued, "maybe she didn't get receipts."

I shook my head. "These were check withdrawals, not withdrawals straight from the bank. They weren't even counter checks because the check numbers were right there next to the withdrawals, and weren't all sequential. Sherry didn't have her checkbook; Carla did. If Sherry was asking for this much money, it seems like Carla would have asked about it and then made the appropriate adjustments to Sherry's taxes when she prepared them."

"Exactly," Dru said. "So all that money, Sherry wasn't spending it, at least not in any obvious way. It should have been going into a savings account or a mutual fund or something. Something that would generate interest that Sherry would have to claim on her taxes. Yet there's no interest income, no capital gains, no nothing. So the money wasn't invested. At all. Not even in a Christmas club account."

"And that," I said, "leaves us with the question of where the money is. Unless she was hiding large sums of cash in her freezer. . . ."

"I wouldn't rule that out," Sean said. "She was an

odd duck. Besides, as long as her bills were getting paid, what would Sherry care about interest income?"

Dru held up her hands in mock surrender. "I'm not saying there was anything hinky going on. I'm just saying that's how it looks. And all the question marks Sherry drew all over these papers lead me to believe that Sherry thought there was something hinky, too."

But what did it all mean?

CHAPTER
Twenty-five

The following day, I set aside all thought of investigation of Sherry's death and focused on my business. The Halloween Howl was a mere day away, and Rena and I had to put together hundreds of favor bags—both canine and feline—stuffed with toys and treats, and we needed to do it before Ingrid Whitfield's going-away gathering that evening.

But, first things first, I got myself up at the crack of dawn, put on my Sunday best, and headed to the courthouse, planning to be there right when they opened so I could obtain the forms I needed to counter Richard's challenge of the rezoning on 801 Maple Street. The Halloween Howl would hopefully increase goodwill in the community and traffic in the store, but if I didn't get the zoning issue straightened out, there would be no store at all.

Winter's cold had settled into Merryville's bones, and we wouldn't shake it until spring. But so far, the snow had been relatively light, not enough to make driving hazardous, and the weather forecasters promised the first big blizzard—currently sweeping across the Dakotas—would hold off until after the Halloween Howl.

I bundled Packer into a studded leather jacket lined with faux fur and put on his "motorcycle" boots before leashing him and heading out into the elements. Given Packer's penchant for outdoor romps and sniffing new places, I tried to take him on as many errands as I could.

We arrived at the courthouse at five past eight, just after they opened, but already the place hummed with activity. A long line of haggard-looking men and women lined the benches outside the courtroom. I knew from Lucy's work tales that they were likely the folks who had been picked up overnight for DUI, drunk and disorderly, or domestic violence, all of them hungover and exhausted from a night on a jail cot, and now awaiting arraignment. Beyond them, at the clerk's office, a line had already formed, both citizens and attorneys waiting to file court documents.

But the real action was down the hallway in the city offices, where I was heading. Just past the doorway to the zoning and planning board's office, a cluster of men had gathered. Someone beyond them, whom I could not see, was rattling off prices while the crowd hooted and yelped to designate their bids—an auction.

Curious, I looked on for a few minutes. Packer, at my side, would occasionally yip along with a bidder, but I tugged gently on his leash to hush him up. Whatever they were auctioning off, I didn't want my dog to inadvertently place the highest bid.

Finally, someone in the center of the small crowd whooped with delight, and the rest of the men started to peel off, their expressions ranging from dejected to downright hostile. When the dust settled, one man remained:

Hal Olson.

He looked like the cat who swallowed the canary, his lips thinned in a smug smile and a light of pure glee in his eyes.

"What was that all about?" I asked, sidestepping a disgruntled bidder to reach Hal's side.

"I just bought the Anderson property for a song," he crowed.

"The Anderson property?"

"The old Soaring Eagles campground. The Andersons stopped maintaining the place and paying their taxes years ago. I was able to pick it up for back taxes and a measly few thou." He waved his hand toward the rest of the group, now trudging unhappily down the corridor, hands in pockets and heads down. "Those guys, they were total amateurs. None of them had the cash to make serious bids."

"The Anderson place, huh? So are you and Pris moving out to the lake?" I asked.

Hal laughed, his big booming laugh. "Ah, heck no. Pris doesn't really do nature."

"What about her gardening club?"

"Aw, that doesn't count. She goes to those meetings in full makeup and mostly shows off what our landscapers have done while she's been safely tucked away in our climate-controlled house. When she *does* go with them to plant bulbs and such, she wears full makeup, padded gardening gloves, and takes a waterproof cloth to kneel on. No, right now the place is nothing but weeds and dilapidated cabins, not exactly Pris's scene."

"Then why buy it?"

Hal gave me a sidelong look, as though I was maybe just yanking his chain with my question. "Well, right *now* the place is a disaster, but in about two years it will be The Woods at Badger Lake, a high-end resort community complete with spa and five-star restaurant."

"Really?"

"Yep. I've got a couple of investors who are itching to throw in with me. Should make us a mint."

And, I thought, if Hal won his bid to be mayor, his political pull might grease the wheels to ensure that nothing derailed the new development.

"I've already lined up Ken West to be our executive chef at the restaurant. I know it's been a while since the Blue Atlantic closed, but he's still got a reputation. Having him on board means instant publicity for The Woods."

Here was more evidence to back my theory about why Ken West lied to cover up Hal and Sherry's affair. Hal was Ken's ticket out of catering and making pastry and back into the world of fine dining. With Hal's backing and a little help from Aunt Dolly, maybe a few others, Ken would have all the capital he needed for a smooth start on a new restaurant.

I wondered whether Hal knew about the personal issues Ken had alluded to—the ones that had led to the Blue Atlantic's demise. I figured it wasn't my place to mention any of that, so I simply smiled and nodded.

"Well, congratulations on the purchase. I'm surprised there weren't more people here to bid on the property. Lakefront property, even out here in Merryville, has to be worth a pretty penny."

Hal colored beneath his golfer's tan. "So much of this auction stuff is just knowing about the opportunities and being in the right place at the right time." Meaning, of course, that Hal had an in with someone somewhere, and he'd found out about the auction through back channels. "The sales are posted in the *Merryville Gazette*, and on the courthouse walls. So anyone can participate; they just have to look for the opening."

I read the *Merryville Gazette* every morning. I'd seen the page with the public notices, all in print so fine it looked like ant tracks. I never bothered to try to decipher what those notices said, and I surely didn't haunt the halls of the courthouse looking for auction notices.

No, like so many things in life, you had to have connections to learn about opportunities like this one.

"What brings you down to the courthouse this morning?" Hal asked. "Can't imagine you spent last night in the hoosegow," he joked.

I waggled Packer's leash. "No, last I checked the jail doesn't allow pets. I'm here because my neighbor has filed a complaint with the planning and zoning board arguing that the building in which I operate Trendy Tails is zoned residential, not commercial."

Hal laughed. "Let me guess: Richard Greene. Old curmudgeon got his own variance to open up the Greene Brigade, but he doesn't want any of his neighbors to do the same. Virginia Harper had to fight the same fight when she opened the Grateful Grape."

"I didn't know you and Virginia were close," I said.

He rocked up on his toes and jingled the change in his pockets. "We're not. Word gets around, though. Small town and all that."

Of course. Hal wasn't close to Virginia, but he *had* been close to Sherry. She was probably the source of his intel.

"It certainly is a small town. And if Richard has his way, I'm going to get squeezed right out of it."

Hal laughed again as he clapped a giant paw on my shoulder. "Don't worry about it. The zoning board wants new business. Richard will make you jump through the hoops, but if you're patient, you will prevail. Virginia did." He winced. "But then, Virginia had Carla to help her. Carla had moved back home by then, moved right in with her mom to help her out. Helped her out with the paperwork and all that stuff for the zoning board."

Great, I thought. Virginia had a dutiful daughter to help her with Richard Greene's legal hurdles. If I were going to have legal help, I was going to have to rely on Sean . . . and I still wasn't sure whether we were actually friends again, or if he was merely tolerating me for Rena's sake.

When I returned to Trendy Tails from the courthouse, my troubles weren't nearly over. I arrived to find Richard standing outside my door, a broom in one hand and a flyswatter in the other.

"It's now or never," he said, shaking his implements of rodent war in my direction. "Either you get rid of that damned rodent today, or I call an exterminator."

"We just set the humane traps two days ago," I said,

following him into the Greene Brigade. "It takes a while for them to work. Give them a week. Please, I'm begging you." I couldn't bear the thought of Gandhi going up against an exterminator.

"Too late. Your traps didn't work." Richard Greene sounded smug, as though he'd known all along that our nemesis was too crafty to be caught in something so banal as a humane trap.

Sure enough, I made the rounds of the traps situated in out-of-the-way corners of Richard's shop—so as not to alarm his customers. Each stood empty, its carrot nubbin bait miraculously gone, but the trap door unsprung.

How had he done it? I was beginning to suspect that the pig could outsmart us all. Gandhi would go down in the annals of guinea pig history as a champion, a lion among pigs.

"Richard, I don't know what to say—"

"Hush! Do you hear that?"

I froze, listening intently. At first, I could hear nothing but the occasional rumble of a car passing by outside. But then I heard it, a quiet rustling.

"Where's it coming from?" I whispered.

Richard glared at me and shrugged, his message clear: How the heck would I know?

Carefully, slowly, I crept toward the opposite side of the store, pausing occasionally to listen, but the rustling grew more faint. Richard followed behind me, his makeshift weaponry raised in case he caught sight of Gandhi. I don't know what, exactly, he planned to do with either the broom or the flyswatter, but I prayed I'd see Gandhi before he did.

I changed tack, moving inch by inch toward the back of the store. Richard had torn down all the walls of the first floor of his converted house, leaving only broad archways between the front door and the back.

Step, step, pause, listen. Step, step, pause, listen. Richard started to grumble something about hunting blinds, and I hushed him. The rustling grew louder. I was getting warmer.

Suddenly, a flash of movement caught my eye. There, on a box right by the back door, sat Gandhi, contentedly chewing on the edge of the cardboard.

"Get him now, Miss McHale," Richard hissed, "or I'll sic MacArthur on him."

I kept up my slow progress, doing my best not to draw the pig's attention.

I was a mere three feet away, Gandhi seemingly oblivious to my approach, when the back door to the Greene Brigade flew open.

"Ta-da!" Aunt Dolly struck a pose in the doorway. "Richard Greene, I've come to take you out on the town!"

For me, the next few seconds unfolded in slow motion: Dolly swept her arms in a grand gesture, knocking over the box on which Gandhi sat, startling the pig from his perch, and—before I could get the word "no" out of my mouth—he scrambled out the back door and into the night.

"Gandhi!"

But it was too late. Once again, the pig was in the wind.

"Oh dear." Dolly's face fell. "Did I do something wrong?"

"Wrong? Dorothy Johnston, you are the bee's knees!" Richard reached out to pull Dolly into the store, spinning her in a surprisingly deft dance move that sent the skirt of her pale rose dress swirling about her legs.

Dolly's mouth formed a startled little "oh" before she giggled like a teenager.

"My heavens, Richard! Whatever has come over you?"

I suspected Richard wasn't so much happy to see Dolly come as he was to see Gandhi go.

CHAPTER
Twenty-six

Even with the prospect of a blizzard coming, Ingrid was determined to leave the day after the Halloween Howl, so that evening—after my trip to the courthouse, my misadventure with Gandhi, and an afternoon of stuffing goody bags for the Howl—I closed Trendy Tails a few hours early and we threw a small party in my apartment to send her off.

"Merryville won't be the same without you, Ingrid," Taffy Nielson said, raising a glass of cider in a toast.

"Good heavens," Ingrid said. "You'd think I was gonna die. I'll be back in May, like Persephone, bringing the summer with me."

"Are you suggesting that Boca is Hell?" I quipped.

"Not at all," Ingrid said with an uncharacteristically coy smile. "Wherever my Harvey is, that's heaven."

"He's a lucky man, your Harvey. You've been a good neighbor," Richard Greene agreed in a voice hoarse with emotion. "Better than most," he added, glancing pointedly in my direction.

"Oh be quiet, old man," Dolly said, nudging him in the ribs. She looked up at him through her lashes, a knowing smile gracing her lips. After Dolly had inadvertently sent Gandhi back into the wilds of the alleyway, I'd expected his sudden rush of affection for her to fade away, but it seemed my aunt had found her way into Richard Greene's musty, dusty heart. They'd already followed through on my aunt's plan to dine together at La Ming, and Richard had asked Dolly to accompany him to the Halloween Howl the next night.

I had my fingers crossed that some of his affection for my aunt would spill over onto me and Trendy Tails, and maybe she'd be able to convince him to drop his zoning board complaint, but so far, his warmth toward Dolly had not thawed his ire at me.

As though reading my mind, Richard turned his full attention on me. "Young lady," he said, his rich baritone voice vibrating with command, "a business is a serious endeavor. Legalities must be observed. Don't think a trim ankle and a pair of big, beautiful green eyes will sway me from my civic duty to enforce all the terms of the social contract."

I sputtered on my cider for a second, before I realized that the trim ankle and beautiful green eyes belonged to Dolly and not me.

"Yes, sir," I replied. "I filed my paperwork with the zoning board this morning."

Ingrid took a seat on one of my overstuffed chairs. Packer trundled out of the kitchen and flopped forlornly across her feet, whining pitifully until she lifted him to her lap. "Sweet boy. I'm going to miss you, too, buddy." She slipped him a tiny piece of the smoked sausage Richard had brought, but she wasn't so quick that I didn't see.

"Oh, Ingrid." I sighed. "You're going to spoil him."

"I'm like his grandma," Ingrid huffed. "I'm supposed to spoil him."

Ingrid ruffled Packer's wrinkly head, and he scrunched himself into the space between her hip and the side of the chair, his front paws and head on her lap, a blissed-out expression on his face.

"So, did you see Edna Malicki while you were at the courthouse?" Edna Malicki was the head clerk at the Merryville courthouse, and Ingrid and Edna had a longstanding feud. I think it started over a hinky hand of euchre. Or possibly over a raffle at the Elks Lodge annual Christmas party. Whatever its genesis, the dispute had ended a years-long friendship.

It struck me as sad, but people in glass houses and all.

While Ingrid sniped about Edna all the time, she also asked about Edna every chance she got, hitting up my sister Lucy, who worked at the courthouse, for all the dirt. I suspected Ingrid would miss her old nemesis once she moved to Boca.

"No, I didn't see Edna. But I did see Hal Olson," I said. "He bought the old Soaring Eagles camp at auction this morning."

While Dolly perched on the edge of one of my kitchen chairs, Richard stood at attention by her side. "Was that today?" he asked. "I'd heard they were auctioning off the land, and I wondered who'd snap it up. Hal Olson, eh?"

"Yep. He's planning to turn it into a resort of some sort."

Richard huffed. "The Harper men must be rolling over in their graves. To think of the pristine view from the Harper lake house marred by a bunch of condos and shops."

"I can't see the young ones getting fired up about it," Dolly said.

"Who, those two pups—what are their names? Veal and Tartan?" Richard asked.

"Teal and Tarleton," Rena corrected.

"Right, Teal and Tarleton. What kind of names are those for grown men? I mean what's wrong with Steve or David or Mike?" Dolly reached up to pat the hand he had rested on her shoulder, and her touch seemed to soothe him.

Ingrid shook her head. "I think I'm getting out of Merryville just in time. First, we're going to end up with that jackass Hal Olson for a mayor, and then he's going to clutter up our lake with some cookie cutter development. And that's going to run off all the deer, maybe the birds. The whole place will go to heck in a handbasket, you mark my words."

Rena, nestled in a corner of the couch, tucked her feet up under her. "Sad. If ever there was a cause for Sherry to take up, this would have been it."

Sherry did like a good cause, I mused, and protecting the land near her family home, the land that she had played on as a child . . . well, that would have been a humdinger.

I sipped my cider.

Yes, it was too bad Sherry hadn't lived to fight this battle.

I took another sip of cider, and let my mind drift. One by one the pieces began to swim into focus.

I'd always thought Hal and Sherry were an odd pair. From what Rena had said about Hal, anything with two X-chromosomes would light his fire. But Sherry? I wouldn't say Sherry had good taste in men, but Hal represented everything Sherry despised. What was she doing with him?

I thought back to the night Sherry'd died. She'd yelled at Nick, called him a loser, but then she'd looked at the guests of the grand opening and almost pleaded with him, saying he was going to ruin everything. Ruin what? Ruin her relationship with Hal? Surely she wasn't in love with him. I couldn't fathom those two worlds colliding.

If Nick was a reliable source—and there was a pretty big question mark there—Sherry had said she was dating someone with connections, that she didn't really hate Nick, that someday he'd understand why she had been keeping her distance. Someday, he'd understand why she was dating Hal.

What was it Hal had said that very morning, about how he'd managed to snag the Anderson property at pennies on the dollar? He had connections, inside knowledge. Sherry had implied to Nick that she needed or wanted connections, and Hal sure had them. But what did a loner like Sherry need with the type of connections Hal could provide?

Eight a.m. at the courthouse. Sherry had marked today on her calendar, something to do at eight a.m. at the courthouse. We'd all assumed it was another protest, maybe a protest of the auction?

That made no sense. Why would she cozy up to Hal and try to learn about his business acumen if she planned to protest Hal's own big money play at the auction. No, she didn't want to just protest the sale of the land; she wanted to buy it out from under Hal. That's why she'd been trying to get inside information on what Hal was planning. That's why she planned to hit the courthouse at eight a.m.

It was all pure speculation, except for that notation in her calendar—eight a.m. at the courthouse. What if Sherry had decided to save the Anderson property by buying it herself? Her life spent making signs and marching in the rain would suddenly pay off, produce some real change, if she could buy the Anderson property and stop its development.

Then I remembered the book I'd found in Gandhi's baby sling—a book on wetlands conservation. A claim that development of the Anderson property would affect the wetlands and throw the lake's ecosystem out of kilter would hold up construction for years. That might have been her Plan B: If she couldn't outbid Hal for the property, she'd tie up his attempted development for years with environmental challenges.

We had assumed Sherry's text to Carla saying she needed money was just talking about living expenses. But it was more than that. She was calling in her chits for the big bucks . . . the money she would need to buy the Anderson property at auction.

But if Dru was reading Sherry's financial documents

correctly, there wasn't nearly enough money to with-
draw. Sherry's account balance was woefully low. Normally, Sherry might not have done anything about that,
might not have even cared that the coffers were a little
low. But with the land auction looming, she needed the
cash right away. She would have been pushing Carla
hard, demanding answers.

"Rena," I said, "I think I know who killed Sherry,
and more importantly, I think I know why."

CHAPTER
Twenty-seven

I'd already made a fool of myself by accusing two inno-cent people of murder. This time, I was going to find some actual evidence before I started pointing fingers.

First thing in the morning, I made my way to the Silent Woman. If it's possible, the bar smelled even worse, seemed even seedier, in the bright light of morn-ing. I found Nick snoring away in a booth near the jukebox.

"Nick," I said gently, trying not to startle him awake. "Nick, wake up."

"Wha—?" he muttered as he sat up and rubbed his eyes with the arm of his black hoodie.

"Nick, it's Izzy," I said, as though we weren't a mere two feet apart. "I need a favor."

"Again?"

"Just a little one, and I promise this will be the last."

He glared up at me through eyes a demonic shade of red. "Okay, what do you need?"

"Did Sherry write you any notes, letters, anything like that?"

"All the effing time. Sherry was a real romantic, you know." To my surprise, he dug into the pocket of his hoodie. "This is the last note she wrote me."

I took it gently, aware that this note obviously meant a lot to Nick. I quickly read it:

"Spaghetti and a can of spray cheese, Sherry."

Very romantic indeed.

"I know it's a lot to ask, but could I borrow this for the day? Just the day, I promise. And I'll take good care of it."

He narrowed his eyes, like he wasn't inclined to trust me, but then he nodded.

I scooted out of the bar as fast as I could, and hoofed it to the First National Bank, where I called in a huge favor from Lois Owens. Huge. With my evidence in hand, I called Sean with my hypothesis.

I thought Sean would want to talk to Carla alone, but he insisted Rena and I come along.

"I'm sure there's a perfectly innocent explanation, and I want you to hear it for yourselves."

I wanted to hear that explanation, too, but I suspected we had very different reasons. Even after I explained my reasoning to Sean, he was clinging to his belief that Carla was on the up-and-up. But if Dru thought the returns were hinky, they were hinky. It might have never come to light if not for Sherry's sudden need for the money to buy the Anderson place. But if Carla was mishandling Sherry's money, and Sherry was threatening to expose her, that gave Carla a motive for murder.

Carla's office was as crisp and tailored as she herself was: a glass-and-metal desk, sleek ergonomic desk chair, abstract prints framed in silver on the walls.

"This is a pleasant surprise," she said as she rose to greet Sean with a quick buss on the cheek. When she extended her hand for Rena and me to shake, I could see the hint of confusion in her eyes.

She gestured that we should all sit in the camel-colored leather side chairs in front of the desk while she returned to her seat behind the desk.

Sean wasted no time.

"We've seen Sherry's tax returns and bank statements."

For an instant, Carla looked off balance, like she might tip over in her chair. But in a heartbeat she was steady again, her mask of cool indifference firmly in place.

"And?" she drawled.

"And there's a lot of money missing from that account," Rena snapped.

"What do you mean? Sherry's life wasn't free. Trust money went in, living expenses came out."

"I mean that we saw her checking account statements for the last five years."

"Since you took over her finances," I added.

"Right," Rena continued. "And there are a large number of extremely unusual withdrawals. Big ones. Withdrawals that seriously sapped Sherry's savings."

"She should be loaded," I chimed in. "She maintained a thrifty lifestyle. She should have tons of money in her account."

I handed Carla a copy of the bank statements, the unusual check withdrawals highlighted in yellow.

Carla glanced at the papers, and shrugged.

"Maybe she invested it," Carla said.

"Maybe," Sean said. "But she hasn't claimed any capital gains income. Ever."

"So she didn't tell me about her income. That's her fault, but not mine."

The look on Sean's face was killing me. He was clearly torn between what he wanted to believe and what he was starting to realize.

"Come on, Carla, you were the one writing the checks. Sherry didn't have her own checkbook, so she would have had to come to you for the money. You mean to tell me you never followed up with Sherry about those huge sums of money when you did her taxes?"

"She was a grown-up. It wasn't my job to follow up."

"Carla. You would have followed up."

"Well, I don't know," she snapped, all pretense of civility gone. "For all I know, she gave her money away to those filthy hippies and druggies she was always hanging around with. Nick Haas. You." She indicated Rena with a narrow-eyed glare.

"Maybe," I said, "but that's not what I think happened at all."

"Oh, really. Please, do tell me what you—a tailor for dogs—think about my cousin's finances."

"Carla," Sean warned. "There's no call for that."

"Really? These two have somehow robbed you of your senses, Sean. They've convinced you to come in here and accuse me of something."

"No one has made an accusation," Sean responded, the "yet" suspended, unspoken, in the tense air of the office.

"So," Carla said, "what are you *not* accusing me of?"

"Look," I said. "Sean's been standing up for you. He's here because he's certain you didn't do anything wrong. I'm the one who's not so sure. I don't think the withdrawals were for Sherry at all, because she'd taken the initiative to get copies of her bank statements and made little question marks all over them. Sherry had no idea what those withdrawals were about."

"I think you're giving Sherry too much credit. Just because she doesn't remember the withdrawals doesn't mean she didn't make them. She couldn't manage her own life. Half the time, she didn't remember what day of the week it was."

"That's not fair," Rena said, her tiny chin lifted in defiance. "Sherry was a little scattered, a little off the beaten path, but even Sherry would have remembered giving a hundred grand to someone."

"I'm telling you," Carla ground out, "I have no idea what Sherry did with that money or why it even matters."

I exchanged a look with Sean. He swallowed hard. I recognized his expression: mingled anger, confusion, and hurt. The expression he'd worn all those years ago when he'd tried to save me from my own foolish self. After a moment, he sighed and nodded, then turned his head away as though he couldn't bear to watch.

"Carla, Sherry didn't do anything with that money. We have these." I held out three documents: Sherry's grocery-slash-love note, the last page of one of the tax returns, and the cancelled check Lois had given me. A check—made out to cash—for $100,000 dollars, drawn on Sherry Harper's account. I laid them on Carla's desk, lined up so that all of the signatures were visible.

Carla leaned forward, and the color drained from her face.

The signatures on the tax form and Nick's note were childish scrawls, barely legible. But the "S" and the "H" on the larger check were completely clear.

"Sherry didn't even sign this check." I said.

"I handled her finances," Carla answered, a tremor in her voice. "Sometimes, she'd disappear for weeks on some crazy protest trip or yoga retreat. Sometimes I had to sign the checks."

She glanced around at the three of us, our matching grim expressions letting her know that we weren't buying the load she was trying to sell.

Carla looked stricken, but then her full lips tightened into a stingy line.

"Sherry was a fool. Teal and Tarleton took their payouts from the trust and managed their own business. But not Sherry. She insisted she didn't believe in banks and checks and such."

"Nick said she was responsible with her money," I said. "Paid her rent up front every three months."

"No, *I* paid her rent every three months. *Me.* And her utilities, and her cleaning service. Where did she think her rent was coming from? Magical fairies? It came from the bank, paid by a check, just signed by me instead of her. And I gave her cash every month so she could eat." She laughed. "Enough cash for her to buy the poster board for all her protest signs. No, Sherry wasn't responsible with her money; she just didn't care about it. I had to handle all of her affairs or she would have been out on the street."

"So you helped yourself to a little piece of her pie?" Sean said.

"Why not? My mother gave her entire youth to this family, marrying my dad when she was only seventeen. They always treated her like the hired help, just because she didn't have the great good fortune to be born rich. And then after years of suffering, married to my stone-hearted father, he dies and she discovers that all the money is wrapped up in the trust. There's nothing for her. She's middle-aged and broke. She deserved to have something of her own. Deserved it more than Sherry deserved to have someone else paying all her bills. So what if I took some of Sherry's mad money—money she didn't even want—and invested it in my mother's business?"

"'So what'?" Sean said, his voice tight with some emotion . . . frustration, anger, betrayal. "'So what'? It's illegal. You're an officer of the court and the trustee of the estate. You had a fiduciary duty to Sherry. You weren't supposed to help yourself to her money."

"But that's just it. Why was it Sherry's money? What did she ever do to earn it? Nothing. Heck, she called it blood money." She tipped her chin down and went on in a mock serious tone. "'Money earned on the back of the working man. Torn from the earth itself.' What a load of malarkey. If she thought the money was dirty, she shouldn't have taken it. She had no principles at all. At least I wasn't squandering the money on woo-woo crystals and fake psychics and harebrained causes. If she was so concerned with the working man, she would have given my mother the money herself."

"You're right," Rena said. "Sherry could be a raging hypocrite. But did you even give her the chance? I mean, did you ever go to her and say 'Sherry, my mom's business is failing. Could you pitch in some cash?'"

Carla sighed. "No. I didn't. Because if I had asked, Sherry would have said no. You know how contrary she was. If I suggested she buy a condo, she insisted she should rent. If I suggested she buy a car, she'd insist her bicycle was just fine . . . even if it meant riding it through four-foot drifts of snow. If I'd suggested she invest in the Grateful Grape, she would have had some reason why she shouldn't: because we didn't pay the dishwashers enough, or because we didn't use locally sourced wines, or because our cheese plates weren't rennet-free."

She had a point. Sherry did have a marvelous knack for finding something wrong with everything. But this time she'd been in the right and trying to do something genuinely good. She'd been trying to save Soaring Eagles from being turned into a bunch of condos.

"What I don't understand is why you didn't just give your mother your own money," Sean said. "You got the same disbursement as Sherry. Why risk everything to take Sherry's money?"

"I don't start drawing on the trust until I'm thirty. Next month. Right now, it takes every dime I have to pay my own bills. When my dad was alive, he was the recipient of the trust, and he didn't exactly share. I have my entire private college tuition and my entire private law school tuition to pay back. Hundreds of thousands of dollars in loans, some of them held by private banks. And then I went to work for a white-shoe law firm in Chicago, and I was expected to live up to that image:

the thousand-dollar suits, the fine jewelry, the swank apartment. I put all those expenses on credit cards, thinking I'd be making big-law-firm paychecks for years to come.

"But instead, I got called back to this backwater to take care of family business. I can pay my debts, but just barely. Why do you think I'm still living with my mom? I can't afford to rent a place of my own. I certainly can't afford to supplement my mother's income."

"So you stole money from Sherry," Sean said, his voice filled with fury. "I can't *believe* you would steal."

Carla's affect changed, softened, and her eyes pooled with tears. "Sean, I didn't steal. I borrowed. I would have paid her back eventually. I thought she'd never know. But my mom just kept needing more and more, and the amount I owed her just kept getting bigger and bigger."

I leaned in to speak gently to Carla. "When Sherry decided she was going to buy the Soaring Eagles camp, she came to you for the money," I prompted.

"Yes. And I just didn't have the cash to give her. Even if the land went for back taxes alone, it would cost a small fortune. If I'd written a check—on her account or mine—it would have bounced."

"What did you tell her?" I asked.

"That there wasn't enough money in the account."

"How did she respond?"

"She didn't believe me. She thought I was holding on to the money because I didn't approve of her plan to buy the Anderson property and turn it into a wildlife preserve."

"That's why she sent you the text," Rena said.

"And that's why she ended up in a screaming match with the bank manager," I added.

"Yes. It was all going to come out."

Sean pinned her with an icy stare. I did not envy her being on the other end of that look.

"Did you kill her?"

"What?"

"I said, did you kill her? Did you kill Sherry to cover up your crime?"

"Lord, no. You have to believe me."

"Why should I believe a word that comes out of your mouth?"

"Because it's the truth!"

Rena jumped in. "We'll go to the police with this. They'll audit your accounts, prove that you embezzled the money. And they'll prove that you killed Sherry."

"They won't because I didn't." She didn't spare so much as a glance for either me or Rena. All her attention was fixed squarely on Sean, eyes filled with pain, as though she could keep hold of him as long as she didn't look away. "Sean, you have to believe me. I know I did a stupid thing."

"A wrong thing," he said.

"A stupid, wrong thing," she amended. "I will have to learn to live with what you must think of me, but I cannot live with you thinking I would kill my cousin to cover up my mistake."

"Dammit," Sean said. "It wasn't a mistake. It was five years of continued criminal behavior. Of course you would kill to cover it up."

"Sean, you know me better than that!"

"Apparently I don't. I never guessed you could abuse your position like this."

"You have to believe me: I didn't kill Sherry."

"Why? Why should I believe you? Do you have an alibi? Something that will exonerate you? Because right now it looks pretty bad."

"I . . ." She trailed off, and I could see the indecision in her eyes. Was she going to manufacture an alibi? Offer some reason why she couldn't possibly have been the killer? Finally, her inner struggle ended with a sigh.

"I was home. Right where you left me."

"Home alone, I suppose," Sean said, the words falling like gravel from his lips.

Carla glanced off to the side and caught a tiny breath. Sean's tone must have hurt.

"No. I wasn't alone. My mom was with me." Sean opened his mouth to cut in, but Carla held up a restraining hand. "I know. I'm a lawyer, too. As alibis go, 'home with my mom' hardly even counts. But it's the truth, and you'll just have to trust me."

"I don't," Sean said.

I thought I should break in, suggest that we call the cops sooner rather than later. But before I opened my mouth, I glanced at Sean, who sat stoic and still in the leather side chair, his usually expressive face devoid of emotion.

"Rena, Izzy, could you give us a few minutes? Carla and I need to have a talk."

CHAPTER
Twenty-eight

On the one hand, I knew that Sean and his love life were really none of my business. I'd given up my right to pry about fifteen years earlier, and even though we'd been spending time together over the last couple of weeks, I didn't think we'd gone back to being confidants. On the other hand, I'd seen that look of betrayal on Sean's face, and I knew that feeling only too well.

I sent Rena back to Trendy Tails to help Dolly and Ingrid mind the store. I trusted Ingrid to rein in the worst of Aunt Dolly's reckless enthusiasm, but I expected business to pick up that afternoon as people stopped by to get last-minute costumes and accessories before the Halloween Howl.

I, on the other hand, decided to wait for Sean outside Carla's office. I only went as far as the hallway before I slid down the wall to sit and wait. As I did, I went through what we'd gleaned from our conversation with Carla. We'd learned she was a thief, that she'd stolen money from Sherry in order to bankroll her mother's failing business and her own overextended financial situation. We'd learned she had a *motive* for killing Sherry, and not much of an alibi. But that was it. We still had nothing connecting Carla to the water hemlock, nothing placing her in the alley that night. When it came right down to it, we'd ruined Sean and Carla's relationship, but we hadn't exactly gotten Rena off the hook.

And once again, I had this sense that something wasn't quite adding up. It was like having a splinter in my finger: I could feel it, it was definitely there, but no matter how hard I looked I couldn't see it.

Sean nearly tripped on me when he emerged from Carla's office.

"What the heck are you doing here?" he snapped.

"Waiting for you."

"This is not the best time, Izzy."

"It's exactly the right time, Sean. I've been where you are right now. You shouldn't be alone."

He laughed dryly. "Well, fine. I'm going back to my place for a hot shower and a stiff drink. You want to tag along, I don't have the strength to fight you."

I clambered up from the floor and scrambled to catch up to him as he shoved open the door to the building and made his way to his car. It wasn't a typical lawyerly car. In fact, the car reminded me of teenage Sean: a vintage Dodge Charger. The passenger-side door squealed in protest as I pried it open and slammed it shut, right as Sean started pulling away from the curb.

We rode to his apartment in silence, me watching

Sean, Sean staring hard at the street before him. When he came to a stop, we were outside a two-story Victorian with wraparound porches on both levels. I suddenly realized I'd had no idea where Sean lived until that very moment.

He led the way to the front door.

"Watch the step," he muttered, pointing at a spot where the concrete of the third step had started to crumble.

When he opened the door, Blackstone trotted out to see him, ears flopping and tail wagging. Sean dropped to a knee and grabbed the dog's face in his hands, resting his own forehead on the top of Blackstone's noggin.

He stood up again, whisked off his coat to hang on the hooks by the door, and held out a hand for mine.

"Make yourself at home."

He disappeared down a hallway, and a few minutes later I heard the groaning of the old house's pipes coming to life.

I wandered into his living room. I felt like a spy, like a peeping Tom, getting this glimpse into his life all on my own. With Blackstone waddling at my heels, I made a circuit of the room. The walls were a creamy white, hung with black-and-white prints of Tucker ancestors and Southern landscapes—endless-looking bayous, trees draped with Spanish moss, a piece of wrought-iron railing that might have been plucked from the French Quarter. Despite their old, almost haunted subjects, the pictures were all matted in stark white and framed with modern black metal.

A magnificent tiled fireplace dominated the room, built-in bookshelves on either side. I ran one finger over the books as I passed, catching the occasional author or title: James Ellroy, Tom Clancy, a handful of biographies of Supreme Court justices.

Despite the austerity of the walls, the furniture was welcoming and well-loved. A large green sectional sofa, scattered with rust-colored pillows and tawny woolen throws, curled around a coffee table topped with a horizontal slice of some massive oak. By the large front window, two more chairs and their ottomans stood sentry. Bronze and glass lamps were scattered around the room, so you could easily cuddle up with a book in any nook or cranny.

I finally settled in a corner of the sectional. Blackstone sat at my feet, his big head resting against my leg. I gently rubbed the fold behind his ear. As simply as that, Blackstone and I became fast friends.

When Sean returned, he'd changed into a pair of jeans and a fisherman's sweater. His still-damp hair formed clean, precise curls that fell in his face. I don't know how he resisted the urge to tuck those tendrils behind his ears.

"Would you like a drink?" he asked, making his way to a small credenza in the dining room onto which the living room opened.

"Actually, yes."

"Scotch okay?" He poured a couple of fingers of deep amber-brown liquor into a tumbler.

"Sure." I'd never had Scotch, but I'd heard it was good.

He poured another glass and brought it to me before flopping down on the far end of the sectional.

I sniffed the drink and took a tentative sip. I gasped

and nearly choked. It was like drinking moldering tree bark, except that it also burned like fire.

I looked up to find Sean smiling that crooked smile at me. He raised his glass. "Skoal."

I breathed out a small laugh, feeling some of the tension in the room drain away.

"Sean, I'm really sorry about Carla," I began.

He held up a hand. "Stop. I know your intentions are good, Izzy, but I don't want to process my feelings or hug it out or anything. Let me just live with this for a bit. Then you can make those sad eyes at me and tell me it'll all be okay."

"Fair enough."

"So," he continued, "as completely crappy as this day has been, I don't think we've actually succeeded in getting Rena off the hook."

"I had that same realization while I was waiting outside Carla's office. What are we going to do?"

"We're going to keep on doing what we've been doing. You're going to run your business, I'm going to represent some clients, and we'll spend our spare time trying to find some actual evidence of what went down in the alley that night.

"Now, speaking of your business, don't you have a costume party to plan?"

I peeked down at my watch. "Oh dear, yes. We're basically set, but there are always a few last minute details to take care of. I should probably go." I paused. "Will I see you there tonight?"

"I didn't get Blackstone a costume," he hedged.

"I run a pet boutique, Sean. I think I can come up with a costume. In fact, I have just the thing in mind."

He shrugged.

"Come on. I know you don't want to talk about what happened with Carla, but you can't wallow in it either. Trust me, wallowing does *not* help. You should come, mingle, be sociable."

He laughed softly. "Between the two of us, we could write a book about bad breakups." He sighed. "But you're absolutely right. You bring Blackstone a costume, and I'll be there."

Merryville's Halloween Howl kicked off at dusk, just as the stars began winking coyly in the indigo sky. Dakota Park hummed with excitement as jack-o-lanterns flared to life and the shrieks of sugar-amped children pealed into the night.

As people meandered through the maze of brick-lined pathways, they could fill up on pasties from the Thistle and Ivy, imbibe mulled wine and cider from the Grateful Grape, enjoy tiny tarts and petit fours from Taffy's tea shop, and collect candy from dozens of local businesses. Even grumpy Richard Greene had donned his own vintage dress blues and showed up with my aunt Dolly at his side, dressed in a fifties swing dress, saddle shoes, and her hair pulled up in huge barrel curls. They strolled hand in hand, each carrying a bucket of old-fashioned penny candy for the kids: Mary Janes, fireballs, caramel creams, butterscotches, and Neapolitan Coconut Squares.

As hosts of the pet contest, Pris, Rena, and I didn't have much time to mingle. We were busy setting up the seats for people to watch the parade of costumed pets, laying out the goody bags for our entrants, and checking the dozens of tiny details that kept any large event afloat.

Both Pris and I had decided to leave our cats at home, for fear that we wouldn't be able to keep our eyes on them. Packer, though, was doing his best to help us. Wearing a black widow's peak cap and a black-and-red satin cape, my dorky little dog made a dashing Dracula. Rena had brought Val, of course, but the ferret—dressed in the brilliant silks of a court jester—was hiding in the inner pocket of Rena's huge overcoat. Packer, on the other hand, was right under our feet.

I was pleased to catch a glimpse of Sean. While I'm sure he wasn't in a particularly festive mood, he'd made the effort. He had brought Blackstone with him, too, and the dog wore the tiny deerstalker cap I'd had Rena deliver from Trendy Tails.

"Virginia, we'll get the contest started in about twenty minutes," Pris said.

We'd left Carla at her office that afternoon, the threat of criminal charges hanging over her head, but apparently she had yet to break the news of her imminent downfall to her mother. I couldn't imagine Virginia showing up if she knew that we'd confronted her child that very day.

"Can I get you anything before we start?" I asked carefully, on the off chance Virginia was actually seething inside and just a master of hiding her emotions.

"No, dear," she said with a smile, and I exhaled hard in relief. She chuckled. "You look as tense as I feel," she chided.

Indeed, Virginia did look tense. Not angry or distraught, just wound a little tighter than usual. It definitely wasn't the reaction of someone who'd gotten news that her daughter would lose her livelihood, be utterly disgraced, and might possibly go to jail. Still, something was off kilter with her.

Before I could give it much more thought, my sister Lucy and her wacky border collie bounded over to the band shell. Wiley wore a pointed and pom-pommed clown hat and a bright yellow ruff around his neck, while Lucy had managed to pull together some sort of sexy circus ringleader outfit, complete with top hat, gold braid, and—holy cats—a whip.

"What's up, buttercup?" she said. Lucy loved a good party, and Lucy loved candy. Put the two together, and she was in heaven. I had no idea how many handfuls of candy corn she'd downed to produce her current sugar high. "I'm still miffed Wiley can't enter the contest, by the way."

"It wouldn't look right. Especially if you won." Some of the animals wandering the park with their owners wore adorable costumes: a cat dressed as a doctor in tiny surgical scrubs; a pug dressed like a pumpkin with a green stem hat, leaves curling on glittering tendrils (that outfit was my own handiwork); even a rabbit dressed up like a French parlor maid. But Wiley's clown suit ranked right up there on the cuteness scale.

"Why don't you take Wiley and Packer for a quick run around the park, let them burn off a little energy?" I thought the run might settle Lucy down, too.

"Sure thing." Lucy took Packer's leash from my hand and clicked her tongue against her teeth to try to get the dogs moving.

Wiley took the hint and began bounding, straining

at the leash, raring to go. But my sweet boy was distracted by something rustling in the dark beneath a molting shrub. He waddled his way over and began snuffling around in the fallen leaves.

"Careful," Virginia said. "Don't let that dog play in those leaves."

Lucy, never one to simply do as she was bade, narrowed her eyes at Virginia. "Why not? He's not hurting anything."

Virginia sighed. "I'm not worried about the plant, I'm worried about him. That's a deciduous azalea. The leaves are toxic to dogs."

Lucy tugged Packer's leash, and scuffed her toe sheepishly. "I didn't know."

"Me either," I said. "That's good information to have. Packer and I take walks in this park all the time."

Virginia shrugged one shoulder. "We had a lady from the Extension office come out to speak to the garden club. She was advising us about pet-friendly landscaping."

"Well, if she comes back, let me know. Sounds like it was a useful lecture."

"Listen," she said, "do I have time for a smoke before we get started?"

I checked my watch. "Sure. Plenty of time."

Virginia stepped away from the band shell, retreating into a cluster of small oak trees, so she could smoke without bothering the rest of us.

I watched the tip of Virginia's cigarette, its glow pulsing in the twilight dark like a firefly. It was almost hypnotic, and as I watched it—unable to tear my eyes away—I began letting thoughts drift through my head.

What if Carla didn't kill Sherry?

Carla had motive to kill Sherry, and she was certainly smart enough to pull off a poisoning. Only two possible killers had motive to take Sherry's phone from the scene of the crime: Hal and Carla. We knew Hal was innocent because he wasn't at Sherry's funeral when Valrhona found the phone. All that pointed to Carla's guilt. And I didn't find her alibi particularly convincing.

But why *then*? Why in that alleyway in the middle of the night? How did Carla even know that Sherry was back there? By all accounts, Carla had had dinner with Virginia and Sean at La Ming, had a glass of wine at the Grateful Grape, and then gone home . . . with Sean watching her enter the house.

Virginia took another drag on her cigarette, and the scattered thoughts coalesced in my mind. The splinter of a thought that had been worrying me all day finally surfaced.

The night we'd taken Xander to the Grateful Grape, Diane Jenkins had mentioned that Carla and Virginia didn't leave together the night of Sherry's death. Virginia had stuck around after Sean had taken Carla home so she could share a toast with her staff after the bar closed.

Carla's alibi was definitely a lie. But she wasn't lying to protect herself. She was lying to protect Virginia.

Virginia, who took regular smoke breaks in the alleyway and might have seen Sherry out there the night of the party. Virginia, who had led Sherry herself on nature walks through the marshy shoreline of Badger Lake, where water hemlock grew wild. Virginia, whose only child was threatened by Sherry Harper's threats to go public about the misappropriation of funds. After all, we knew about the text Sherry had sent to Carla, but how many phone calls had she made . . . calls perhaps not just to Carla's cell phone, but also to the home phone Carla and Virginia shared? Or perhaps Carla had confided in her mother once Sherry's demands had become too insistent.

I waved Sean over, and filled him in on my thought process.

"I suppose it makes sense," Sean said. "But I can't imagine Virginia killing anyone."

I tipped my head to the side. "Today you were willing to believe Carla capable of murder. Surely you realize everyone has a breaking point. Even Virginia."

"Actually," Sean said, "I could have believed anyone in this town except for Virginia. I've never met a gentler, more nurturing soul."

"Well, there's only one way to find out if she's a killer."

Sean raised a questioning eyebrow.

"We ask her."

Before we talked to Virginia, I wanted to have a quick tête-à-tête with Pris.

"My, don't you look intense," Pris said. "Is there some scandal afoot? You know how I love a good scandal."

"I actually just have a question and a favor to ask of you."

"Go on. I'm intrigued."

"Virginia said someone from the Extension office

gave a talk to the gardening club about pet-friendly landscaping."

"Ugh. Yes. What a snooze."

"Do you remember the woman talking about hemlock?"

"Hmmm. Yes, actually. It caught my attention because I'd always thought it was Queen Anne's lace."

I shared a quick glance with Sean. I could see the resignation in his eyes.

I laid a hand on Pris's arm. "Thanks. And now, the favor."

Sean and I made our way to Virginia's side, just as she snubbed out her cigarette.

"Hi, Virginia," Sean said. "Could we have a word with you?"

Her lips twisted in a small smile, her expression caught somewhere between sadness and regret.

"Of course," she said.

Sean cleared his throat.

"I guess you heard about Hal Olson buying the Soaring Eagles camp at auction yesterday."

"Yes. Small town. Word travels fast."

"How do you feel about that?" Sean asked gently.

"Sad," she said. She lifted the tail end of her crimson scarf and wrapped it round her hand. "I hate to see the land developed. The best memories of my marriage and family are all out at that house, many of them the hours I spent with Sherry and Carla."

"So you don't support the development of the lake?"

"Of course I don't support the development at the lake. If Hal Olson does what he says he's going to do, builds condos and high-end shopping centers along the waterfront, then the tranquility of the Harper lake house is gone forever."

"Did you know Sherry was thinking about buying the campground herself?"

Virginia stared off into the distance as she answered. "Yes, she'd mentioned it. But she couldn't have stopped the development. Sherry has no head for business. Eventually she would have ended up right where the Andersons did, and Hal would have bought the place anyway. There's something to that old saying: If you can't beat 'em, join 'em."

"But that's the thing. Sherry wasn't ready to join because she didn't think she'd been beat. She thought she could finally use her share of the trust to buy the Soaring Eagles camp and stop the development in its tracks," I said. "She'd been reading up on wetlands conservation, too, ready to use the law to stop the development if she had to.

"But all of that—trying to purchase the camp out from under Hal Olson, waging a court battle to stop the development—all of that cost money. And the money—Sherry's money—is all but gone."

"Virginia," Sean said, "we know about Carla. We know she stole money from Sherry's accounts and funneled it into your business."

She winced as though she'd been struck. But she did not look surprised.

"You knew what she had done," I said, my words a statement, not a question.

"Not at first," Virginia said. "Not until it was too late."

"Too late?"

"I never should have taken a dime from my child, but I wanted the business so badly. And she offered the money with a smile, every time I so much as hinted at needing it. My beautiful, talented daughter kept writing checks for my new business. New furnace, no problem. New roof, no problem. A fully stocked wine cellar, no problem. A perfect, temperature-controlled vault for the wine, sure thing. I was so used to the trust being this bottomless well of money like it was when I was still married to Carla's father, but gradually I began to worry that Carla was draining her share too quickly. And then, one day, my young Jeff made a comment about how Carla would be turning thirty soon, and he'd be the only one without access to the trust. That's when I realized that *none* of the money she'd been giving me was hers. She was in deep.

"The only way we were going to be able to pay Sherry back was to get the Grateful Grape turning a profit. But so far, we haven't had the traffic we need. Deer season didn't bring in the wine bar crowd. Maybe if we'd been able to hold on for the holidays, when the real tourists come back. . . ."

"But Sherry created a ticking clock."

Virginia laughed softly. "More like a ticking time bomb. I don't even know how she first learned about the campground going to auction. Must have been through one of her conservation groups. But once she got it in her head to stop that development, nothing would stand in her way. At first, she just asked Carla for money. But when Carla had to start saying no, Sherry got belligerent, demanding. Finally, she asked to see her taxes. I have no idea how she ever thought to ask."

Probably another pearl of business wisdom she picked up from her fling with Hal Olson.

"Carla didn't think there was any harm in giving her the forms, because, by themselves, they didn't mean anything. But Sherry somehow figured out that she was missing a whole lot of money. And that's when the threats started."

"Threats?"

"To go to the police, to go to the papers. Heck, Sherry threatened to go to the governor . . . as if he would care."

Virginia shrugged. "She was going to hurt Carla, and all Carla had done was try to help me."

"What Carla did was wrong," Sean said.

She lifted a hand to cup his cheek. "Oh, Sean. Carla always said you had an overdeveloped sense of morality. Black and white, right and wrong. What Carla did was certainly illegal, but it came from a good place. So was it really wrong?"

While I didn't think Carla should be let off the hook, I had to admit that I'd done a few shady things to help my friend. Nothing truly illegal, but arguably unethical. I'd taken advantage of Nick Haas's perpetual inebriation, I'd exposed Hal's affair to Pris, and Sean and I had *both* held on to Sherry's phone when we found it. I could sort of see Virginia's point.

"Is that when you decided to kill her? When she started making the threats?"

Virginia tapped another cigarette from her pack and lit it. "This is where I'm supposed to deny everything, right?"

"You could. But it's just us here, so why bother?"

Virginia heaved a sigh. I remembered how sad she'd seemed when I visited her at the Grateful Grape. She'd been close to Sherry and her actions weighed heavily on her soul.

"I suppose you're right. I knew Sherry would never give up. I'd always admired her persistence, you know, but once she turned on Carla . . . I'd always known about water hemlock and knew it grew wild down by Badger Lake, but the lady who spoke to the garden club reminded me. I figured Sherry ate so much of that nasty dried ginseng root, I could find a way to slip the hemlock to her. I'd been carrying around a bag of the poison for a week, trying to find the right time, trying to find my nerve. And then, the night of my birthday, I was waiting for the staff to cash out the last of our customers when I went out to have a smoke. And there she was. Fighting with that awful boyfriend of hers. He left, and she was alone, and it was like a signal from the universe."

She shook her head, and I could see there were tears in her eyes.

"She smiled when she saw me. She took the bag of poison from me and said 'thank you.' I couldn't believe how easy it was. I could walk right back into the Grateful Grape and no one would ever be the wiser."

"Except you messed up," I said. "You took her phone because of that one suspicious text to Carla, and you tried to take the ginseng bag back from Sherry after she'd eaten the poison and stuffed the bag in Gandhi's sling."

"Ridiculous, carrying around that rodent in a harness. Blasted thing bit me." She held up her finger, still wrapped in its bandage. Apparently she'd lied about the uncorking accident.

"But I don't see how that was messing up. Even if my print is on that scrap of packaging, it won't prove that I'm the one who tampered with it, or even the one who gave Sherry the bag. And the phone . . . I don't have the phone anymore, and there's no way to prove that I ever did have it."

"No way except this." I held out my fist and un-curled my fingers to reveal Pris's tiny digital recorder. "I'm afraid you just confessed on tape."

CHAPTER
Twenty-nine

Sean swung by Trendy Tails the following evening, just as we were locking up. Rena was wiping down the big red table where she'd spent the day cutting fish-shaped kitty treats, trying to restock after the huge glut of treats we'd given away at the Howl.

In a rare show of camaraderie (undoubtedly brought on by the icy wind slipping over our window sills and finding cracks in the hardwood floors), Jinx and Packer were curled up together in Packer's fleece bed. Technically speaking, Packer was being held captive by the gigantic cat that had draped herself over his head. I occasionally saw his foot twitch, but there was no way he'd risk getting up and disturbing the sharp-clawed behemoth above him.

Outside, snow fell in small, icy crystals. All day the pace of the downfall had been picking up, as had the wind, and the forecast called for blizzard conditions before midnight. I silently said a prayer that Ingrid's plane had taken off before the weather hit and that she was happily winging her way toward her Harvey, her last Minnesota winter fading in the distance.

"It's a bad day for the Harper family," Sean said, shaking snow from his scarf. "Mother and daughter were both arraigned today, one for murder, the other for fraud, theft, and a host of other more minor charges."

Rena, who had been positively ebullient all day, whooped with joy, then quickly sobered. "Oh, Sean, I'm sorry. I shouldn't be celebrating. This must be hard for you."

"It's okay," he said. "Given the cloud you've been living under, you're entitled to a little celebration."

She threw her arms around him, dragging him down to give him a big smacking kiss on the cheek. "Tomorrow, I take you out for dinner at La Ming to properly thank you. Uh, uh, uh," she said as he opened his mouth to protest, "it's the very least I can do.

"For now, though, I need to get home before I'm socked in for the night. Last I checked, Dad had eaten all the canned ravioli, so I need to swing by the store on the way home, or we'll turn into the Donner party before the week's out."

She hugged me tight. "I'll see you tomorrow, assuming the roads are clear."

And with that, she was gone, leaving me alone with Sean.

"So," I said.

"So," he replied.

Tension crackled in the air between us.

"Ready to hug it out?" I asked, hoping to break the tension.

He said nothing.

"Too soon?"

"Definitely too soon."

I lowered my chin and studied him through my lashes. The ghost of that boy who'd proclaimed his love outside my bedroom window was still there, just beneath the surface of the handsome man who stood before me. Even his stance was the same: legs braced apart, hands clenched at his sides, body rocked forward on the balls of his feet, as though he were preparing for a fight.

My heart yearned to take his hand, run off to my parents' basement, and play a game of gin rummy while laughing over the stupid little details of our day. My heart yearned to unwind all the years I'd lost tailing Casey around. My heart yearned to be eighteen again and say yes on a stormy summer night.

"It's been great catching up with you these last couple of weeks," I said, and then mentally kicked myself for the banality of it. I'd found a body in my alley, he'd lost his girlfriend, and together we'd caught a murderer. We hadn't just been "catching up."

Thankfully, he took pity on me. "Yeah," he agreed, a note of surprise in his voice. "It actually has been good seeing you."

"You know," I said with forced cheer, "Rena and I were planning to have a movie night at my place next Saturday. Screwball comedies, pizza, just hanging out." I cleared my throat, trying to keep my tone light. "You should join us."

"Izzy." He sighed. "I can't just suddenly be your friend again."

"I didn't know we ever stopped," I said.

He leveled a "get real" look at me.

"Look, it was just one night, one mistake."

"That's just it. I didn't say anything until that night outside your bedroom window. But for me, we'd stopped being friends long before that."

"Well, thanks for that."

"That's not what I mean." He paused to run his fingers through his disheveled hair. "Look, that night had been a long time coming for me. I'd hit a point where I couldn't be *just* your friend a long time before that night."

"It's been fifteen years. You've moved on," I argued.

"Sure, I've moved on with my life, but that doesn't undo what happened. I told you I loved you, Izzy. I was a teenage boy, and I told you I loved you. Do you have any idea how hard that was? And you tried to tell me I was *wrong* about my feelings . . . and then you tried to go on like nothing ever happened."

"I was young and stupid. Dizzy Izzy. Lord, if you had any idea how many stupid things I've done, before and after that night. But that was fifteen years ago," I repeated, emphasizing each syllable, imbuing it with all the significance of a life spent missing that boy and the man he had become.

"Not to me. To me, it feels like just yesterday. I can't just slip back into your life like a puzzle piece."

"So, what, we go our separate ways and never speak again?"

"Of course not. I can't slip back into my old place in your life, but I can create a new one. I don't know what that will look like, but I'm willing to find out if you are."

"How do we start?" I asked.

"How about this: Hi, my name is Sean Tucker."

"Nice to meet you, Sean. I'm Izzy."

About the Author

Annie Knox doesn't commit—or solve—murders in her real life, but her passion for animals is one hundred percent true. She's also a devotee of eighties music, Asian horror films, and reality TV. While Annie is a native Buckeye and has called a half dozen states home, she and her husband now live a stone's throw from the courthouse square in a north Texas town in their very own crumbling historic house.

RECIPES

Human Chow

Rena's sweet cereal mix is a surefire winner for choco-holics of every age!

   1 14.5 oz. box chocolate crisp rice squares cereal
   1½ c. candy-coated peanut butter drops
   1½ c. powdered sugar
   ¼ c. cocoa powder
   1 c. chocolate chips
   ¼ c. peanut butter
   ¼ c. butter
   1 tsp. vanilla

In a large mixing bowl, combine the cereal and candy. In a smaller bowl, combine the powdered sugar and cocoa powder.

In the top of a double boiler (or a bowl set over a pot of simmering water), combine the chocolate chips, peanut butter, butter, and vanilla. Allow the ingredients to melt together, stirring often. Remove from heat and pour the chocolate mixture over the cereal mixture. Stir to coat evenly. Place half of mixture in a 2-gallon sealable bag, add half the powdered sugar and cocoa mixture, and shake until well-coated. Repeat with the second half of the cereal and powder.

Spread coated cereal on a large cookie sheet covered with parchment paper, waxed paper, or foil. Allow the chocolate/peanut butter coating to cool until set. Break up any pieces that have stuck together and serve!

Rena's Spinach Lasagna

This easy spinach lasagna makes a great midweek treat for the family, but it's also decadent enough for a weekend dinner party. Serve with a crisp green salad and a side of golden garlic bread for a hearty yet simple meal that will satisfy year-round.

2 15 oz. containers skim, low fat, or fat free ricotta
1 egg
½ tsp. fresh ground black pepper
1 tsp. salt
¼ c. grated parmesan
12 oz. frozen chopped spinach, thawed
1 package oven-ready (no boil) lasagna noodles (for a
    9" x 13" pan)
3 c. shredded mozzarella

Sauce:

1 Tbs. olive oil
2 tsp. crushed garlic
2 28 oz. cans tomato puree (use a good brand)
1 tsp. dried oregano
1 tsp. salt
1 tsp. sugar
2 tsp. dried or ¼ c. fresh basil
1 Tbs. balsamic vinegar

Preheat oven to 375°.

To make the sauce, heat olive oil in a medium saucepan over medium heat. Add garlic and sauté until the garlic is fragrant. Add remaining ingredients. Bring to a low boil, then reduce heat to low and allow to simmer gently, covered, until the filling is prepared.

For the filling, press as much water out of the spinach as possible. Combine the ricotta, egg, black pepper, salt, parmesan, and spinach in a large bowl.

Spread ½ cup of the sauce in the bottom of a 9" x 13" pan. Top with one third of the lasagna noodles, covering the bottom completely. Spread half of the filling on the noodles, then add 1½ cups sauce and 1 cup of shredded mozzarella. Add another third of the lasagna noodles, the second half of the ricotta filling, 1½ cups sauce, and 1 cup of shredded mozzarella. Finally, top with remaining noodles and remaining sauce, making sure none of the edges or corners of the noodles are exposed. Cover with foil and bake for 30–40 minutes, until the noodles are cooked and the sauce is bubbling. (Test the noodles by inserting a sharp knife straight down in several spots; the knife should not encounter any resistance.)

Remove foil, top with remaining cup of mozzarella, and bake another 10 minutes.

Remove from oven and allow to set for 10 minutes before cutting and serving.

Read on for a sneak peek at the next book
in Annie Knox's
Pet Boutique Mystery series,

GROOMED FOR MURDER

Available in print and e-book from
Obsidian in September 2014.

"**W**hat do you think of the meatball?" Ingrid Whit-field handed Harvey Nyquist a tiny paper plate bearing a single bite-size meatball speared with a tooth-pick and resting in a small pool of creamy brown gravy.

Harvey shoved his well-used handkerchief into his pocket and reached up from his seat on my sofa, careful not to shift my dog, Packer, who was snoring loudly in his lap. As he grasped the plate in his liver-spotted hand, I detected a faint tremor, and he grabbed at the toothpick with the sort of lunging movement of a per-son whose fine motor skills were deteriorating.

He chewed the meatball thoughtfully. "Good," he said. Packer snorted softly and raised his head, his doggy dreams distracted by the rich scent of meat.

"Good? Don't you think the nutmeg's a little strong?"

"Maybe."

Ingrid heaved a long-suffering sigh. "Well, do you want them as is, or do you want less nutmeg?"

"Ya, sure." He rubbed the end of the toothpick in the

leftover gravy and sucked it off, his eyes closed and a contented smile gracing his face. Packer whined and licked his chops, Harvey held out the plate for him to clean, and Packer looked up at Harvey like he was the king of dogs. My little four-legged traitor.

" 'Ya, sure'? What kind of answer is that? Pain-in-the-ass old coot," Ingrid muttered, but there was no heat to her complaint, and she gave Harvey's shoulder a flirtatious little shove before she returned to my galley kitchen. No doubt about it, brusque and brash old Ingrid had a soft spot, and its name was Harvey Nyquist.

When the couple had first arrived in Merryville, I couldn't figure out why Ingrid was so smitten with Harvey. They'd been high school sweethearts torn apart by his family's decision to send him to military school, and before Ingrid had flown off to join him in Boca Raton, I'd seen pictures of the lithe, handsome man he had been. Ingrid had rhapsodized about the love notes he had written to her and the numerous times he had serenaded her in front of God and everyone.

But Harvey Nyquist sixty-some years after the serenading stopped? The man didn't say boo, he had some sort of chronic sinus problem that produced earsplitting sneezes on a regular basis, and he looked like someone had stuffed a madras sack with sunburned potatoes.

When I had met Harvey, I decided Ingrid's determination to live happily ever after with him was driven by nothing more than the memory of a love long ago.

But during the week since their arrival, I'd watched

Harvey as he watched Ingrid bustling about my apartment, rearranging my knickknacks, finding hidden deposits of dust to clean away, and cursing about the little details of their upcoming nuptials. He looked at her as though she were his last mooring to this earth, all the light in his face reflected from her vitality. He didn't just love Ingrid. He needed her. And having someone need you is a powerful aphrodisiac.

"Well?" I asked, pointing at the meatball-filled tinfoil takeout box on my counter.

"I guess they'll do," Ingrid groused.

Ollie Forde, who'd made literally hundreds of thousands of Norwegian meatballs for the residents of Merryville over the years, would be delighted to learn that his spherical masterpieces would "do."

"That's good," I said, struggling to hide my frustration. "The wedding is tomorrow, after all, and we should probably finalize the details today."

As if to punctuate my pronouncement, Harvey whooped and sneezed. I heard Packer whimper from the bluster of it all, and Jinx—perched on the passthrough between my kitchen and dining nook—swished her tail in annoyance.

In truth, we should have finalized the details the day Ingrid and Harvey rolled into town, with absolutely no advance notice, and declared they were going to get married in Merryville within the week.

Ingrid had decided at the last minute that she wanted to get married in her hometown, in Merryville, instead of the Cherub Chapel of Bliss on the Las Vegas Strip. More specifically, she and Harvey were getting married in my store, Trendy Tails, the space Ingrid had called home. Trendy Tails occupied the first floor of 801 Maple, a house Ingrid had owned for decades. The second floor had been Ingrid's apartment, and I still lived in the third-floor apartment. Ingrid and Harvey's announcement had turned the entire house on its head.

The wedding plans got off to a rocky start when Ingrid had discovered that the tenant I'd found for her apartment was still in residence, so she and Harvey had to bunk with me. "There goes the nooky," she'd complained.

The plans had only gone downhill from there. Soon she was chafing under the froufrou influence of my mom and aunt Dolly. If Ingrid had had her way, she would have dressed in her best plaid shirt, signed the paperwork, and been married in ten minutes. But Mom and Aunt Dolly had managed to find her an actual wedding dress, had ordered a huge bouquet of lilacs, and had even stitched a deep purple lace-edged pillow to one of Packer's harnesses so he could serve as a canine ring bearer. "It's just me and Harvey," she'd muttered, "not the damn royal wedding."

Yesterday, we'd hit a new snag. Ingrid, who was usually perfectly happy with a bowl of canned soup and some soda crackers, suddenly became hypercritical about all the food options we had (which were scarce, given our short timeline). "Not as good as mine," she griped about every single dish we proffered. For someone who claimed not to want a fussy wedding, she had become quite a demanding bride.

Now she looked at me with narrowed eyes. "You know I love you, Izzy McHale, but I don't appreciate the sarcasm. Ollie Forde makes a good meatball, but you have to admit the man can be a little heavy-handed with the nutmeg. We'll have the wedding tomorrow with or without meatballs, but I'm not paying through the nose for a plate of crapola."

I narrowed my eyes right back. "You know I love you, Ingrid Whitfield, but you've become an irascible old biddy."

Ingrid's frown melted away, and she threw back her head in laughter. " 'Become'? I've been an irascible old biddy since the day my mother birthed me. That's precisely why you love me."

I snickered. "True enough. But you know what they say about too much of a good thing."

"Well, if it wasn't for that interloper on the second floor . . ."

"Hey, no fair. You asked me to rent out the apartment, and when Daniel asked for an extra couple of weeks, I had no idea his stay would interfere with your wedding. You weren't due back for another month. A little notice would have helped," I added pointedly.

Ingrid plucked another meatball from the small tray. "So, what's up with this Daniel Colona guy?" she asked before popping the morsel in her mouth.

"Honestly? I don't really know. He pretty much keeps to himself. He comes down to the shop pretty regularly to buy Rena's treats for his Weimaraner, Daisy May, but he doesn't talk about himself much at all."

"You said he's a writer?"

In the other room, Harvey sneezed again. I waited until he was done trumpeting into his hankie before answering.

"That's what he said when he called about the apartment, but he's never given so much as a hint about what he's writing."

"I can't believe the crew around here hasn't figured out all his deepest secrets by now. You and your friends are pretty nibby."

"Oh, believe me, it's not for lack of trying. We've had some long conversations about Mr. Colona over dinners, drinks, card games—you name it. I think he's a novelist, maybe a J. D. Salinger kind of guy, and he's hiding out while some sort of sex scandal blows over."

"Really? Why do you say that?"

"I don't know. He's got these dark haunted eyes and long black hair. He could play Heathcliff in a remake of *Wuthering Heights* if he grew just a few more inches. He's got to have a troubled past and a broken love story."

"You get all that from his hair? I think you're being overly romantic."

"That's what Rena says." My best friend and business partner had been teasing me mercilessly about having a crush on my tenant, as though I needed another wrinkle in my strange personal life.

A week after Harvey and Ingrid's wedding, Trendy Tails was playing host to a doggy wedding . . . puptials, if you will. The dogs in question were Hetty Tucker's retired greyhound, Romeo, and Louise Collins's pudgy beagle, Pearl. Hetty and Louise had always been close, so they hadn't been difficult to work with. But their sons . . .

Neither Hetty nor Louise could drive, so each depended on her son to get her to our planning sessions.

Sean Tucker and Jack Collins were night and day. Sean was intellectual, reserved, a true romantic. In a past life he might have written lots of poetry about sheep or painted women frolicking through the woods in diaphanous gowns. Jack Collins was a cop. A man's man. In a past life, he was a cop. At our meetings, the two men danced around each other like alley cats with their backs up, hissing and spitting at each other at every opportunity. They were different, sure, but I'm not sure where the animosity came from. I honestly didn't know what to do with either one of them.

"Anyway," I continued, "Rena thinks he's a retired crime boss who's writing a tell-all book. She says that once you get past his polished shoes and perfectly pressed dress shirts, he looks a little rough around the edges, like maybe he's broken a few knees in his time. Meanwhile, Lucy and Xander both think he's an investigative journalist doing an exposé on . . . Well, they don't exactly know what he plans to expose. And of course Sean and Dru, the practical members of our little gang, think we're all crazy and we ought to let the man have his privacy."

"Sean and Dru are probably right." Ingrid leaned forward and called into the living room, "Don't you think so, Harvey?"

"Ya, sure."

Ingrid chuckled. "It's nice to be right all the time," she said.

"I know we shouldn't be such busybodies, but honestly, our speculations are perfectly tame compared to Aunt Dolly's. She's come up with far more harebrained theories than the rest of us. She's completely obsessed with the man."

"Your aunt Dolly is a nut job," Ingrid huffed.

I shrugged. "Yeah, well, she's our nut job. She fancies herself quite the sleuth after the hubbub last Halloween."

Last fall, my friends and I had found ourselves in the middle of a murder investigation, trying to keep Rena from being hauled to the hoosegow. Ever since we'd sussed out the killer, Aunt Dolly had taken to watching and taking notes on true-crime shows. She'd even suggested she might try to get her private investigator's license.

"She's dragging me right behind her, straight to the loony bin," Ingrid complained. "All this stuff with the wedding: favors and veils and nonsense."

I gave Ingrid a sidelong glance. "Come on, I know you're not a girly girl, but you must be enjoying all the attention just a little."

Ingrid grinned at me around a gravy-stained toothpick. "Maybe just a little," she said with a wink.

Lord help me, I thought. Between Ingrid blowing hot and cold, Dolly blowing plain old crazy, and Harvey endlessly blowing his nose, this wedding might be the death of me.

That afternoon, I set to work making favors for the wedding, listening to Rena humming out of tune while she worked on cookies for Ingrid and Harvey's reception. I sucked in a big lungful of vanilla-and-sugar-scented air.

At the tinkling of the bell above our doorway, I looked up to find Aunt Dolly using her rear end to bump open Trendy Tails's door. She managed to maneuver herself into the shop with her arms filled with boxes of white tissue wedding decorations. Thankfully, I'd already ordered decorations for Pearl and Romeo's doggy wedding. We could give the decorations a dress rehearsal, using them to perk up Trendy Tails for Ingrid and Harvey.

"How's the blushing bride today?" Dolly asked, her voice brimming with high spirits and good cheer.

I set the last little packet of Jordan almonds, bundled neatly in a circle of white tulle, and raised a finger to my lips. "She's upstairs," I mouthed.

"Gotcha," Dolly mouthed back.

I stretched my back and answered her in a voice that wouldn't carry up to my apartment on the third floor, where Ingrid Whitfield had gone to sulk. "Take your pick," I said. "Irritable, grumpy, annoyed, occasionally hostile. She's spent a lot of time storming up and down the stairs, muttering that she and Harvey should have just gone to Vegas like they originally planned. At one point she bellowed at Harvey that they should call off all this 'stuff and nonsense' and just keep on living in sin."

Rena sauntered out of the kitchen to join us during my explanation. "We've been having a great time," she deadpanned. "Maybe we should get Ingrid on that show about bridezillas. I bet she'd be their first postmenopausal bride."

Dolly snorted a laugh as she carefully lowered her

load onto the giant red worktable in what used to be the dining room of the gingerbread Victorian house. She shoved aside the tangle of ribbons and fabric swatches that littered the table, the detritus of my early morning efforts to create "cat's pajamas." The unfinished results hung on a wooden cat-shaped form I'd had made special by a carpenter in Bemidji. Eventually I would try the jammies on Jinx, but she was too feisty to serve as a model during development.

"I guess we shouldn't be surprised," Dolly whispered. "Ingrid's always been a pill, and a bride must be an awkward hat for her to wear."

Dolly made a good point. Our octogenarian friend would pick corduroy over cashmere any day of the week.

Still, I thought Ingrid's irritability went deeper than that. She seemed uncharacteristically vulnerable. I had a sneaking suspicion why.

Ingrid had spent most of her adult life running the Merryville Gift Haus in the space now occupied by my store, Trendy Tails. She'd supported me in starting up the business right before she left for Boca, but it must still have been difficult to come back and see no trace of her own well-loved shop left. What's more, the second-floor apartment in which Ingrid had lived for over four decades was now occupied by a stranger, a renter she'd never even met. It's hard to deal with the fact that life in your hometown could continue on without you.

"Well," Rena said, "one way or another it will be over tonight."

"That sounds ominous," Dolly said with a shiver.

Rena laughed. "You haven't seen ominous until you've seen the thundercloud that gathered over Ingrid when she found out Jane Porter was bringing a plus one to the wedding."

"It's not like Jane's marrying Knute Nelsen," Dolly huffed. "They just gad about town together."

Rena started pulling rolls of crepe paper and tissue paper wedding bells from the box Dolly had brought. "Why would she care about Jane's love life, even if she was going to tie the knot with Knute?"

Dolly hummed thoughtfully. "I think the whole reason Ingrid invited Jane was that she had a vision of Jane curled in a puddle of misery while she walked down the aisle with Harvey. Jane having a date takes some of the fun out of it."

"Geesh," I muttered, fanning out a honeycomb bell and slipping the plastic clips in place to hold it open. "Ingrid's always been brusque, but I've never known her to be mean-spirited. Other than a few sour grapes over a canasta hand, what does she have against Jane, anyway?"

"You don't know?" Dolly gasped.

Rena's eyes lit from within as she leaned in for a good dish. "No, we don't. . . . Spill it."

Dolly hummed nervously, studying the ceiling as though she could pinpoint Ingrid's precise location there. "Well," she finally whispered, "Jane and Arnold Whitfield dated in high school, when Harvey and Ingrid were together. Everyone thought Jane and Arnold would get married and Harvey and Ingrid would live their own happily ever after. But then Jane moved to Chicago to do some modeling, Harvey got sent to military school, and things just sort of happened the way they happened. . . . Next thing you know, Arnold and Ingrid were engaged.

"Then back, oh, thirty some years ago now, when Arnold was still alive, Ingrid spent a few months up in Duluth looking after her sister, who'd broken a hip. When she got back, she and Arnold had a big blowup, and he ended up spending a month or so with his brother in St. Paul. When he came home, he brought Ingrid a fancy new dishwasher. I don't think either one of them ever told a soul about that fight, but we all knew. And we all knew its cause: Jane and Arnold had, uh . . . well . . ."

Rena squealed. "Oh, no, they didn't! Arnold Whitfield and Jane Porter had a fling?"

"Hush," Dolly urged, glancing up at the ceiling again.

"Man," I whispered, "Jane picked the wrong woman to betray, didn't she?"

"You bet she did," Dolly continued. "Ingrid seemed to forgive Arnold, but she never forgave Jane. What's more, without so much as a word she made sure everyone in Merryville remembered that Jane's morals were a little loose. I know Ingrid never hung her head in shame over the affair, but this . . . well, this was her big chance to beat out Jane in the love game once and for all."

I slipped a ribbon through the grommets on the tops of three of the honeycomb tissue bells, making a little cluster to hang from the chandelier in the front room. "Wow. I never would have guessed. I can't imagine Ingrid putting up with a tomcatting husband. I guess everyone has secrets."

Dolly finished nestling the bundles of Jordan almonds in a lace-lined basket. "That they do, my dear. That they do. Don't you ever forget it."